110686497

IT IS I, JOSEPH

Cynthia Davis

Americana Publishing Inc.
303 San Mateo Blvd. NE
Suite 104A
Albuquerque, NM 87108
(888) 883-8203

Copyright by Cynthia Davis

All rights reserved. No part of this book may be reproduced
or transmitted in any form or by any means, electronic or
mechanical, including photocopying, recording, or by any
information storage or retrieval system, without the written
permission of Americana Publishing Inc., except where
permitted by law.

Davis, Cynthia.
    It is I, Joseph / by Cynthia Davis. -- 1st ed.
    p. cm.
    ISBN 1-58943-004-2

    1. Joseph--(Son of Jacob)--Fiction. 2. Bible. O.T.--History
of Biblical events--Fiction. 3. Biographical fiction.
4. Religious fiction. I. Title.

PS3604.A857I85 2001   813'.6
                                    QBI01-701271

AMERICANA PUBLISHING, INC.

AUDIE AWARD WINNER
BEST NEW AUDIOBOOK PUBLISHER 2001
AUDIO PUBLISHERS ASSOCIATION

To request a catalog or to order books and audiobooks
from Americana Publishing, please call or visit our website.

www.americanabooks.com

Titles from other publishers are also available
through AmericanaBooks.com.

Americana Publishing, Inc.
303 San Mateo Blvd. NE, Suite 104A
Albuquerque, NM 87108
Tel: (888) 883-8203 / (505) 265-6121
Fax: (505) 265-0632

Thanks to Rhonda McIntire for her encouragement. And, thanks to my husband, Ken, and daughters, Julie, Joyce, and Ruth, for their love and support.

Prologue

Word that the Lord Governor was coming sent the household into a whirlwind of activity. When it was rumored that the King would be accompanying him, the men agonized in fear and sought out their father. Without waiting to wash the dust of the road and sheepfold from their garments, they hurried to his tent. Squatting in the midst of the fertile Delta lands, the Hebrew tents seemed strangely out of place so near the pyramids, the white washed towns, and shipping lanes of the Lower Nile.

"Father, what can be the reason for this visit?"

"My sons, have no fear; your brother is coming to visit me. I have here his words." The old man held up a papyrus scroll. "At my request, he comes to tell me all that God has done in his life."

"But is the Great One, King of Egypt, coming also?"

"Yes, he, too, desires to hear the story."

"What shall we do? We have but poor hospitality for such as the Lord Governor much less the King of all the land!" The brothers looked wildly at one another, the same thought racing through their minds. "And, our father will hear of our treachery."

"Silence!" the patriarch angrily commanded, as he struggled to his feet. "The hospitality of the tent of Israel is known from Haran to the Great Sea!"

The men subsided in the face of his anger.

"Besides, your brother has sent slaves ahead to prepare a place for the king and his retinue. Not a mere tent for the King of Egypt." Jacob smiled slightly ironically. "Haven't you seen the pavilion that has been erected?"

Following their father's gesture, the brothers stared at the elaborate pillared hall just down the road from the tent where they stood. Constructed of alabaster marble and ornamented with paintings and gold etchings, the building gleamed in the mid-day sun. Ostentatious and fit for a king, the building caused the eleven brothers to stare in amazement. An army of workmen swarmed over the structure, putting the finishing touches on the brilliant paintings covering the pylons that formed the gate.

"Now, my sons, put your minds at ease. Our royal visitors will arrive within the week. Bring the finest of the animals in close so they can be prepared as needed. Your brother has sent additional cooks to help prepare such foods as the Pharaoh enjoys. All is ready and my heart rejoices that at last the time has come to hear of your brother's adventures."

With murmurs of "Yes, father," the eleven men drifted away to form small groups.

"What will our father say when he learns what we did thirty years ago?"

"Surely now our brother will ask the King for vengeance on our lives."

"If not the King, then our father will curse us."

"Hasn't our brother said many times that God used the evil you planned for good?" The youngest spoke up, but his brothers ignored the words as they tried to predict what would happen when the King and their Father, Jacob, heard of their actions. Haunted by guilt, the brothers talked long into the night.

Trumpet fanfares and the noise of many horses and men announced the arrival of the royal entourage. A litter with silken curtains stopped before the tent of Jacob. Standing erect beside the litter, Ctah, chamberlain of the King of Egypt, proudly intoned: "The Great Pharaoh, King of the Nile, Blessed of the gods, Ruler of all Egypt from the Great Sea to the Cataracts, from the Sahara to the Red Sea and beyond, greets Jacob, sheik of Canaan and patriarch of the house of Israel."

Jacob made obeisance to his regal guest. His sons threw themselves to the ground in total abasement and fear. "My Lord Pharaoh, welcome to my humble tent." Five years in Egypt had improved his Egyptian, and an interpreter was no longer needed. He gestured to the newly woven rug now spread for the king.

The chamberlain hurried forward to direct a slave in positioning Pharaoh's gold and ebony chair on the carpet. The claw feet sank into the lush weave of the rug. Bending at the waist, Ctah awaited the King's descent from the litter.

"Our thanks to you, Sheik, for your hospitality." The man who stepped from the litter inclined his head to the old man. Even without the crown of Egypt on his head and the crook and flail he carried, there was no doubt that this man was King. He wore royalty like a second skin, aware of the power he had over people's lives and proud of the lineage he inherited. Everyone present bowed to acknowledge his presence as he made the short walk to his throne.

"I look forward to speaking to you of your son," he announced, as he seated himself.

With great rattling of harnesses, the wagons moved toward the pavilion. Jacob personally offered a platter of choice sweetmeats to the royal guest. But, his eyes still sought his son in the multitude of wagons passing.

Again, the trumpets sounded. A chariot, drawn by a matched team of blacks, drew up before the tent. The early morning sun reflected off the gold trimmed wheels and shone in the eyes of the eleven men just rising from their position on the ground. Immediately, they prostrated themselves again. Jacob's heart leapt as Ctah announced: "Zaphenath-Paneah, Lord Governor of Egypt, second only to the Great Pharaoh, Preserver of the Black Land, Protector of the People, Great …" Before Ctah could finish the introduction, the man vaulted out of the chariot to embrace his father.

"My son, at last we will have time together. I prayed God would grant me this final favor before I am gathered to my fathers." Unashamed, both men wept as they embraced. Pharaoh looked on, smiling benignly.

"My father, now that the famine has ended, I can come to you. I am eager for you to hear all that God has done for me to carry out his promise to Abraham and to Isaac and to you!"

Finally, he released the old man and turned to the eleven men now standing nervously nearby. He walked to them. As one man, they fell to their knees.

"Have mercy, Great Lord!" The plea came from many lips.

Sadly, Joseph shook his head, "My brothers, you still do not understand. I bear you no ill will, for God turned to good what you meant for evil. Hear my story and see how great is our God."

Chapter 1

I was the special, the beloved, and the youngest son of Sheik Jacob of Canaan. I grew up coddled by mother and father. Vaguely, I remember my grandfather Laban setting me on his knee in Haran and telling me that God planned great things for me. "You will be greater than your brothers. Those born to the barren are doubly blessed by God."

I was often reminded that my mother, Rachel, had been barren for ten long years before I was born. Even the birth of my baby brother, Benjamin, in Ephrath didn't diminish my status in my father's eyes. If anything, we grew closer through our shared grief. Rachel, his beloved wife and my mother, died. A five-year-old boy feels the loss of his mother deeply.

My father provided a tutor for me as soon as we settled in Hebron, because everyone believed that God had destined me for greater things than herding sheep.

"My son, you are an answer to prayer. You are the son of my first and only love, Rachel. Leah and Bilhah and Zilpah have given me many sons, it is true, but you are special to my heart." Hearing these words regularly from my father, I soon began to act as though I was better than my older brothers. In youthful arrogance, I never thought of their jealousy. Even when they tried to ignore me, I pranced before them, always eager to display some new favor of our father.

My seventeenth birthday dawned clear and bright. The tents nestled comfortably in the valley and were protected by the size of the camp and the prestige of Jacob. I awoke with great anticipation, expecting something extraordinary for this special day. I was not disappointed. My father called me to him early in the morning. "My son, see what I have for you!"

Despite their pretended indifference, I could feel eleven pairs of eyes following me as I strutted over to my father. I took the neatly folded item from him. With a hug, he told me, "Joseph, today you will begin to fulfill all that your mother and I have planned and dreamed for you!"

Curiously, I unfolded the gift. A wonderful and elaborately embroidered linen coat with long, flowing sleeves rippled in my hands. I ignored the collective gasp of outrage from my brothers. Joyfully, I hugged my father. "This is the most wonderful gift. See my brothers! Is not Father kind and generous?"

Slipping into the coat, I whirled before my brothers. With an eye on father, they made the appropriate but un-enthusiastic congratulations. The symbolism of the princely robe was not lost on me or the rest of the family. "And that explains why I had the dreams I have had." I thoughtlessly added fuel to their rage.

"What dreams?" Jacob asked when no one else responded.

Standing proudly in my grand, new coat before my brothers and the rest of the family, I explained, "I dreamed that we were all in the fields. All twelve of us." Looking around at my brothers, I saw that they were concentrating on finishing their meal. Undeterred, I continued, "The harvest was done and we were binding up the sheaves. Suddenly, the most amazing thing happened!"

Turning to look fully at all the brothers, I told them, "Your eleven sheaves *bowed* down to *mine*." With a proud toss of my head, I stood staring down at them. Their instantaneous reaction was one of anger.

Reuben, the oldest, jumped to his feet. "*You* think I would ever bow to you!"

"Nothing but a spoiled brat," Judah snarled.

"Big dream for a little man," big Gad sneered.

"My sons," Jacob intervened before I could answer, "dreams can mean many things."

"But wait, my father and brothers." Unable to drop the subject, I plunged on. "I had a second dream, like the first!"

"Really?" Simeon affected a yawn.

"Truly, listen!" I grabbed his arm. Roughly, he shook me off, but I careened on. "My second dream was of all our stars."

"Our stars?" Levi was almost interested.

In Haran, we all learned of our natal stars and the control they held over our lives. Taking his response as encouragement, I continued, "Your eleven stars and the sun and moon all gathered around my star!"

Excitedly, I turned to my father. "Then they all bowed and made obeisance to my star!"

His anger surprised me. "You think that not only your brothers, but your mother and I will bow to you?" Robes swirling, he stamped away.

Stunned, I could barely stammer, "It was only a dream."

He made no response and my brothers mocked me as they left to take the sheep to a far pasture.

"Dreamer, dream again."

"Not so special, are you?"

"Bow to you? Never!"

I wandered off to be by myself, away from the whispers and titters of the women. The dreams were vivid in my mind. I had no doubt that they foretold what God had planned for me. "Everyone knows that when a dream comes twice, it is determined by God." I told myself, reviewing again in my mind the picture of sheaves and stars bowing to me. "My brothers, you *will* bow to me. God will fulfill what He has promised," I muttered after the dust cloud that hid them on their way to Shechem.

Jacob and I never again mentioned my dreams. There was a reserve between us that had not been there before. I refused to apologize and so the tension grew. One day he called me to his side. "Joseph, my son, go and see how your brothers are doing."

"Yes, my father."

"Your tutor can go with you."

Seeing a way to be totally free and alone, I said, "No, Father, let him stay here. I can go more swiftly alone. You know that Ebrot is not happy traveling."

It took some arguing, but finally Jacob agreed to let me go alone. Wearing my grand coat, which I treasured all the more now that my father was cooler toward me, I set out. Striding briskly over the hills and through the wadis I arrived at Shechem. My brothers, however, were not to be found in the fields.

"Who are you looking for, my lord?" A shepherd approached me.

Gratified that he believed me important, I replied, "I seek the sons of Jacob, sheik of Canaan."

"They have gone on. I believe they went to Dothan."

"Thank you, my man," I replied grandly as I tossed him a piece of silver.

"Generous lord, may you find those you seek," he called after me with many a salaam.

Head high, I proudly strode off toward Dothan. Clearly, my God-given status was obvious to all but my own family. I spied the sheep and brothers camped in the valley near Dothan. Eagerly, I waved to them from the hilltop. They turned their backs to talk to each other. After scrambling carefully down the hill, I hurried toward them.

"My brothers, Father sends his greeting and blessing."

"Why, look, brothers," Simeon drawled, "it's our little brother, the grand dreamer."

"Father wanted to know how you are doing." Oblivious to the undercurrent, I babbled on. "Are the you all and the herds doing well? I had to follow you from Shechem."

The ominous lack of response finally made me fall silent. For the first time, I looked into their eyes. Hatred and jealousy were plainly seen. Taking a step back, I bumped into Napthali. He grabbed my arms, but not to steady me. Encircled by my brothers, I felt fear for the first time. Angry hands ripped my coat, the precious gift from my father, off my back.

"Not so special now, away from Father!" Levi sneered in my face, his own face contorted with rage.

Their bottled up fury exploded into vicious beating and kicking. Helpless against so many, I fell to the ground, and futilely tried to protect my face from their blows. Only barely conscious, I heard Reuben say, "Wait, let us not kill him. He is our brother. Throw him into the empty cistern there. Then our hands will not be stained with his blood."

Rough hands dragged me across the ground. I felt myself lifted and then falling. The last of my consciousness left me as I crashed to the bottom of the pit. How long I lay in the mud I don't know. Gradually, pain told me that I was alive. Dimly, I heard laughter. My brothers were celebrating my death. Horror washed over me. With a groan, I reached out in the blackness. My hand felt the damp mud I lay in. Agonizingly slowly I stretched further. Pain shot through me, but I managed to reach out. I felt the wall of the pit. By gradual, slow movements I was finally able to stand up. Leaning against the side of my prison, I gasped in pain. By looking straight up, I could see that it was night.

Sobbing in despair, I sank into the mud. My head pounded with the knowledge that my brothers, my own flesh and blood, had attacked me. They were going to leave me here to die. Aching in every joint, I bowed my head onto my knees.

"Where is the God of Abraham, Isaac and Jacob?" I cried into the blackness. "Why have You let this happen if You are so great? Am I not the son of the promise? Your promise? The dreams You sent? God, are You going to let me die here?"

The night was spent in hopeless rage against God. Eventually, a little light filtered down from above and I knew it was day. I could hear nothing. Had my brothers left already?

Painfully, I stood up. My head ached from the beating and from my lack of sleep. I could feel cuts and bruises all over my body. My throat was parched from lack of water. Panting from the exertion of dragging myself to my feet, I leaned against the wall of the well. Then I heard the jangle of harness and voices approaching. Hope glimmered in me.

"Help!" My voice was barely a whisper.

I tried again. "Help!"

It sounded louder to my ears. Desperately, I repeated my cry, wishing for a concerned face to appear over the rim of the cistern.

Instead, Issachar's angry voice called down to me, "Shut up, fool!" as his head blocked out the light.

"Brother, help," I started to beg, but he was gone. The murmur of voices went on for a long time but I couldn't make out the words. Suddenly the light was blotted out again. Judah called down.

"Are you still there? Tie this rope around your waist and we'll lift you out."

Joy and hope surged through me. My brothers had repented and were rescuing me. Eagerly, with the strength of renewed trust, I grasped the rope and wrapped it around my waist, ignoring the jabs of pain in my body. Almost before I was ready, they began hauling me up. Unable to use my hands and feet to steady myself along the sides, I was swiftly and roughly, with many bangs against the stone lining of the well, brought to the surface and dragged over the edge. Blinking in the morning light, my swollen eyes squinted around. I rose to my knees and found myself looking into the impassive eyes of a huge man I did not know.

"So this is the merchandise?" His voice rumbled deep in his chest. Still not understanding, I turned my head, only to have his huge hairy hands grasp my chin and pry open my mouth.

Indignant, I struggled and raised a fist only to receive a kick in the ribs from Levi. Gasping for air, I fell forward when my jaw was released.

"Looks healthy," the big man said to the anxiously waiting men. Then to me he said, "Can you indeed read, write, and figure?"

A clay tablet was thrust at me. Struggling back to my knees, I stared wildly at my brothers, seeking some explanation.

Like wolves, they stared at me. Big Gad leaned over and hissed in my ear, "Do what he asks or it will be back in the pit." The threat chilled my soul. His eyes told me that this was not a joke.

I took the tablet and at the big man's directions, wrote out an order for grain – first in Sumerian and then in Egyptian.

"Now, figure the price for six omars."

I wrote the sum and gave the clay pad back. My mind still did not comprehend what was happening. It was not until the trader pulled out a purse and began counting silver into Judah's hands that I understood. I was being sold into slavery.

With an almost animal cry, I sprang to my feet. Anger caused me to forget my bruises. "How dare you?" I charged into the midst of my brothers. Their faces were blank and

stony as I frantically begged for help. "Judah, how can you do
this? We are brothers! Simeon, have you nothing to say? Levi,
Napthali, how have I harmed you? Asher, Zebulon, will no
one help me? Dan, will you not spare a thought for Father's
sorrow?"

No one responded and the trader laughed. Feeling much
like a hunted animal, I darted a glance around. Where could I
run? Seeing what I thought was an opening, I made a dash.
The flick of a whip around my ankles brought me to my
knees. Swift, strong hands bound my hands behind me. A
rope around my waist was tied to the camel saddle. A quick
command and the caravan moved off. I was forced to run
behind or be dragged. My final sight of my brothers was the
circle they formed to divide the coins they got from selling
me. The rest of the day became a blur of heat and thirst,
stones and stumbling, curses and blows. Evening saw us
camping near a pool of water halfway to Migdal after trekking
down the dry wadi from the fields of Dothan.

Hands still bound, I was untied from the camel and led to
the water. Gratefully, I plunged my face into the murky water,
gulping it in great swallows. A strong hand gripped my
shoulder and pulled me back.

"Don't let him drink too much at first. He will be sick."

"Yes, Father," the boy who held my rope replied. He was a
sturdy lad and only a little younger than me.

Too exhausted to even argue, I sat on the sand with my
head lowered. The boy squatted nearby watching me as if I
was some exotic beast. Eventually, the big man came back
and untied my hands. The muscles complained as I
straightened my arms. The trader handed me a chunk of
bread. It was dry and hard, but it was the first food I had seen
in over a day. Ravenously, I gnawed at it.

"Go on to the fire, lad, and get your meal," he told his son.

"Boy," I realized he was addressing me, "you will find me not a harsh master, if you do as I say. Your brothers tell me that they beat you for disobedience."

I threw up my head in denial. His upraised hand silenced my angry response.

"Whether that is true or not, I don't care. Normally, I do not even trade in slaves. But I know a man in Egypt who is seeking a scribe. If you can learn humility and obedience, you could serve him well. You seem young and smart. It is up to you, boy. I will be watching."

With this combined threat and promise, the man stood up and relinquished my rope to his son. "Let him wash off some of the blood and dust before tying him up for the night." The man gestured toward the camel line.

It felt good to splash the water, dirty though it was, over my body. The grit stung my cuts, but in the end I felt better. Wearily, I followed my keeper back through the camp, barely seeing the stares of the other traders. Carefully, the boy tied me between two camels. Exhaustion of body and soul claimed me and I slept.

The next day, I learned that Borz was the trader's name. His son, my guard, was Abdul. Plodding behind Abdul's camel, I had plenty of time to rage inwardly at God and my brothers. Sullenly, I followed Abdul's camel day after day. There was no point in trying to escape. I did not know where I was, except that the Great Sea lay to the West and the mountains of my home were fast receding to the North and East. My cuts and bruises were healing, but the deeper hurt to my heart grew larger as I again and again relived my brothers' treachery.

Sitting alone one night, I stared up at the stars. "God of my Fathers, why did you desert me? You let me be sold to slavers, bound like an animal. You allowed my brothers to beat and betray me. God, are You even there? Do You even care?" That night I resolved to work out my own redemption. Shaking a fist at heaven, I swore, "You may have visited Abraham and Isaac and my father Jacob. But You have turned your back on me. Since You will not save me, I will save myself."

The next morning, rather than silently stalking beside Abdul, I engaged him in conversation. He was not much younger than me and lonely amid all the grown men in the group. It was his first time to travel with the trade caravan. I learned that their main trade items were the spices, balm, and nuts from further east. In return, I told him of the many flocks and herds of my father Jacob.

Borz was at first suspicious of my changed attitude. But when I did not try an escape, he relaxed and even let me teach Abdul some letters and numbers each evening by the firelight.

During the days that followed, I was allowed to have free run of the camp and was no longer tied between the camels at night. When the men learned that I could tell stories, they encouraged me to entertain them in the cool evenings. I know they thought that I was making up the anecdotes. All I had to do was remember the tales Jacob told of his time in Haran. I told them how God made his flocks flourish no matter what Laban did. One night I told of the wonderful coat my father gave me and the dreams I had.

"You are a great storyteller," Abdul told me the next day as we walked through the sand. The Sea now lay to the North and I was told that the Wilderness of Shur lay to the South. "I don't believe half of what you say, but you have a way of spinning a tale! I'll bet you could entertain Pharaoh himself. Father says we will be in Egypt in a week," he continued.

The thought was sobering. I was reminded again that I was not a free man two days later when Borz informed us that we were crossing into Egypt.

"Our first stop will be Succoth. They are always anxious for the spices we bring." I overheard the trader telling his son, "Then I will journey South to On for that is where Captain General Potiphar lives."

"Father, why can't Joseph stay with me, as my slave and tutor?" Abdul tried to plead with Borz.

"You knew from the start that I purchased the boy only to please my lord Potiphar, Captain General of Pharaoh's army."

"But he is not a slave. He should not have been sold by his brothers." The boy was near tears on my behalf.

"Younger sons have been sold before this and will be again. My son, I know it seems harsh, and I am sorry that you became friends. You know I rarely deal in slaves and only did it this time as a favor."

Abdul was no longer listening. He ran away. I found him behind a palm tree angrily beating his fist against the trunk.

"Thank you." The simple words made him stop and look at me questioningly.

"I heard you talking to your father." My explanation made his brows draw together.

"He is so unreasonable!" the boy exclaimed angrily. "I know ... we can run away together!"

For a brief moment, I considered the option, then common sense reasserted itself. "We would be found in a day," I pointed out. "We hardly look Egyptian and our accent would betray us the first time one of us spoke."

"Do you want to be sold? Don't you want to be free?" His frustration turned to anger at me.

"More than anything!" I replied, knowing it was true and that I was probably a fool for throwing away this chance. "But you would be beaten and I would be sold to the galleys, and from there, there is no return."

"You are a coward! And a fool!" Turning his back on me, Abdul strode back to camp. I followed sadly, knowing I had lost a friend.

That night, I slept restlessly, only to be roused by a sandal clad foot in my ribs. Abdul stood over me, once again the slave guard of our first meeting.

"We will reach Succoth today where I will be rid of you," he informed me, his snarl covering up the tears that threatened.

Abdul refused to speak to me during the final day of desert travel. Silently, he rode while I plodded behind. I mourned that our friendship ended in such a way.

I had no idea what to expect, but my first sight of an Egyptian town astonished me. There were few towns in Canaan, but all were built of mud brick, squatting against hillsides or cowering in the valleys. Here was a city rising out of the grasslands of the Nile delta. It was hard to believe that it was built of mud brick, too. Many houses were two stories and covered with some kind of whitewash that reflected the orange and crimson colors of the setting sun. The official buildings and temples were ornamented with dramatic paintings of life in Egypt. I know my mouth was open as we wove our way through the city. Borz was well known to the city officials who came to welcome the caravan. We camped in the fields belonging to the local royal counselor.

Early the next day, the traders set up their booths, adding their shouts to the din in the marketplace. Borz put me to work keeping track of the sales. Pride compelled me to do a good job, although I knew that this was his final test of me before our journey to his friend Potiphar.

Next morning, we left behind the rest of the caravan. Borz woke me before it was light. "Come, Boy. It is time to set out for On."

From Succoth we traveled straight West to the Nile and then boarded a boat bound for On. As the wind and boatsmen's poles moved us rapidly upstream, I stared in wonder at the rich, narrow river valley. Fields lined both sides of the river. The green of the crops contrasted with the golden sand stretching to the horizon in both directions, just beyond the reach of the Nile's water. Further on, we saw some of the great Pyramids built, Borz told me, to hold the bodies of the Pharaoh's for the afterlife. On itself was an amazing sight. The temples on the West bank were dedicated to many different gods. I stared at the representations of the many gods depicted on the pylons and walls of the temples. Borz told me that the city of On was the home of Ra, the sun god of Egypt. Everywhere I looked, there were gold tipped obelisks to reflect the sunlight and statues of Ra with the sun disk on his head. The pillared limestone halls were awe inspiring for their sheer size and the grandeur of the carvings and murals I glimpsed.

When we were almost to On, Borz pointed to an estate gleaming in the sunlight. "That is the home of Captain General Potiphar," he told me.

Chapter 2

My heart was in my throat as I followed Borz down the road. We skirted the edge of the city on our way to the house that I had already begun to consider my prison. We passed the bulrushes by the boat landing and then walked past fields and fields of grain. My feet moved slower and slower until the trader turned with an angry command accompanied by his hand moving toward his whip and a jerk of my bound wrists.

"Come, Boy, let us not keep Potiphar waiting! I sent him word that I had a special piece of merchandise. He is a very important and wealthy man here in Egypt. You will make him a useful slave with your ability to calculate and write."

As we approached the gate, I breathed a quick prayer. "God of my fathers, if You care, help me."

I'm not sure that I expected anything, but nothing happened. Borz was greeted by the gatekeeper. We entered through the servant's entrance. Inside the walls was an entire town. I saw grain silos, stables, and many other buildings I could not identify. The main house sat on a small rise like a queen above her subjects. The pillared porch surrounded a house larger than my father's whole camp. I even glimpsed a roof garden before we went inside the main hall. The size of the room brought me to a halt. Twice the size of Jacob's tent, the walls were covered with murals depicting many battles. A huge figure of a man in a chariot dominated each frame of the paintings. More pillars topped with representations of the ever-present lotus blossoms lined the hallway I could see beyond the room. The rich colors on the walls and pillars reminded me vaguely of the temples in Haran, which I remembered dimly from my childhood.

Still staring, I stumbled forward as Borz wrenched the rope.

"Borz, you old rascal!" The voice was booming, used to uttering battlefield commands.

This was Potiphar, master of the house, I realized when I looked from the paintings to the speaker. Even in person, the man seemed larger than life. Older and with a ragged scar running from his cheek to his chest, this was still the warrior whose valiant deeds were emblazoned on the walls. I had thought Borz large, but he seemed almost dwarfed by the height and weight of the owner of this magnificent house.

"What have you brought me that is so special? You sent a messenger a day ahead to tell me the news and ensure my interest. But wait, where are my manners? Before we discuss business, let us drink to fair trading and good friendship."

The steward was already standing by with a tray bearing a gold goblet. Taking the cup, Potiphar offered it to Borz with a ceremonial bow. Touching his lips to the rim, Borz handed it back with an equally elaborate salaam. Potiphar then replaced the goblet on the tray. The steward removed the tray and returned with a pitcher and two silver cups.

"Now, to our friendship." Potiphar handed one cup to Borz and took up the other.

"Does your son require a cup?" the man asked in an offhand way.

"He is not my son," Borz replied.

"No?" For the first time, Potiphar looked at me. Noticing the rope, he remarked, "Ah, then this is the merchandise." He turned to the trader with a look of contempt after his keen soldier's eyes looked me up and down.

"This is the special merchandise? A boy hardly grown? I have no use for striplings needing training. I wouldn't even take him on if I needed foot soldiers against Nubia." Grasping the goblet, he drained it in one gulp, then held it out to be refilled as he threw himself irritably into a chair.

Borz lifted his goblet in salute to the man.

"You are right, he is nothing to look at. Too skinny by far to be good for much," he shrugged. "I had thought of your desire for a slave with the ability to keep track of your many projects. But no doubt, great Potiphar, you have already found such a man. I should not have troubled my lord."

Setting his goblet down, Borz rose, bowed, and turned to leave.

"Hold, you sly thief!" Potiphar was sitting up with a look of interest on his face. "You say the boy can write and tell numbers?"

"Well, mighty lord, I have observed that he has some small skill in that area. The men I purchased him from indicated that he could read and write both Sumerian and Egyptian. I have seen for myself that he is quick with sums. Why, in Succoth, I put him to work keeping records of the sales."

"And he knows Egyptian?" The lift of his eyebrow in my direction plainly said that he doubted that a ragged person such as myself could possibly have intelligence.

"Some. It is odd, is it not? A lad from the Hebrew riffraff in Canaan that knows Egyptian."

My blood boiled at the slur and I straightened, lifting my chin proudly. Potiphar hefted himself out of the chair. A hand made strong wielding a sword and battle-ax tilted my head back. I refused to look away as his eyes stared at me and his hands probed my muscles.

"Proud and with a look of intelligence. I do not like the fact that he looks so thin. But his muscles are wiry and he is not sickly looking." Suddenly, he rounded on me. "Boy, do you understand what we are discussing?" This was said in Egyptian.

"Enough," I replied through gritted teeth, still smarting from the Hebrew riffraff statement. "Borz, the trader, wants you to buy me to keep your accounts. I learned writing and numbers in my father's house in Canaan, among the Hebrew riffraff." I couldn't resist the comment.

The slightest twitch of his eyes showed that Potiphar caught the gibe. He glanced at Borz, who scowled.

"Proud and insolent, too," Potiphar commented. "Where did you say you bought the lad?"

"Nine brothers offered him for sale. He claims that he is indeed their brother. Who knows, he may be. But the hills of Canaan are a long way from the Nile. I must add, to his credit, the boy never tried to escape."

"I will try his skills." Potiphar signaled to the steward still hovering nearby. "Clep, fetch a papyrus scroll and writing tools."

At the time, I was amazed at the speed with which the items were brought. I was to learn that Potiphar brooked no delay when an order was given.

"Here, boy. Sit and write as I tell you."

For the next half-hour, Potiphar tested my writing and calculating abilities. Finally, when my fingers were aching from the rapid dictation, he took the scroll. First he reviewed the figures. Nodding, he rolled the scroll to read the order he had dictated.

"What is this?" His finger pointed to a Sumerian glyph among the Egyptian.

"My apologies, my lord, I could not remember the Egyptian for that word, so I inserted the Sumerian."

"Hmm." Potiphar leaned back in his chair, staring into the distance and face expressionless. It was a characteristic attitude when he was thinking.

"My lord Potiphar is pleased?" Borz asked as the silence stretched out.

"I believe the boy can learn and be of use," he finally said. "What is your price?"

The trader named a price over five times what he paid my brothers.

"Quite a profit," I muttered in Hebrew, causing him to cuff me and order silence.

"Insolence, my lord," Borz explained to Potiphar's raised and questioning eyebrow.

"Perhaps, like me, the lad feels the price too high. I think I will pay seventy shekels of silver."

"My lord, I have had the care and feeding of the boy for months. I will have no profit." With his voice taking on the singsong whine of a master trader, Borz began to wheedle. The bartering went back and forth. Watching my life's worth being weighed out for a price felt very strange. I felt my control of who I was disappearing into the years of slavery that stretched ahead. Finally, the money changed hands and Borz rose with a deep bow to the Captain General of Egypt. "Boy, serve your master well," were his last words to me.

Potiphar ordered the steward to take me and get me washed and clothed.

I found myself following the man down a long tiled hallway to the slave baths. The steward, whose name I learned was Clep, told me that I would not be allowed into the main house except on Potiphar's command. "My lord Potiphar will designate your duties," he informed me. "Here is the bath." The door opened into a pool filled with water and fed by water flowing from a carved pitcher on the wall. Desert born, I was unused to such extravagant use of water.

"What is your name?" was the next question as he handed me a slave's rough, linen loincloth.

"Joseph bar Jacob. My father is Sheik of Canaan. If he did not believe me dead, he would have searched for me and destroyed the slave trader with his men," I replied proudly, clinging to my heritage in the midst of all the Egyptian trappings.

His words ignored this last claim to myself and reminded me that I was a slave with no say in my life. "No, you will be called Hebiru, for that is what you are. Remember this and it will be better for you here. You are no longer the son of a powerful father. Here you are the slave of the Captain General of Pharaoh's Army. A greater honor you cannot wish as a slave. You should be thanking whatever god you believe in for having brought you here."

I opened my mouth to object but closed it again. The steward nodded. "Come, Hebiru, you must bathe and shave. Here is razor and soap. All body hair must be removed. I will cut your hair and then leave you to complete the bath. Shave there," he pointed to a basin set in the wall, "then bathe."

"Now, sit." Clep produced a pair of shears and set to work trimming my wavy brown hair into some semblance of the straight cut favored by all the Egyptians I had seen. Subdued, stunned and confused, I sat dejectedly even after he finished. When I did not move, he prodded me with the point of the shears.

I jumped and swung around in angry reflex before I remembered my new status. His fist in my gut reminded me.

"Wash, shave. I will be back soon." The steward left as I was still gasping air back into my lungs.

Reluctantly, I turned to the basin. A marred bronze plate hung above for a type of mirror. I was reminded of the polished bronze mirror my mother had used and a wave of homesickness and sorrow almost reduced me to tears. Only the fear that Clep would return kept me from sobbing uncontrollably. Grudgingly, I set about shaving my beard. It felt odd to be clean-shaven. And even odder to shave my body. After rinsing in the pool, I donned the unfamiliar Egyptian clothes. Not a moment too soon, for the steward entered as I completed looping the loincloth into place. Feeling only half clothed, I stood before him for inspection.

He nodded in approval. "Come, I will show you where you will sleep. Tomorrow, my lord Potiphar will see you and explain your duties."

The evening air felt odd on my exposed skin as I walked behind the steward. The night sky and stars told me that the day was over. Exhausted from emotion and feeling very alone, I curled up on the bulrush mattress in the slave quarters. My last waking thought was that God had truly abandoned me.

Early morning light was barely on the horizon when I was wakened along with all the other slaves in the room. Together we stumbled out to meet the day. It was my first as a slave in the house of Potiphar, Captain General of Pharaoh's army. As we grabbed a hasty meal of flat bread, I looked at my fellow slaves. Some returned my stares with curious looks of their own but most simply gazed ahead, caring nothing about the new arrival. I wondered at the story behind each face.

Three figures especially caught my attention: the tall, muscular man with skin the color of ebony wood whose left arm hung virtually useless from a sword stroke that left a long scar down the length; the wrinkled, old man whose back was permanently bent from bearing others burdens; and the dwarf man with skin and hair almost white also caught my eye. I wondered that a man of power such as my new master would keep such useless slaves. In the days to follow, I learned that Potiphar indeed had no useless slaves. He used each man for his abilities and cared nothing for his appearance.

The old man bore in his mind the history of the house. The dwarf acted as a spy and reported all that he saw to Potiphar.

The Nubian warrior, despite his useless arm, was a formidable fighter and trained the household guard.

The steward, Clep, came in as we finished eating. He issued orders to all the household servants who moved off to accomplish their daily tasks. I was left with the three men I was even more curious about. They had received no orders. But I had little time to wonder because Clep turned to me.

"Hebiru, come with me, my lord Potiphar wants to see you. He has decided what you are to do."

Without waiting for my response, he turned and walked out the door and started across the open courtyard to the main house. Following his lead, I again was awed by the wonders in the house. There were wonderful ebony and gold inlaid tables scattered along the length of the hall. Each table had a small statuette of some Egyptian god. More murals were etched along the stairway to the upper, family level of the house. My eyes ached from trying to see everything. Finally, Clep stopped and opened a carved door that was twice my height. He bowed as he entered. When I still stood amazed, the application of the steward's staff to the back of my knees caused me to crash to me knees.

"So," the booming voice was amused. "The lad is still showing spirit. Come here. I have a task for you."

Carefully, I got to my feet, half expecting Clep to strike me down again. I knelt before my master. His nod showed that he was still amused by my response. "You will be writing my memoirs." It was a statement and he continued. "Not the grand and glorious story depicted on these walls, but the life I really lived. Phu, here, will tell you what to write. He has lived with me from my youth."

I looked up to see the old man from breakfast smiling and nodding.

"I will call on you to read what you have written. Phu and Clep will provide you with all the supplies you need."

Phu bowed and left the room followed by Clep and myself. My pride, as well as my legs, stung as I followed the two men in a daze. How could all my dreams and my father's hopes have come to this? No governorship or high position; rather, I was to be a slave scribe to an aging warrior who wanted his exploits recorded.

Angry as I was, I was just wise enough not to voice my rage. It must have shown in my face because I overhead Clep instruct Phu. "Keep your eye on the boy. He still thinks he's some princeling."

"What if he is?" Phu glanced toward me.

"What of it? If he doesn't work well, Nukor will take him in hand."

We had descended the stairs and now entered another large room. The entire room was lined with cupboards and piles of scrolls. I guessed it was the library although I had only heard of such places from my tutor.

"Here is where you will work." Clep removed a map from the low table near a window and gestured for me to sit.

"Work well and you will find my lord Potiphar is a generous master. But remember this, Hebiru, my lord Potiphar expects excellence in what he commands. He will brook nothing shoddy or half-done. Nukor is a master with the whip as some have learned to their distress."

With this warning, the steward left me with Phu. The old man was quite excited. He rubbed his hands together. "My boy, this is wonderful! You have the skills to write and I have the story in this old head. The gods must have sent you!"

I sneered bitterly, "No god cares whether I am here writing some scroll or still in my father's tent."

"Ah, when you have lived the years I have, lad, then you will understand the gods will is strange. Why was I born a slave and not a free man? The gods know. But, my lord Potiphar is a good master. My brothers were not so fortunate.

Sold to other masters, their lives were short and miserable. Here I have become as free a man as a slave can hope to be. As my master's confidant and conscience, I have seen things and been places I would never have experienced as a poor, free man. You would do well to heed Clep's words. He, too, has been in service to my lord Potiphar for many years. A soldier first, his loyalty was so strong that he lowered himself to steward in the household rather than serve under another captain.

I turned away to gaze out the window. Far away I could see the sands of the desert to the East. Somewhere, miles away, was my family. My voice was low and filled with emotion when I replied. "If you have never known freedom, how can you compare even good slavery to being free? Free to come and go as you please. Free to have dreams and family." I stopped as I heard my voice clogging with the tears clutching my throat. "The God of my Fathers has taken all that from me. My father will never know what has happened to me. My brothers dare not tell him that they sold me. Of all men, I am most bereft."

"Who knows what the gods have in store? I have learned to be content with where I am." The old man's hand was gentle on my arm. "Let us start to work. Perhaps my lord Potiphar's story will give you insight. It will at least take your mind off your troubles." He added as an aside.

With a shrug, I settled to the task. Sitting at the table, unrolling a clean scroll, and sharpening the quill, I waited for Phu to begin.

Chapter 3

Day followed day in a soon predictable routine. Rising
before dawn to bathe, shave, and eat with all the slaves
of the house was followed by a brief time of exercise in the
stable yard, led by Nukor. My lord Potiphar insisted that all
his slaves maintain good health and strength. On rare
occasions, he himself joined us in the yard. Mostly, I learned;
he exercised privately with Nukor and rode the magnificent
war stallion regularly. Only Nukor and Potiphar were allowed
near the animal that lived in a separate stable with his own
private field.

When the sun rose higher over the eastern desert, Phu and
I would walk together to the library. The ornate carvings and
furnishings ceased to awe me, as I became familiar with the
house. Even sitting in a chair and using a table became
commonplace, replacing the old familiarity of sitting and
working on mats and cushions on the ground. Canaan
seemed further and further away with each sunrise.
Sometimes I could hardly remember who Joseph bar Jacob
was and what his dreams had been.

As the days rolled by, I actually became engrossed in the
story of my lord Potiphar's life. Phu was able to make the
tapestry of his life come alive. From the vivid descriptions of
all parts of the "Black Land", as I learned Egypt was known
because of the annual flooding which left the land black and
fertile, to the loving depiction of my master, the old man was
a master storyteller. The words flowed off the reed onto the

papyrus scroll in the stylistic hieroglyphics. The more I learned of his life, the more impressed I was. From a humble beginning as the son of a minor landowner, Potiphar was conscripted into Pharaoh's army. As a foot soldier, he not only survived but also distinguished himself by saving his commanding officer's life. This led to his promotion to charioteer. Phu explained to me that through it all, Potiphar never forgot his father. He told me of the monthly runs he made from the army location to report to his concerned father.

Because Phu and Clep used the phrase constantly, I, too, fell into the habit of referring to my master as "my lord Potiphar." One day I asked if my lord Potiphar had any family left.

Phu shook his head, "Sadly, no. You know his mother died when he was away on the first campaign. There would have been a sister, but the baby died, too. His father died before he could see how greatly my lord Potiphar would prosper. There is, of course, my lord's wife, the lady Dala."

I raised my head in surprise. "I didn't know my lord was married!"

"She has her own apartments and only joins him on state occasions. He loves her dearly, but ..." Phu paused to consider how best to proceed. "But her love is not as constant," he concluded shortly. "Now back to the business at hand."

I accepted the reed he held out and rolled the scroll forward. I had much to ponder. My lord Potiphar must be a lonely man with no family and a wife who, according to Phu's veiled words, was unfaithful. For the first time, I felt a kinship to the man who was my master.

Phu was continuing with the story. "It was after the battle near the headwaters of the Nile that my lord Potiphar received his next promotion. The Nubians were threatening our southern border and Pharaoh ordered the troops out to stop the advance. The fighting was bloody on both sides. The Nubians were fighting for freedom and home. Pharaoh's troops were trained warriors, but against the fervor of the Nubians they fell back. The army was backed against the river with the attackers on the hillsides pouring down fiery arrows, rocks, and spears. The day looked bleak indeed, until my lord Potiphar approached the general with a flanking plan.

'Let me take a dozen hand picked men around the back of the slope. I think we can get above them and pin them down. Meanwhile, you can concentrate on the east slope.' The general could see no other plan and agreed to let my lord take the men he wanted. He gave us clear instructions. We each took a sword and spear. One by one we slipped out of camp, going north, then west. Just as my lord thought, the Nubians didn't notice our departure and we crept, scrambled, and clawed our way up the far side of the slope until we were above the warriors. It was a straight run down the hillside, broken only by a few outcroppings of rock. From the vantage of our location, we could see that the general and Pharaoh's troops were not faring well in the crossfire. But, my lord Potiphar waited until the setting sun shown in the eyes of the attackers on the eastern slope. The fighters on our side were in the shadow. Then giving the war cry, 'In the name of Ra!' we rushed down the hill. We could only hope the general took advantage as planned for we became much too busy to look. Although taken by surprise from above, the Nubians fought like furies. But our swords and spears were superior and the slaughter was almost complete. At the end, I saw my lord Potiphar engaged in hand to hand combat with a tall, muscular, young Nubian warrior. They were evenly matched until my lord was able to slash the arm with his sword."

I looked up. "Nukor?"

Phu smiled complacently, happy with the surprise in my face.

"Yes, Nukor was the leader of that Nubian resistance. My lord Potiphar found him such a gallant opponent that he brought him home. Most people think Nukor is a slave. In reality, he is a favored associate and ally of my lord Potiphar."

"Like yourself and Clep," I ventured, the answers to my questions falling into place.

Phu grinned, "So you have noticed. The lad is not as oblivious as he looks. A lot goes on in your mind doesn't it?"

I felt myself flush guiltily. "I have noticed that there is something unusual about the relationship you and Clep and Nukor and even Melmintah, the dwarf, have with my lord Potiphar."

"We are all useful to my lord in various ways. He saw in us certain abilities that he can use. I believe he sees something special in you also."

"Me?" I was astounded. "What could he see in me?"

"How can I say? I do not have my lord Potiphar's discernment. But don't think that he bought you from the Ishmaelite just to write these memoirs. Speaking of which ..." He gave a meaningful glance at my reed and papyrus.

I did not want to let the subject go. "But how did Clep and Melmintah come into my lord's service?"

"We'll get to that," Phu stated and then his voice took up the singsong of the recital. "The defeat of the Nubians led to a royal commendation from Pharaoh and promotion to second in command. Pharaoh also gave my lord this estate in the city of Ra and the permission to use the colors of Ra on his chariots. Egypt had peace for a time and my lord Potiphar had work started on the murals here. His father died soon after and so never saw the full grandeur of the house. He never got to see his son rise to become Captain General of Pharaoh's army. But, that is a story for tomorrow. The light is fading and my stomach tells me it is time to eat. Roll the scroll carefully."

I followed Phu out of the library. As we walked down the hall and across the courtyard to the slave quarters, I marveled that the son of a small landowner in Egypt could become so great, while the son of the greatest sheik in Canaan could have fallen so low.

That evening, as I sat on my bulrush mat, I prayed, "Lord God of my Fathers, God of Abraham, Isaac and Jacob – the God I believed in once – can it be that these gods of Egypt are stronger than You? I have asked You to free me; yet, I remain here as a slave. Show me, if You can, Lord God, who is greater." I felt only silence and my dreams seemed to mock me. I dreamed again of the bowing sheaves of grain, only this time, the fields were the rich Egyptian fields that I saw daily.

Next morning, Clep told me, "Write well, Hebiru. My lord Potiphar desires to see your work tonight."

Phu was thrilled. "My lord will be delighted with how much we have done!"

I was nervous. "Will he like it, do you think?"

"If you wrote as I instructed, my lord Potiphar will be pleased. Come, let us begin."

The old man was almost trotting down the hall in his excitement. He barely waited for me to sharpen a fresh reed before he began.

"The next great campaign was to the west. We are rarely threatened from across that great desert, the Red Land, but certain marauding bands had combined under one leader to make forays into the temples and tombs at Thebes.

Pharaoh's general told my lord Potiphar to plan the strategy. My lord asked for two days. This was agreed to. My lord took his three trusted associates to lie in wait and watch for the thieves."

"Who did he take?" I asked the question as much out of curiosity as for the memoirs.

"Didn't I say?" The old man looked slightly taken aback. "Why it was myself, Clep, his trusted lieutenant, and Nukor, his friend from the Nubian battle.

While we waited on the outskirts of Thebes that night, I learned that my lord Potiphar's mind never rests. He spent the evening sketching ideas in the sand for improving his estate. Suddenly, we heard the swishing of the sand as when men are trying to make no sound. You can only hear it in the still of the night and only if you are close to the ground. We trailed the robbers back to their lair. The next day, my lord Potiphar took a small group of soldiers to surround and destroy the encampment. All went as planned, except that a stray arrow struck the general in the throat. My lord Potiphar went a little mad when he saw his friend and mentor die in such a meaningless fight. He personally led the charge into the camp. Swinging the curved sword, he mowed down man after man and even his wounds did not stop him. We hewed down every man in the robber camp. Finally, Nukor and I came upon my lord. He was standing in the center of the carnage, blood streaming from his wound. If he had not been holding a spear that pinned one of the thieves to the ground, he would have fallen. With Clep's help, we got him to a litter. Even then, he raised himself to say, 'If any are still alive, bring them to me. Search the camp.' Nukor and Clep remained to carry out that order. The only person found alive was Melmintah. He was only slightly injured and had, with his characteristic flexibility, rolled under a trough to hide. If Clep hadn't seen the tiny movement of cloth out of the corner of his eye, Melmintah probably would have escaped. They dragged him out and brought him to my lord Potiphar. The priests had used their skills to stop the bleeding and bandaged the wound. You have seen the scar it left from face to chest."

Nodding, I said, "I wondered how my lord Potiphar came by that scar."

Phu sighed, "It is not a battle scar he is proud of. My lord Potiphar would rather not remember that episode at all, but daily he is reminded of it."

Silent for a minute, the old man continued, "By the time Melmintah was brought to him, my lord was calmer. We all expected him to execute the survivor on the spot. However, he sent us out of the room and questioned Melmintah about his role in the bandit troop. Because of his size, Melmintah used to infiltrate homes and temples to find where the greatest treasures were stored. My lord Potiphar saw the possibilities for a man with such talents. He gave him the chance to live and be his personal spy. For fifteen years, Melmintah has loyally served my lord. Pharaoh, while displeased with the loss of his best general, was nonetheless pleased that the marauders no longer ravaged Thebes. My lord Potiphar received a promotion that placed him over others with longer service. Pharaoh named him 'Captain General of Pharaoh's Army and Defender of the Priestly Cities, Councilor and Confidant of the King'."

Phu waited while I completed drawing the titles with a flourish. He then expounded on several other battles where my lord distinguished himself.

"All the enemies of Egypt heard of his valor and the land had peace. My lord Potiphar was able to retire to this estate. The lady Dala was given to my lord as a bride. Young, spirited, and beautiful, the lady Dala was a niece of Pharaoh. Potiphar found her entrancing and captivating. He fell in love with her and can see no fault in her. Not long after they were wed, she requested that he install apartments for her and her ladies at the far end of the house. She claimed that the coming and going of the daily business was disturbing. A separate entrance was installed so the ladies could come and go in privacy. There she and her ladies live and conduct their lives. Rarely does my lord Potiphar see the lady, his wife."

Phu paused. A look of disgust revealed what he thought of my lady's way of life.

"I may as well tell you. You will eventually hear it anyway. It is rumored in the town and at court that the lady Dala takes lovers. Any man who strikes her fancy, from the garden lad to a royal courtier. No one, it seems, can refuse her."

"But my lord Potiphar?" It seemed inconceivable that a man like my master would overlook such actions in his wife.

"He will not believe evil of her. Once he found a stable lad in her chambers. The boy was executed that night. On another occasion, an aide to the local governor was seen leaving the premises. He disappeared into Pharaoh's dungeons and hasn't been heard of since. Hebiru, I say this partly in warning. Hear what I say. I have come to like you. Stay away from the lady Dala. You are just the sort of young, handsome man she seeks out."

It was the first time that Phu had actually called me by my new name. I was touched by his concern but could not see how Potiphar's wife would affect me. I certainly didn't plan any dalliance, even with the slave girls. Some of them had rather blatantly hinted at their willingness to share my bed. Certainly the sparseness of the Egyptian clothing left nothing of what they were offering to my imagination. But, I knew that slave romances were doomed. The story of my great-grandfather Abraham and his concubine, Hagar, taught me that even a slave bearing the master's son can be sent away.

Nightly, I still prayed for rescue, but the hope dimmed with each passing week. I became more Egyptian and less Hebrew. The gods of Egypt, while strange, were present. I told myself that one god was as good as another and surely Ra, the sun god, chief god of On and Egypt, was like the One God of my

Fathers. In any case, it seemed that the God I had believed in had abandoned me.

Just as Clep had said, Potiphar sent for me that night.

"Take the scrolls." Both Clep and Phu were quite anxious. I was too, although with the bravado of youth, I tried to hide it. The three large scrolls contained much of my lord Potiphar's life. Some of it quite different than that depicted on the walls. The scrolls in my arms held the reality of the life and dreams of the man waiting on the rooftop to see what Phu and I had accomplished.

Clep opened the door, and bowing, announced us to my lord Potiphar. A brief glance around this cool evening retreat was all I allowed myself before falling to my knees. In that quick moment, I saw an airy apartment with vines growing up the latticed walls. The floor was some smoothly polished light colored wood. My lord Potiphar reclined on a long, low couch with carved lion heads at one end and a lion's tail curving over the foot. The legs were beautifully executed lion paws. The furniture was placed comfortably near the pool in the center of the room. Behind him stood the fan bearer who languidly moved the ostrich feather fan over his head, augmenting the slight breeze from the river that cooled the room.

"Come in, let me see what you have completed," his booming voice bade us enter.

I moved forward, keeping my head lowered and presented the scrolls to my master.

"Sit here." He pointed to a stool at his feet. "I would like to look on as you read. Take the scroll and start." He randomly pointed to one of the rolls.

It was the final scroll, completed just that afternoon. Remembering what it contained made me hesitate.

"My lord, that is the last scroll. Would it not be better to begin with the first?" Bravely I had voiced my concern.

"No, I will hear what you have written about these years."

"Yes, my lord Potiphar." I took the linen wrapping from around the papyrus and unrolled it to the beginning. A quick look at Phu showed that he was gripping his wrinkled hands together in nervousness or perhaps fear.

"My lord," I began but had to clear my throat and start again, for a lump of fear choked me. I took a breath and began again. "My lord, this begins with the western campaign against the Thieves of Thebes."

I paused for a brief sideways glance at my lord. He didn't seem angry, but leaned back on the couch, quite at ease. So, I began reading. I think that the empathy I had begun to feel for the man who was my master came into my inflection. I could see the story of his life come alive off the page, and when I dared look at him, my lord was leaning forward reliving the battle again. His hand traced the path of the scar from cheek to chest.

The man leaned back when I stopped after the discovery of Melmintah. "Boy, you have a gift for storytelling. I never thought to like that episode in my life. You have made it live again and," he mused half to himself, "you have made it bearable."

"So, that is how you got the scar." A soft seductive voice came from the curtained couch beside him. The curtains parted and I immediately looked away. The glimpse was all I needed to realize that the woman, surely the lady Dala, was wearing only the most filmy and transparent of linen. I was still very uncomfortable with the fact that highborn or slave, men and women in Egypt wore scant clothing. Even the rough linen of the slaves was thin and revealed more than it concealed. The memory of my first sight of a noble Egyptian lady in Succoth still had the power to embarrass me. Borz had laughed at my open mouthed amazement and told me that the thinner the linen, the richer the wearer.

I now looked helplessly toward Phu and Clep, who both stood with heads bowed and eyes downcast. Slaves were forbidden to look directly at a noble woman.

"My lord, we will leave you now," Clep spoke in a low tone.

Before he could answer, the lady spoke. "Nonsense, I want to see the lad who is the talk of the house. A bearded, robed, wild desert dweller is what I expected." There was a slither of her garments against the bed and curtains and she slipped to the floor. "But what I find is ..." her hand unexpectedly came under my chin. With surprising strength, she lifted my head. I forced my eyes to stay closed, knowing that to look at my lord Potiphar's wife would mean a beating or worse. "I find a lad quite like all the others in Egypt. Perhaps the hair is a bit thicker and more wavy and his skin is a shade lighter." Her hands ran through my hair and over my face. One finger trailed down my bare chest, sending chills and heat through my body. The woman laughed, soft and silky, then stretched over my seated figure to Potiphar. "But in you my lord, I see strength and power."

Her filmy gown and heavy perfume in my face were stifling. I had to escape somehow. By moving to the right, I slide away from her body. Carefully keeping my body bent at the waist and hands extended forward beside my lowered head, I backed across the room until I felt the door at my back.

Clep repeated, "We will leave now, my lord." Together we retreated into the hall.

I discovered that my hands were shaking and I felt ill.

"You handled that well, Hebiru." Clep patted my shoulder.

Phu took my arm. "Come outside, you look pale."

Realizing that night air was indeed what I needed, I fled down the two flights of stairs and out the door. Beginning to run, I did not stop until I plunged into the Nile water itself. I had to wash off the scent and feel of the woman.

"Stay out of her way." Phu's words rang in my head. I did not need the warning. All my senses told me that she was danger.

Chapter 4

I barely slept that night. Equal parts of fear and revulsion kept me awake, staring into the blackness. The memory of the stable boy who had been executed and the government official buried in jail were not comforting. If Potiphar had dealt so with men the lady Dala was only suspected of seeing, how would he view her blatant seduction attempt in front of him? But as much as I feared Potiphar's wrath, the lady's tactics repulsed me. She had a strong and honorable man who loved her, but she seemed bent on destroying him.

Daylight came, just as I slipped into a dream where hundreds of Egyptian women, all looking like the lady Dala, pursued me down the riverbank toward a gapping pit. I awoke just before I pitched headlong into the pit. My morning prayers were confused and desperate. "May the God of my Fathers and the gods of Egypt protect me from the wrath of Potiphar."

Phu looked at me with sympathy, noting my lack of sleep.

"Hebiru, my lord Potiphar is a just man. He will not hold you responsible for what you took no part in," he murmured in an attempt to be heartening.

Clep entered the kitchen and immediately strode to me. "When you have bathed and changed you are to see my lord Potiphar," he ordered, his words giving no hint of the reason.

Seeing my fear, he continued more gently, "My lord is pleased with what you wrote and would like to hear more, I believe. Anything else is best not talked about." With these words he gave encouragement and warning.

Feeling somewhat like a prisoner hoping for a reprieve, I rapidly bathed and shaved. Then summoning all my courage, I walked past the murals and pillars, down the hall to my lord's private chambers. Without Clep to announce me, I was unsure how to proceed. I knocked on the heavy wood door. The sound echoed in the empty hallway. Potiphar's booming voice bade me enter. Taking a deep breath, I opened the door and stepped into the room, stopping to bow to the floor. Nukor stood next to my lord Potiphar. Both men held a sword. It was not a comforting sight until I realized that they had been practicing swordplay. I almost laughed in relief and had to bow my head to hide the smile.

"Come, boy, what is it they call you?"

"Hebiru," Nukor supplied when I did not respond.

"Of course, Hebiru, come here. You have done a magnificent job on my memoir. I read more last night and I am quite pleased. Have you ever learned to fight?"

His sudden change of tact caught me by surprise so that I was only able to shake my head and stammer, "No, my lord."

"Here, let's see if you have any skill in that area." He tossed a short, curved sword to me. I caught it clumsily, barely escaping cutting myself.

Potiphar sat down and Nukor stepped forward. The black man had never seemed so tall before. The thought crossed my mind that this might be Potiphar's way of killing me. But I discarded the idea as uncharacteristic of my lord.

Nukor took a stance and invited, "Do you have any skill? Try to cut me."

Recklessly, I charged forward, slashing wildly. Nukor easily deflected every move and then with a flick sent the sword tumbling out of my hand.

Potiphar laughed, "The lad has spirit, if not much skill."

Nukor nodded as he retrieved the sword. "I could make him into a soldier. With his energy, the boy could be devastating in battle once he learned how to land the blows."

I stood panting, listening again to my life being discussed as though I was not present.

"However," Potiphar looked at me finally, "I did not pay good money for a soldier but for a scribe. Hebiru, I want you to come here each morning at this time. Nukor will teach you enough skill to defend yourself and me when we travel. For you will be going with me to keep accounts and record conversations."

The remainder of the morning was spent in drill with Nukor under Potiphar's critical eye. The sun was high before my lord called a halt. "That will do for today. Tomorrow we will work more. Take these scrolls to the library and send Clep to me."

I re-rolled the open scroll and wrapped it in the linen covering. Then, bowing I left the room. My ears caught a final comment from Nukor.

"My lord Potiphar, the lad is a fast learner and within a week should be ..." The rest of the sentence was lost as the door closed.

When Clep returned from my lord's chamber, he informed me that my afternoons would be spent learning the details of keeping the master's accounts. There were many and I had to memorize certain amounts and codes.

"These can never be written down." Clep stressed daily as we reviewed the information.

My days settled into a new routine. Mornings were spent with Nukor and my lord Potiphar learning fighting skills. Each afternoon I poured over numbers and details with Clep. I wrote long reports for my lord Potiphar to send to Pharaoh. Time flowed past me like the Nile flowed past the monuments and towns in Egypt. Each day I became less

Hebrew and more like the people around me. One day I stopped to think about who I was.

"Where is Joseph?" I wondered as I took a break from the records and reports I was transcribing from my notes. My lord Potiphar and I had just returned from a tour of all the army posts in Upper and to the very lowest of Lower Egypt. Most of the guard posts were North of us in the Delta to defend the access into the country. A few were scattered along the Nile to protect the towns and temples that lined the river. In the far South, Nukor and Potiphar showed me the battleground where they met. Now all the information had to be compiled and forwarded to Pharaoh.

I stood looking out the window into the private garden of the estate as I thought about who I had become.

"Joseph bar Jacob," I repeated the name to myself. It felt strange and the person who wore that name proudly no longer existed. In his place was a young man, not really a slave, but not free. No longer the proud, arrogant younger brother but rather a humble scribe and assistant to a powerful official in Egypt.

"How long have I been in my lord Potiphar's service?" I thought back and realized that nearly five years had passed. My lord had promoted me to his chief aide, just below Clep, only a year after I came into his service. I remembered the day it happened. It was the first time Potiphar had been summoned to report to Pharaoh since I came into his service. Clep came to me as I bathed.

"Hurry, my lord Potiphar has had a message from the mighty Pharaoh. You will be leaving this afternoon."

I hurried to his chambers and found Nukor and Phu directing the packing of suitable ceremonial garb.

"There you are. You will be attending me on this trip to report to Pharaoh." The man's booming voice greeted me. "I

will need the scrolls you just completed about the army
numbers and equipment."

"Yes, my lord." I was thankful that I had completed a clean
copy the evening before.

"Come here. As my scribe, you will need to be more
suitably garbed. Clep, where is the man? Clep!" impatiently
my master looked around the room.

"Yes, my lord," the steward seemed to materialize in front
of us.

"Have you brought it?"

"Yes, my lord." Clep held out the tunic and the collar made
of leather and beads. I recognized the symbol of Ra and
remembered that my lord Potiphar was allowed to use the
symbol because of his victory at the cataracts.

"This will identify you as my special deputy," the master
explained, fastening the collar around my neck. My mind
tumbled back to just a year before when my father had given
me the rich coat. The memory of the dreams carried in that
gift made me forget where I was. Lost in thought, I stood
silent for a long moment, until Clep nudged me.

Recalled to the present and seeing gathering displeasure in
his face, I prostrated myself at my lord Potiphar's feet.

"My lord, you do me too great an honor. I will humbly
strive to serve you and be worthy of this trust."

Standing in the library, I now fingered the collar. "It is both
a symbol of the regard of my lord Potiphar and the insignia
of my slavery," I thought. "Joseph, son of Jacob, the Hebrew
of Canaan, no longer exists. Who have I become? I have
become not a Hebrew and yet not an Egyptian. The dreamer
is gone and is replaced by the man who mindlessly obeys and
follows his master. The God of my Fathers no longer sends
me dreams, for they would be of no use. Gone are the plans
of my youth. How being sold into slavery could be part of
God's design I cannot understand. Once I thought that

perhaps the God of my Fathers had a plan for my life. Now I see the future stretching out in service to Potiphar. My father and brothers believe me dead. Truly, I am as one dead, for all I believed in has deserted me. How different my life is from my dreams and my father's plans. He planned marriage to a girl from my mother's kin in Haran, then a government post in Ur. How well our plans had fit together. But, all the planning went for naught because of the jealousy of my brothers. Here I live miles away from my home and months travel away from Ur."

Standing in the library, I remembered what Phu had said before that first trip with my lord Potiphar. "The gods are smiling on you. You may think slavery is an awful way of life; but in this house you are to be more than a slave."

Now, staring unseeing out the window, I tried to recall the tents of my father. Tears came to my eyes when I could barely recall the shadowy outlines. "Joseph is no more." The thought gave me pain. "The man called Hebiru, slave scribe, assistant to my lord Potiphar, Captain General of Egypt, is who I have become."

I heard the door open and swung around, embarrassed at being caught daydreaming. My first thought was fear that it would be the lady Dala. Only rarely did I see her; but, now that I had free use of the house, sometimes I thought I felt someone watching me. It was not long after my lord Potiphar and I returned from that first visit to Pharaoh that I turned around suddenly and saw the flutter of a linen gown disappearing around the corner. "The lady Dala," I thought. I realized it was more likely one of her ladies sent to watch my movements. The idea did not give me much comfort. Who could I ask for counsel?

That evening I sought Phu. We had not spent much time together since the memoirs were completed. His obvious joy at seeing me caused me a twinge of regret. "My lord Potiphar has been keeping you busy, lad. It is as I said. He has great plans for you."

I sat down with a smile. "I guess you were right." Now that I was with him, I didn't know how to broach the subject to my friend.

"Is something troubling you?" With the experienced eye of a lifelong listener, Phu sensed I had not sought his company for a simple visit.

Even though we were outside, I glanced around. There were bushes and a low wall nearby that might have ears. "Can we walk toward the river?" I suggested.

Phu rose. "If you don't mind the slow pace of my old bones. Some days they feel quite stiff."

When we reached the beach, I spoke of my concerns. "I think the lady Dala is spying on me."

When Phu didn't seem surprised, I continued. "I've felt eyes watching me all week, and today I caught the glimpse of a gown retreating around a corner."

"It would not be the lady herself."

"No," I agreed, "but one of her ladies could be watching me on her orders."

Phu nodded. "She is not likely to let you out of her sight. You are not only a favorite with my lord Potiphar but I fear the lady has her eye on you too."

"I have no interest in her," I protested. "I would not treat my lord Potiphar in that manner."

"Lad, Hebiru, I am fond of you and would die for my lord. For both your sakes, keep out of her way. Stay with others as much as possible. When you are alone, don't do the same routine, or she may find a time to waylay you. Above all, give my lord Potiphar no cause for concern."

"Thank you, my friend, I knew you would have good advice."

And I had been very careful in the ensuing months to avoid being anywhere near the women's quarters or present when the lady Dala was with my lord. I was grateful that we had spent so much time away from the house on my lord Potiphar's official business. However, she had found ways to pursue me, trying to tempt me with her charms.

This time it was not the lady, but Phu himself. It was as though my thoughts conjured him up. "Here you are, lad. My lord Potiphar is waiting for you. He has received an order to attend Pharaoh. There is to be a meeting with ambassadors from many countries around the Great Sea. My lord bids you bring the scrolls you have completed for him – the plans for the estate." Phu's eyes met mine with a question.

Neither of us understood why my master had me working on a document and drawings to present to Pharaoh about work on the house and fields. My lord Potiphar had said we would be going to Memphis where my skill would be tested in a meeting with the Great King of Upper and Lower Egypt, the Morning and Evening Star, the god Ra personified, Pharaoh himself.

"Yes, I was just getting the scrolls." Adding one more to the pile, I reached for the bag to put them in.

Phu handed me the linen wrapping and then helped me put the papyrus in the leather bag to keep the writing safe. Few things were more important than the written word in Egypt. A scribe had a special obligation to make sure each hieroglyph was perfect and understandable for the word became the essence of the idea. The worst punishment possible was to have your name erased from all documents and buildings. I had learned that the name of the government official found with the lady Dala had been removed from all government records. Phu explained that this meant that when he died, his *ka* would be lost with no name to rest on.

Together we walked from the library up the stairs to my lord's chambers. Just before we reached the rooms, Phu came close to me with a low warning. "The lady Dala will be accompanying my lord Potiphar to see Pharaoh."

I felt a chill that had nothing to do with the cooler air in the hall. Resolving to stay as much out of her way as possible, I hurried to attend my lord Potiphar.

Chapter 5

The entire house was a hive of activity centering around my lord's chambers. I was used to this now having accompanied my lord Potiphar several times. Slaves hurried to and fro packing the chests. Nukor was giving the armor a last polish so that the leather and bronze gleamed. Melmintah was present. Potiphar was giving him instructions regarding information he wanted about the others at the meeting.

I immediately went to the table and began rolling and wrapping the scrolls we had worked on in his chambers. The oiled leather would keep them dry even on board the barge. In the bustle, I had not noticed the lady Dala until I smelled her perfume and felt her leaning against my back. Her hand covered mine on the scroll.

"I feel so useless. My ladies urged me to leave so they can get my things together. So I came here, but there is even less for me to do. Let me help with these." Her silky voice held a note of petulance.

"My lady, I do thank you," I responded, moving away from her and gathering the last scroll into the goatskin bag. "But I have just finished. I must see what my lord Potiphar has need of."

Her hand tightened on my arm. "Look at me, slave. I have needs, too, and you will be able to fill them all." The voice softened at the end as her hand moved up my arm and across my back. From the corner of my eye, I saw her slowly moisten her red lips.

Bowing, I moved away from her without looking at her.
"My lord has need of these."

I saw her gold sandal-clad foot tapping with impatience as I
crossed the room to my lord Potiphar.

"So, the scrolls are ready." It was a statement, not a
question.

"Yes, my lord Potiphar."

"Good, they are in your charge until I need them." He
turned to other matters and I turned to help Nukor. My
lord's authoritative voice called me back.

"Hebiru, you will sit at my right hand during the council.
All men will know that you are highly favored in my sight. All
my household slaves are yours to command for you have
proven yourself worthy in small tasks and will be faithful in
great things." In his hand was a new scribe collar with onyx
and turquoise stones. He removed the old collar and replaced
it with the new gift.

"My lord Potiphar, I am unworthy." Truly overwhelmed, I
fell at his feet. To sit at his right hand meant he was publicly
proclaiming his patronage. He was elevating me from slave to
associate. Before he could reply, I felt the brush of linen as
my lady stepped over me. She remained standing with one
foot on each side of my body.

"And my lord, if he, this slave you have made your deputy,
is seated at your right, where do I sit?"

"My dove, my love, the council is no place for a woman."

"But I am Pharaoh's niece." She tilted her head with a
smile just for him.

"Truly, you would be bored." I heard the weakening in his
voice as my lord Potiphar tried to think of a reason to keep
the lady from attending the council meeting.

She heard it too. "Then I may attend!" The woman clapped
her hands like a girl.

Her husband sighed and like an indulgent father agreed, "Yes, my dearest, my lady Dala, my wife, you may attend. But, don't blame me if you are bored."

"Then I shall leave. I will now go to be sure my ladies are ready."

As I heard her footsteps receding, the blood stopped pounding in my head from her heavy perfume. Rising to my knees, I saw Potiphar watching the lady leave the room. His adoration of her shone from his eyes. Then he looked at me. "Hebiru, we have much to do. We will talk more on the journey of your duties."

Accepting the dismissal, I gathered the scrolls. With a bow to my lord, I turned to secure them into a special trunk. Nukor accompanied me to the wagon. He stowed away the armor as I set in the box with the scrolls. His silent sympathy meant more than words. Clep, Phu, and Nukor knew how many times I had made excuses to avoid being in the lady Dala's presence over the last five years. I was afraid that she would try to get me alone during this visit to Pharaoh's palace and resolved to be vigilant.

Before Ra reached the top of the heavens, we were on our way south. My lady Dala and my lord Potiphar were each carried in a litter borne by four slaves. A wagon filled with cushions held the lady's women and her chests. The wagon of equipment and supplies followed, driven by Nukor and surrounded by selected household guards. Lastly, came the slaves and servants necessary for the comfort of the travelers. I assumed I would walk with them, but Nukor invited me to sit with him.

After a few minutes of silence, Nukor nodded to the collar that I was fingering. "Quite a promotion, Hebiru. Although I thought for a minute you were going to refuse."

I looked up to see his teeth gleaming in a smile.

"To tell the truth, I was stunned into immobility. I never expected such an honor – to set me apart like this. It is a bit," I searched for the right word, "uh, extraordinary."

"You'd be wise to keep in mind that honors can be removed."

"Yes," I agreed, "I well know how fortune can reverse when least expected."

We were each silent. I remembered my brothers who beat and sold me into slavery. Nukor, I suppose, remembered a vicious battle when he went from prince to slave. "Our stories are similar," I remarked. "Both of us were princes in our homeland. Now we both serve my lord Potiphar."

"A good master." Nukor stated, looking ahead to where the litter was. "A great warrior and a good master."

With a nod I agreed, "A wise man and a good master."

A short time later we were at the dock. A large boat that seemed of reeds and pitch awaited our arrival. Although I had taken several trips up and down the Nile with Potiphar, I was still amazed by the reed construction. During my first boat trip, with Borz from the Delta to On, I had been too angry and frightened to observe how the vessel was built and moved. My travels with the Captain General taught me to trust the seemingly impossible buoyancy of the river craft. The captain greeted to my lord Potiphar with a bow and soon the wagons were being unloaded onto the deck. Slaves and sailors rushed back and forth with piles of items. It took the rest of the day to load the luggage and supplies onto the boat. In the morning we would float the short distance up the Nile to the capital of Memphis. Camp was made near the river. The ladies were to sleep on board. Potiphar declared he would like to sleep under the stars as he had as a soldier.

"It is good to sleep under the stars again," he told Nukor when he joined us. "I do miss that about not being on campaign. Do you, Nukor?"

The big Nubian replied, "My lord, sometimes I take my bed outside even in your comfortable home."

"Good idea!" Potiphar's booming laugh carried far. "And you, Hebiru, you had been used to living in tents. Do you miss the sky and the open air?"

"Sometimes, my lord Potiphar, I do long to see the desert sky and stars and the silhouettes of the mountains on the horizon in the moonlight. To hear the sheep and ..." I stopped and laughed at myself. "I sound like a girl sighing for a lover."

"We are men of the outdoors," Potiphar proclaimed. "I feel more alive than I have in many a month. But, tomorrow we will be in the capital. There, Hebiru, you will see sights to make you forget your distant tents and mountains."

Morning came too soon. And after a delay, while my lady Dala sent her ladies in many directions searching for a scarf that was found to be already in the litter, we were on our way.

"Hebiru, come sit beside me," my master ordered as the boat poled into the current. I turned from watching in amazement as with oars, poles, and sail the vessel moved across the water. "We have certain things to discuss."

I hurried to crouch at my lord's feet.

"Boy, the morning sun is in my eyes," he said petulantly. "Sit between us here so that I am not blinded."

With a bow, I complied, all too aware of my lady's watchful eyes behind the curtain covering the adjacent chair. She stretched her leg gracefully until her toes came in contact with my back. I shivered as she began rubbing them up and down my spine.

After a moment, Potiphar spoke, "I want you to write down all that is said."

"Yes, my lord Potiphar."

"But, I want it to be so others cannot read what is written."

"My lord?" I was confused by the demand.

"Sumerian, write the words using Sumerian glyphs." His face had a shrewd look. He gripped the carved arms of the chair. "Few, if any, present will know how to read that. If there is any question, I will simply say that you are not proficient with the Egyptian." The man settled back into his seat, a satisfied smile on his face.

"Yes, my lord Potiphar." I bowed my head in obedience.

"Also, boy, as my scribe and slave, you will be invisible to many at the meeting." He leaned forward again to look at me. "Use that to my advantage. Melmintah is one set of ears. You will be another. Remember all you hear and I will get a report from you each night."

"Yes, my lord." The intrigue seemed excessive, but I had to admit that I knew nothing of court politics.

More instructions followed, only to be interrupted when the boat made a sudden swerving movement to avoid another barge. The lady gave a contrived scream and tumbled forward from her chair. Instinctively, I caught her and set her on her feet.

"Stop!" Potiphar's command brought the oarsmen to a halt. He was out of his chair in an instant. "My dove, are you hurt? Nukor, have the captain beaten! If not for my good Hebiru here, my lady wife would have suffered a nasty fall!"

The lady Dala continued to cling around my neck as though too weak and frightened to stand. I was pretty certain that she had used the sudden movement in order to draw attention to herself. I tried to remove her hands from my neck and she let them slide down to rest on my chest, just below the scribe collar.

"My lord, I was so frightened." She half turned to my lord Potiphar. "The boat changed course just as I stood up. Then I was falling. Why if this slave had not been here I'd have fallen." Tears gathered in the dark eyes as she looked from me to her husband.

"Yes, my love." To my relief, Potiphar gathered her into his arms. "You should go lie down. The captain will be beaten for causing you to fall."

"I must thank the boy for his aid."

The lady Dala slipped from his arms. She threw her arms around my neck and pressed her lips to mine.

Immediately, I stumbled back, again removing her hands. I bowed low to both the lady and my lord Potiphar.

"It is my honor to serve the lady Dala, wife of my lord Potiphar, in any way I can."

"See, my dearest, all is well. Come to your bed." With a tender kiss, my lord installed the lady in her curtained alcove amid the comfortable pillows.

"Nukor, come walk with me," the man ordered.

The Nubian hastened to join us.

My lord Potiphar strode around the deck.

"The oarsmen will be beaten, my lord," Nukor assured him.

"See to it. My lady Dala could have been hurt. I will not have such treatment of my lady, my wife."

Nukor bowed, with a sideways glance at me. I knew he thought, as I did, that the lady herself caused the commotion. But that would not spare the slaves. The realization that neither Nukor nor myself could save our friends from the whipping post was sobering. It reminded me of the fragility of my position. Potiphar could see no wrong in the lady Dala. Even now he continued.

"Lad, take no thought to my lady's actions. She was overcome with shock and relief. Your actions will be rewarded." He put his hand on my shoulder in a gesture of camaraderie.

"Most gracious lord, I need no reward but to serve you." I kept my head lowered afraid my look might betray the disgust I felt for the lady's actions.

"We will see," was his only reply.

The captain approached with fearful bows. He fawned over my master in an effort to preserve his livelihood and ship. With promises to see that every oarsman was beaten and replaced, he appeased my lord.

There was no time for further conversation, for we had reached Pharaoh's private landing. I was disappointed that we would not get to see the capital itself, but had to content myself with the glimpse of many impressive buildings and streets that could be glimpsed from the river.

We were expected. Litters awaited the lady Dala and her ladies. My lord Potiphar would be marching with the troop as Captain General. Nukor assisted my lord into his ceremonial armor while we docked. He looked impressive. Pharaoh's guard welcomed him with salutes and smart attention.

"Come, Nukor, Hebiru!" He snapped the command as he started to ascend the steps from the landing to the palace.

Nukor and I fell into step at his heels. I know my mouth was agape at the splendor that became more evident with each step. Carved columns, topped with the ever-present lotus emblem were not only painted but also gilded with gold. This towering colonnade presented the life of Pharaoh in his god state. For Pharaoh, I knew from what Nukor had told me, was not only king but also the incarnation of Horus, the son of sun god Ra and upon death became Ra himself. On Pharaoh the whole life of Egypt depended. His morning ablutions were necessary to start the cycle of the day and his word was more than law, it was a decree from the gods. Everything he said was recorded and carefully preserved.

At the door, a priest bowed low to my lord Potiphar and held out a silver chalice. My lord took the cup and held it. The priest poured a tiny amount of oil onto the wine, and after studying it, declared that the omens were favorable. We were then escorted into the palace by the steward. Guards stood at attention beside each door and slaves moved unobtrusively back and forth. Finally the steward opened a door and bowed to my lord Potiphar. The chamberlain inside the massive room clicked his staff on the floor and announced,

"The lord Potiphar, Captain General of the Armies of the Nile, Defender and Councilor to Pharaoh, King of the Black Land, Upper and Lower Egypt."

My lord Potiphar entered and made low homage to the King. Following Nukor's lead, I prostrated myself on the floor behind my lord.

From the far end of the room, I heard the voice of an old man. "Come forward, Potiphar, our brave Captain General. It is good to see your face."

My lord stood and moved forward. "I bring you greetings from On, Mighty King. The lady Dala, your niece, will be joining us later." Potiphar bowed again as he came to the throne.

I followed Nukor across the vast chamber feeling overwhelmed by the grandeur and sheer size of the room. Feeling very provincial, I peered around. There were already many people talking in small groups but in the vastness they seemed few. Somewhere I heard musicians. Pharaoh himself was seated on the dais at the east end of the room. On his head was the massive crown of both Upper and Lower Egypt. Behind the throne great gold panels portrayed the conflict between Osiris and his brother Set, god of evil. The journeys of Isis to find her husband's body and the incarnation of Horus were all shown. Naturally, the face of the god was the face of Pharaoh. Even from across the room, I could see the resemblance.

Seated in majesty with the crook and flail crossed in his hands, I could almost believe that this man was a god. On closer view, I saw that Pharaoh was indeed an aged man, not the youth of the murals behind him and on all the pillars and walls. But, he still controlled the destiny of Egypt.

"We see you still have the faithful Nubian by your side." Pharaoh gestured to Nukor as we drew close to my lord Potiphar. "And, who is the slave with the scrolls? It seems you've found some fool from the countryside. Look at the boy, he appears to be totally witless and overwhelmed by our simple council chamber."

Potiphar barely glanced my way. "I bought the boy from Ishmaelite traders. He has some skill as a scribe. He is overcome by your Royal Self, Great One. In Canaan, where he is from, they have no royalty, only sheep."

Once I might have bridled at my family being so discussed and dismissed. But, I had learned better in the past years.

After a brief laugh at my expense, Pharaoh didn't give me another thought. Turning to the priest hovering at his side, he asked. "Who is yet to arrive?"

"Only the delegation from Minoa"

"We will begin to take our places," the King announced. Slaves immediately brought forward seats for everyone and the delegations were seated. Potiphar's place it seemed was just below Pharaoh's throne. I took my place at Potiphar's feet with my scroll ready. Nukor stood behind him.

Expecting the delinquent ambassadors, a bustle at the door caused everyone to turn. But, it was the lady Dala. With barely a bow, she hurried forward to greet Pharaoh.

"My dearest uncle, I have so longed to see you. You don't mind if I sit with your council?" Her painted lips formed a pleading pout.

"Surely such a lovely flower can but add beauty to our gathering."

A toss of her head acknowledged his compliment. "And can I sit here near you? Potiphar, the old spoilsport, said I

would be bored. But next to your Greatness, my King, that
could not be."

The old king smiled, pleased with her attitude. "Sit here
then, by our Captain General."

A chair was brought, and before I had a chance to move,
the lady had seated herself and was resting her slender foot
on my leg.

The meeting began and I had to concentrate in order to
make sense of the many voices all discussing the proposed
alliance of power. I was only vaguely aware of the fact that
the lady Dala persisted in running her foot up and down my
leg and playing with my hair. When Pharaoh called the
meeting to a close, my lord Potiphar ordered me to bring the
scrolls and follow him.

We were escorted to a private audience chamber where
Pharaoh waited. Without the crown and ceremonial robes,
the man looked even more old and frail. A slave was rubbing
salve into the king's neck.

"These ceremonial crowns and jewels are too heavy and
awkward," he commented. My lord agreed as Nukor removed
the helmet and breastplate.

"Unroll the scrolls we brought, Hebiru." Potiphar
commanded. After I did so, Pharaoh and my master bent
over them. Nukor and I withdrew to the side of the room.
My head ached from the noise of the council and my hand
was weary from the rapid writing I had been doing. I envied
Nukor, who only had to stand ready behind my lord. He
could ignore the buzz of words and didn't have to get every
word written down.

All too soon, it was time to follow my lord Potiphar to his
chambers and then to the banquet. The rich food and the
elaborate entertainment made me forget my weariness. Even
Nukor admitted he had never seen a peacock cooked with all
its feathers. It was the dancers and acrobats that shocked me.

I still felt uncomfortable with the scantiness of most Egyptian dress but the entertainers wore nothing more than jeweled belts and bracelets. The scarves and ribbons they used while performing did nothing to conceal their bodies. My desert sensibilities were, I had to admit, offended and excited at the same time.

The lady Dala was in her element. As the loveliest of the few ladies present and as niece of Pharaoh, she received plenty of attention. Many men looked longingly at her and she did nothing to discourage them. I wondered how my lord Potiphar could be so wise in diplomacy and yet so blind where his wife was concerned. Her gown covered her body but the diaphanous material left as little to the imagination as did the dancers' lack of clothing.

After the meal, our master signaled for Nukor and me to accompany him to an antechamber. Here Melmintah joined us. He had been busy and had much to report about the plans of the delegations. Pharaoh listened to the report from his Captain General's slave. "So, it is as you predicted, my wise Captain General," he stated. "I fear that we will not reach an agreement. I had so hoped, but the gods do not will it, despite the positive omens."

Nukor and I remained in the room when Pharaoh and Potiphar rejoined the festivities. From the curtained door, we could see the whole room. My eye was caught by the lady Dala. She was parading on the arm of a young Hittite nobleman. As I watched, she cuddled closer to him and glancing up gave a sultry laugh to something he said.

"Nukor," I said.

"I see." He too was watching. Now she held out her hand to an older man of the Mycenean delegation. "She is pitting them against each other. I have seen it before. Then she will make her choice."

"You mean she will actually encourage them in the royal palace, under my lord Potiphar nose?"

"Undoubtedly." Nukor sounded both disgusted and resigned.

Even as we watched, she seemed to take offense at something the Mycenean said and moved off with the young man. I saw them step out the far door that led to the private apartments.

"Is there nothing we can do?"

"We do not dare," Nukor stated the fact. "My lord Potiphar has chosen to see what he wants to see. To bring it to his attention would be imprisonment at least, if not a painful death."

He gave me a moment to digest the information. Eventually, we sought our beds. It seemed only minutes later I was being shaken awake by one of Potiphar's guards.

"Nukor wants you to join him in the bath house."

Blearily, I found the bath. As I opened the door, I paused, hoping this was not a ploy by the lady Dala. Then I saw Nukor. He was almost dressed.

"Hurry, boy, my lord does not like to be kept waiting. You must bathe and shave."

A few minutes later, still feeling only half-awake, I followed Nukor along another maze of hallways to my lord Potiphar's rooms. He asked us what we had heard the previous night. Since I could not tell him about the lady, his wife, I had nothing to report. Nukor had very little to add. Then Potiphar insisted that Nukor put me through the daily training. "It will never do for you to get soft, just because we are not at home."

The lady Dala entered the chambers just as I disarmed Nukor. A feat that made all three of us partners rather than slave and master. Face flushed with victory, I held aloft my sword. Both Nukor and my lord were congratulating me.

Facing the door, I caught her look of sheer lust as she ran her eyes greedily over my sweat-covered body.

"Why, what sort of victory have I interrupted?" she inquired coming forward to run her hand down my now lowered arm to the hand that held the sword.

"Lady," I said, backing away to bow to her. Nukor also bowed and followed me to retrieve his sword.

My lord exuberantly picked her up to swing her in the air.

"My dove, the shepherd boy has learned to disarm the warrior!"

"How interesting," she remarked, seductively running her hand down her body on the pretext of smoothing her gown. I carefully kept my eyes averted, busying myself with putting away the swords and other training equipment.

"My lord, I will not be attending the council today. My ladies and I wish to visit the markets while we are in the capital."

Potiphar kissed her on the forehead. "Of course, that would be more interesting. I know you will find some wonderful bargain to surprise me with."

"You are so understanding, my husband." She turned to leave. Suddenly, she swung back into the room and to my side. Raising on tiptoe, she pressed against me and caressed one cheek while kissing the other.

"Congratulations, slave boy," she murmured. Then she was gone, leaving me feeling soiled by her touch. I plunged my hands and head into the water basin, washing off not only the sweat but also her touch.

"My boy, what a magnificent move." My lord Potiphar was still gloating over my success.

"Yes, my lord," I responded in a subdued voice, unable to believe that my master saw nothing odd in the lady Dala's actions.

"Come, we must prepare for the council," he instructed.

The day was a repeat of the previous meeting with each delegation attempting to obtain an advantage. The lady Dala again joined the group for the banquet but she disappeared while my lord was meeting with Melmintah and Nukor.

The final day of the council also adjourned with no progress made toward an alliance. Pharaoh was saddened and I heard him tell my lord Potiphar, "I had hoped that I could leave a secure confederation for my son. Egypt has been too long isolated; it is time she looked beyond her borders. Other countries have much to offer us. Look at how the introduction of the horse and chariot has improved our fighting skills. You, my Captain General were the first to see the advantage."

"Great King, you have much time left to reconvene many councils," Potiphar said.

"Faithful friend, the gods have shown me that I will soon join them." The old man raised his hand to forestall further argument. "No, this was my final attempt at forming a coalition with the nations around the Great Sea. I will let you now attend to your duties as my Captain General."

Accepting the dismissal, my lord Potiphar bowed and left Pharaoh staring across the throne room.

Chapter 6

In his room, my lord Potiphar sat down heavily. "Pharaoh had such hopes for this alliance. Would that the gods wanted it to happen."

He sat in silence staring into space. Finally, he looked at me.

"My boy, you have been a good and faithful scribe and an invaluable asset during this meeting. Nukor must attend me as I review the troops around Egypt. My lady Dala will not want to tarry in the capital now that the meeting is done. Pharaoh keeps a quiet court for the most part. I am placing my lady wife under your care to bring her safely home. This is a charge I do not give lightly. Were Clep here, I would send him and keep you to assist me. I will indeed miss your help, but my lady's comfort and safety are more important."

"My lord, I am not … I dare not …please, my lord Potiphar … I cannot." I fell at his feet imploring my lord to release me from this task.

"Do not be so modest, Hebiru." He misunderstood my hesitation. "I would not send you if I did not trust you fully. I know that you will bring my lady …"

The lady Dala herself interrupted him. " 'Bring my lady' where? Were you talking about me? Can you believe that all the emissaries are preparing to leave? I cannot stay here. You know how dull my uncle's court is when there is no council in session." Fretfully, she flounced on the bed.

"Yes, my love, I have thought of that." My lord Potiphar sat next to her and patted her hand. "As soon as the road is passable from today's rain, you will return home."

Partially mollified, she gave a half smile. "And will you be taking me, my lord?"

"No, dearest one, I am sorry. Your uncle, the King, has certain commissions for me to complete as Captain General."

"Then I am to travel unattended?" she tossed her head at the thought.

"You know I would not allow that, my dove."

"Well, then …" She raised her eyebrow in question. "I will not travel with some squad of soldiers."

Potiphar knelt beside her and took her hand to plead my case.

"You may think him too young, but the man I have chosen to accompany you has shown himself faithful. And, he has some skill in arms. Of course, you will have soldiers also for protection."

"Who?" Then even as my master spoke my name, her eyes flew to me.

"Hebiru, my young scribe, will take you safely home. I have no qualms about his abilities."

"Nor have I," her voice purred as she looked me up and down, as though sizing up where to start on a tasty meal.

"My lord," I made a final attempt to forestall what could only lead to disaster. "Please, I do not know the way."

"That is not a problem, faithful scribe, I will be happy to direct your path." The look in her eyes and the slow circling of her lips with her tongue was enough to send a shiver of fear and revulsion up my spine.

"Then it is settled." Potiphar rose. "If the road is dry enough and the river calm, you will leave tomorrow. It would be best if you got a good rest."

"Yes, I wouldn't want Faithful Scribe to be to tired to perform." The voice held a laugh as though she knew my fear and held it in contempt.

"Nukor, go with the boy and see that he is prepared for the journey. Then report to me in the morning."

"Very good, my lord Potiphar." The Nubian replied. We bowed ourselves from the room.

The door barely closed before I grabbed his arm. "Nukor, my friend, what am I to do? You saw and heard ..."

He put a finger to his lips. In silence we walked down the hallway and outside. The rain had stopped but clouds still hovered over the desert muting all the colors on the walls of palace and temple. Well away from the buildings, he turned to me.

"Hebiru, lad, I'm afraid I have no advice for you. The lady is not used to being refused."

I sat down on a bench and put my head in my hands. "God of my Fathers, what have I done? What can I do? My master is a good man. I do not want to shame him. God hear me."

Nukor's hand came down on my shoulder. "Perhaps the gods will help you. It is all that is left to you."

Soberly, we went about completing preparations for the journey. The clouds dispersed by the time we had finished preparing the chests that would be returned to the estate. Bright stars foretold a clear morrow. I slept very little, my mind raced in circles as I tried to figure out how to avoid the lady Dala's tactics.

The morning dawned bright and golden but my heart was too heavy with fear to enjoy the sunlight. My feet dragged as I accompanied my master and lady to the portico where the bearers waited to take the ladies to the boat. I still hoped for some way to avoid attending the lady Dala to the estate.

My lord Potiphar himself lifted the lady into her litter.

"You have my best bearers," he told her. "A strong corps of guards will accompany you and your ladies. All decisions are to be left to my faithful scribe, Hebiru." He gave me a slap on the back.

"You will stay next to my lady. See that she has every comfort."

"Yes, my lord Potiphar." I bowed low and knelt before him. "My lord, believe me, I am unworthy of this honor, but I will do my best to carry out your wishes."

"I have no doubt of that. Get up and be off before the sun is any higher."

My lord gave the lady Dala a final kiss and carefully closed the curtains.

"The lad will see that you have a comfortable trip, my dear. I will be with you before many days pass."

At a salute from Potiphar, the bearers started out. I saw Nukor raise his hand in farewell and waved to him. The boat was waiting and my lady was settled on board with no mishap. Smoothly, the oars carried us across the Nile to the eastern shore. After disembarking, I oversaw the loading of the wagons and then turned to the lady.

"Your litter awaits." I bowed to avoid looking at her.

"Lift me into my litter," she ordered. I desperately wished that she were talking to someone else. But she was standing in front of me, waiting for my assistance.

"Yes, my lady," I swiftly swung her into the litter and stepped back with a respectful bow.

"You will walk next to me, as my lord said," she instructed. "You don't know how lonely it is to be shut in here. You will talk to me of your life."

At my nod, the bearers picked up the load and we set out for On and home.

Carefully, keeping more than an arm length from the lady's litter, I walked beside her.

"Tell me where you come from, boy," she demanded.

"The land of Canaan," I replied, hoping that if I kept the answers short she would tire of the game.

"I've heard rumors that you claim to have been a prince there."

"Some would say so." My answer was carefully neutral.

"And would you?" She insisted on probing the wound.

"My father is the wealthiest landowner and shepherd in the area." I couldn't stop the proud tilt of my head remembering Jacob's prestige in the land.

"Yet," she paused as though considering her words, "he leaves his son to rot as a slave."

"He believes me dead," I replied. With difficulty I contained my anger at the memories her insinuations brought up.

"Really?" The doubt in the one word had the desired effect. The words spilled out.

"My brothers were jealous and hated me because I was our father's favorite. He gave me a tutor that they didn't have. He bought me a splendid coat and I was to travel to my mother's family in Haran for a wife. Instead, ten of my brothers planned to leave me to die in a dry well. Only the passing of the caravan of traders changed their plan. I was sold into slavery for gain."

Pausing for breath, I cursed myself for allowing her to see my pain. With I bow, I left her, saying, "Pardon, lady, I must see to my duties." I strode back along the line of slowly moving litters and wagons. The high sun told me that it was time to find a resting-place. Ahead was a grove of trees. The bearers were directed to set down their loads in the shade. Slaves began to prepare a meal for the ladies. I stood alone on the bluff overlooking the mighty Nile. The scent of the lady's heavy perfume preceded the touch of her hand on my shoulder and chest by only a second.

"Poor, faithful scribe." Her voice and breath were soft and whispered in my ear. "All alone. So much responsibility for one so young."

The lady's caressing fingertips sent conflicting chills and heat through my body. Struggling to retain control of the situation, I removed her exploring hand and turned to face my tormentor.

"My lady, you should be resting." I took a step back.

"Come, then, shepherd prince, take me to my bed." She did not plan to let her prey escape, stepping toward me.

"I could not so treat my lord Potiphar," was my response. It angered her for she drew back.

"Did he not entrust you with my safety and comfort, boy?"

"Yes, my lord Potiphar has given my much honor in escorting his lady wife and love home. He has given me honor in his household above others of my rank. My lord is a wise and noble master who has withheld no honor from his humble slave. The God of my Fathers forbid that I should trespass the trust of my lord Potiphar."

Turning, I summoned one of the guards to fetch one of my lady's attendants.

The lady Dala was not mollified by my words. Lust and rage seethed from her.

"See you don't regret your words," were her parting words to me.

More than ever, I felt soiled and scorched by her words and touch. I wished I could scramble to the river for a cleansing swim, but it was time to set out again. We had not gone far when an ominous crack was heard.

The axle on the wagon had snapped. I sent a slave running to the house, now visible in the shimmering heat. Scanning the surroundings, I could see no shady place to provide comfort for my lady and her attendants. All around were the flat fields of grain belonging to the estate.

"Put up awnings, here, in the shade of the wagons." I instructed. "That will give the ladies some shade."

The lady Dala strolled over to me as I helped erect the tent.

"Faithful scribe, helping his fellow slaves while I suffer in this heat." Languidly, she flipped her feather fan, sending a wave of perfume in my direction.

"We will soon have a shelter for you and your attendants." I told her pulling hard and anchoring a rope.

Her well-known pout appeared. "But I want to be resting in my room."

"Yes, my lady, I have sent a runner for another wagon. Clep will be here to help us in just a short time."

"I don't want to wait!" As though suddenly thinking of a marvelous plan, she smiled happily. The lady looped her arm in mine, pulling me away from the task.

"I have it! You can accompany my litter to the house. My ladies can wait here in the shade you have so thoughtfully provided." The idea sent a chill of fear and danger racing through my blood.

"Lady, truly, help will be here soon. Clep is no doubt on his way as we speak."

"But don't you see," she wheedled, "he still has to get here and then all the equipment has to be transferred. I can't bear to get home after dark." Pulling herself close to me she reminded me. "Potiphar entrusted you with my safety and happiness. This would make me happy and I would tell my husband of your kindness."

In a quandary, my mind searched for some way to postpone the lady.

"Your safety, too, my lady. My lord Potiphar entrusted me with your safety. The guards have to stay here with the wagons. You will have no protection."

Her soft, scornful laugh was my answer. "Surely, the training that Nukor has given you has prepared you to protect me for a few miles. After all, did you not just learn to disarm that great warrior? I have no fear with you as my only guard." A gentle hand caressed my arm muscles.

"As you wish." My bow was an admission of defeat. The lady was set on this plan. "Let me inform the guards of this change of plan."

Bowing again, I moved away to talk to the senior guard. "The lady Dala insists upon proceeding to the house. I must see her safely home. Clep will be here soon. Then proceed with all haste to bring the rest of the ladies and wagons to the house."

The sense of impending doom clutched my heart as I returned to my lady's litter. She stood beside it fanning herself slowly. I made one last effort.

"My lady, would you like one of your ladies to come with you? She could ride with you and be of service when you arrive."

"Silly Boy, it would be too hot and uncomfortable with two in my litter." Her fan flicked my cheek as she laughed at my discomfort.

"Then …" I tried to think of another solution.

"No! Stop dawdling and lift me into the litter. We must be on our way. This heat is terrible." The order was sharp.

I swung her into the seat. Her final words were for my ears only and left my face burning and my heart pounding with fear.

"You will give me all the service I require."

With a salute to the guards, lounging at ease in the makeshift shade, I stepped out beside the litter. We met Clep when we reached the gate to the estate. He had two wagons and a great number of slaves with him.

"The lady Dala did not want to wait in the heat." I explained as we came up beside him. "She insisted that we make all haste so she could rest in her own chambers."

Looking at the number of slaves with Clep, I asked, only half joking, "Is anyone left at the house? Someone will need to attend the lady Dala. As you can see none of her ladies came with us."

His eyes were worried as he replied. "Only the kitchen staff. The rest will be in the fields until dusk. Many hands are needed to bring the river water into the fields."

"Make haste, then, and bring the lady's attendants to her," I urged.

Clep nodded and at his word, the wagons rolled forward. The lady had already started her bearers toward the house. I turned to follow. The closer we got to the house, the greater was my dread. I had not missed Clep's look of warning as he left.

Almost automatically, my lips formed a desperate prayer. "God of my Fathers, God of Abraham, Isaac and Jacob." I repeated the words hoping for some solution to my dilemma. No answer came as we arrived at the house. I slowly approached the litter.

The lady greeted me with her sultry laugh. "I saw you praying as we came along. So, I said a prayer, too. We will see who the gods listen to."

She took my offered hand and daintily slipped out of the litter. The bearers moved away leaving us alone.

"From what Clep said, all the slaves are gone. You will have to assist me." Her smile was meant to be enticing as she ran her hand down my arm.

"Yes, my lady," I barely got the words out past the choking fear in my throat.

"Come, then." Swaying provocatively, she started up the stairs into the house. I followed slowly. The scribe collar placed around my neck by my lord Potiphar felt uncomfortably tight as she led me into the women's part of the house.

"You have never been here before, have you, faithful scribe?"

"No, my lady," my voice echoed hollowly in the empty hall. The place was eerily quiet without the chatter of women and the subdued murmur of slaves at their duties.

The lady stopped before a door, waiting for me to open it. When I did, I realized that this was her private chamber. From the gauzy draperies about the bed to the carved figures of the cat goddess Bast by the door, everything bespoke her presence. The scent of the perfume she used hung over everything even after her absence.

"Come, you will be my maid." In passing, she crooked her finger under my collar, pulling me like a fish into the room. The door slid soundlessly shut and I felt the walls closing in like a jail cell. "Such an innocent." Her eyes were wide as she tilted her head and feigned concern. "Have you ever helped a lady prepare for her bath?"

"No, my lady," my voice came out as a croak. I concentrated on keeping my head bent and eyes on the floor.

"That cannot be helped now. I will not wait for my ladies before bathing the sweat and dust of the road off."

She was very close. I could see the tips of her sandals below the linen gown as I stared at the floor. Her hands took my face and forced my head up until I looked into her eyes.

"Faithful scribe, you tire me with the pretext of disinterest and honor for my husband. He is an old man who doesn't care what I do."

"He loves you." I defended my master against her contempt.

"Oh, he loves the idea that I am young and lovely and *his*, but beyond that," her lips softened and she moved even closer, "he cannot fulfill my needs. You are young and handsome and strong."

Her hands began to play down my chest and I backed up only to come up against the cushions of her bed.

"My lady, this is wrong." My hands closed around hers to prevent their dangerous wandering.

"What is wrong is your refusal to believe me when I say you will serve my needs, slave." The subtle reminder of my position in the household did not ease my fear and disgust.

She slipped her fingers from my grasp. With one hand she loosened the ribbons holding her gown around her neck. I closed my eyes as the light material began to slide smoothly down her skin. But I couldn't stop her pressing her naked body against me. She was forcing me backward onto the bed.

"No, I cannot." Summoning all my strength and a great deal of courage, I grasped her arms and lifted her from me. As I stood, I grasped a sheet from the bed and wrapped it around her shoulders. Even without looking at her, I felt the anger building.

I bowed at her feet. "My lady, forgive me. I cannot go against all that I was taught about loyalty and love." Standing, I turned to leave.

With a hiss, she attacked, "You dare to speak to me of love and loyalty? You, a slave in this house?" Her hand slapped my face so that I stumbled in my retreat. She came after me clawing like a cat. She left a long scratch down one arm as I lifted it to protect my face. Her other hand left a gash in my right side.

As suddenly as the attack started, she stopped, panting, in the middle of the floor. I stood with my hand on the door handle, ready to leave.

"Wait," her voice was tearful and I glanced back. Her next words were a surprise. "Perhaps I presumed too much. No slave has ever refused me before." That pause was my undoing for she crossed the floor between us and jerked

Potiphar's collar from my neck. The force snapped my head against the door.

"And you will regret that you were the first to do so." Her voice was filled with venom. Holding the collar she asked, "Who do you think my loving lord Potiphar, Captain General of Pharaoh's Army, will believe? A slave covered in a woman's scratches or his poor wife who had to defend herself against the assault of that slave. 'Look, my lord,'" she mimicked. "'When I screamed and fought, the man ran, but left this behind as evidence.'"

Her triumphant laugh followed me down the hall. I ran madly and blindly to my room. There I found water to wash the scratches and stop the bleeding, but nothing could conceal them from sight. For the first time in months, I wished I had one of my Canaanite robes.

There was no doubt in my mind who my lord Potiphar would believe. I sat, my head sunk in my hands until Clep came to find me.

"The lady is raising an uproar. She claims you tried to rape her and she was only just able to fight you off."

I looked at him with haggard eyes. "And you believe her?"

"Boy, it looks bad. Just as the lady said, you have the marks of her struggle and she holds the scribe's collar jerked from your neck."

"Yes, jerked from my neck after I refused to lie with her and after she tried to claw my eyes out in her anger," I retorted heatedly.

"So that is the way of it. Hebiru, you know I care for you and will do what I can on your behalf. If you give me your word that you will not run away, I will not have you chained as she demands."

"Where would I go? This land is still strange to me."

"My lord Potiphar will be home in a week. Perhaps by then the lady will have cooled her anger."

"Perhaps," I agreed without a real hope that such a miracle would be possible.

"You cannot stay here with the other slaves, however. There is a room, closet really, where you can sleep. You will have to remain out of sight." My friend was apologetic.

"I understand." Head bowed, I followed him from the room.

Phu was waiting in the hall. "Lad, it looks bad." I saw his eyes scan the scratches. "Where are you taking the boy?"

"The room off the kitchen." Clep shrugged. "There is no other place."

"Put him in my care. We will share the room and I will keep an eye out for him."

Clep looked at me and I nodded in agreement. One place seemed as good as another to await my death.

"He has given his word not to run away, but the company would be good, I'm sure." Clep's eyes were concerned.

So it was that I spent a week sharing Phu's small but airy room in the building next to the slave quarters. In the evenings, he entertained me with stories of my lord Potiphar and his household. I heard about Clep when he was a soldier and how he refused to admit that he was getting a belly when he became steward of the estate. The old man told me stories of his childhood with Potiphar and the early days when my lord was a lonely soldier.

During the day, he kindly left me scrolls from the library and brought me meals at night. I tried to read, but nothing kept my mind from racing in fearful circles. My dreams were no comfort, for in the night wind I heard the mocking voice of the gods of Egypt. The jackal face of Anubis and the crocodile god appeared in my dreams chasing me down an endless river crying 'Are we not stronger than your desert God? Will you not die in the sand of this land? Where are your dreams of power and grandeur now?' The memory of the death of the stable boy and the disappearance of the government official haunted my waking hours. The God of my youth seemed far away and so unreal that my prayers almost stopped.

Finally, one day, Phu told me the news I had been dreading. "My lord Potiphar will arrive tomorrow." His old hand rested on my shoulder in a welcome gesture of sympathy and support.

"Can I walk outside tonight? I would like to see the stars again."

Phu's nod showed he understood and he completed what I left unsaid. "Before it is too late. Perhaps Clep will join us."

He left me alone with my thoughts and my desperate prayer.

"God of my Fathers, for what purpose did you keep me alive in the pit to die a slave, in a land of foreign gods? This is all because of the lies of a woman. Are you not stronger than her gods? You sent me dreams that have come to naught and my father will never know of his son's death. Jacob believed in You. He believed that You gave him the promise of a great nation and that in me it was fulfilled. God of Abraham, Isaac, and Jacob, can he have been so wrong? Do you not care that one who trusted in you is betrayed yet again? God, are you there or is it just the dark desert night that brings mocking promises to my fathers?"

Phu returned with Clep when the moon was high. Together we walked out under the stars toward the river.

"I had come to love this country." I mused aloud. "The river and the people are so different from my own. Still, it is a land and people I could have learned to care about. I thought that perhaps the God of my Fathers sent me here, even as a slave, for some purpose. But that is a desert mirage. My brothers will be the bearers of the promise given to my grandfather and father that the family will become a great nation of blessing to all people. Even though it was their greed and jealousy that brought me here to be abandoned by God and man. Perhaps it is true that the gods of the Nile are greater than the God of my Fathers. Who knows? My fate is in the hands of whatever gods there are and my master who must weigh my loyalty against the words of this wife."

My companions let me talk. The bitter, hopeless words poured out. We turned back toward the house. Even the stars had brought me no comfort, for they only reminded me of the emptiness of the promise to Abraham. Despite the plans and dreams of my father, I would not see the great nation promised to him.

When we reached the house, Clep suggested, "Here is the bath. Shave and bathe, for there may not be time or privacy tomorrow."

Mechanically, I entered the room. I washed, shaved, and trimmed my hair. The week of isolation had given me a good growth of beard. I remembered the first time I had been in the bath and how strange it felt to shave all my skin. Now it felt odd and even unclean to have body hair.

Phu and Clep were waiting and talking in low tones when I emerged. Solemnly, we all went to our beds. Neither Phu nor I slept much. I could hear his fretful sighs even as my thoughts tumbled madly trying to think of what to say to my lord Potiphar.

I heard my lord arrive. The tramping of many feet and his booming voice made the house come alive. How long I would have to wait to be summoned, I had no idea. It was not long.

Nukor appeared at the door of Phu's room. His serious countenance told me that he knew the charge. He entered the room and grasped my hand.

"Hebiru, I have heard the lady Dala's account of what happened. I cannot believe that is the full story."

"It is not." I stated plainly. "I did not attack or attempt to lie with the lady Dala."

"It is not me you must convince, but my lord Potiphar. He has sent me to bring you to him in the great hall. I tell you, as a friend, that this does not look good. My lord is very angry." He finished in an undertone as we walked toward the door.

"I know, thank you for your friendship." I replied, humbled by his continued support.

He bound my hands behind me. We then marched through the house to the same room where I first met my lord Potiphar. Much had changed in me since that day when the angry, shepherd prince became slave to the Captain General of Egypt.

The look of sorrow that was mixed with my lord's anger caused me to prostrate myself at his feet. "My lord," I began.

"Silence!" He roared. "Keep silent, slave, unless I ask you to speak."

My face pressed flat to the floor I cringed as he continued.

"Hebiru, I gave you my trust only to find that you abuse it as soon as you have the opportunity."

I lifted my head, unable to restrain a defense.

"No, my lord."

He bent forward to slap my face and again ordered me to be silent.

"My dove, my lady wife, the lady Dala was in your care. You, I charged with her safety. Yet," here he rose to stride angrily up and down the room, "you are the one who she tells me came to her and attempted to lie with her. Only her screams and fighting deterred you. This she snatched from her attacker in the struggle."

I knew though I did not raise my head, that he held the scribe collar that the lady had ripped from my neck.

"Look at me, boy." My master's rage seemed to ebb slightly. I raised my head to find him seated again, the collar dangling from his hand and looking at me with contempt not unmixed with grief.

"Boy, I held you as almost a son. I gave you honor above your age and station. How is it that you can so betray me?"

"My lord Potiphar, I beg you believe me that I did nothing to bring you dishonor."

"Nothing?" he leaned forward to hold the collar before my eyes. "Then can you explain this?"

A strange calm settled on me as I began to speak.

"My lord, the lady was angered that I was clumsy in assisting her in the absence of her ladies."

"And why were there no ladies?" The man's booming voice was void of emotion.

"My lord, you have been told how the axle cracked on our journey from the capital?"

"So?" The monosyllable didn't give much encouragement, but I plunged on.

"The lady Dala did not want to wait in the heat. I accompanied her to the house to watch for her safety as you, my lord Potiphar, charged me."

"Her safety does not involve her private chambers in this house." The anger was back in his voice and face.

"No, my lord, it is true. I erred in acceding to the lady's request for assistance." I paused and then seeing his impatience I continued. "My lord Potiphar, as I said, the lady became angered at my clumsiness. She was no doubt tired from the journey and my inadequacy was more than she could bear. The lady was forced to strike me and then in frustration she ripped the collar from my throat and ordered me from her sight."

Even to my ears, the half-truth sounded weak. My lord sat, resting his chin on his hand and studying me. I couldn't tell if he believed me or not.

"The lady Dala tells me that you insisted on accompanying her to her chambers. Then you forced yourself on her. It was only by screams and fighting that she was able to stop you."

He suddenly and swiftly, for a man his size, stood and jerked me to my feet. His hand was rough on my bound arm as he turned it to see the scratch, still plainly visible. His eye also noted the mark on my side. I knew he had made his decision when he shoved me down and turned away. It was on my knees that I awaited his verdict.

"Take the slave and put him in bonds. See that he is lashed and his name forgotten by all in this household. Have him committed to Pharaoh's prison until he dies. He no longer has a name in this household. Know that this is how I would reward even one whom I trusted as a son! Truly I am betrayed." He turned his head away from me. It was over. My life was preserved, but to what end? To spend the remainder of my life in Pharaoh's prison seemed worse than death.

Nukor stepped forward and took my arm. In silence, I was marched to the stable. Bound to the whipping post, I waited for the beating to begin, promising myself that I would not be weak. In all the time I had served my lord Potiphar no one had been lashed. I knew this was unusual for some masters used the whip as a regular discipline.

I heard Nukor speak to one of the household guards.

"This slave is to receive the thirty lashes required for attempted rape. My lord says to use the three cord whip."

I had seen the triple whip hanging in the stable. It was a vicious looking thing with three braided and knotted cords rather than a single lash. Bracing myself, I heard the heavy whip sing through the air before it bit into my back. Again and again it came until I was unable to stand and hung against the stake. Finally, the whip ceased but I was left to droop against the ropes holding my hands over my head.

Footsteps receded and I was alone in the empty yard. The sun beat down and the flies circled to settle and sting the gashes on my back. Eventually, the sun set and the evening cool gathered around me. Sometime in the middle of the night, as I hung between pain and sleep, I roused to the smell of the perfume the lady Dala wore. Her hand forced my head up.

"Whose god won? Goodbye, faithful scribe. You could have spared yourself this, but you had to be loyal." Her voice dripped with sarcasm then she was gone. Her mocking laughter rang in my ears for a long time.

Chapter 7

Nukor came for me when the sun lightened the sky in the East. Without a word, he untied me from the post. A wet rope was used to bind my wrists together. It would tighten as it dried and be virtually impossible to untie. He led me out of the yard. A horse waited for him, but I realized that I would be running behind the animal. My lord Potiphar must be in a hurry to be rid of me. It was rare for any Egyptian to use a horse; they were still considered a new and strange thing. My lord Potiphar kept the great stallion in the stable and had a team for the war chariot, but oxen pulled wagons and he rarely rode himself except during wartime.

As I stumbled up the road after the horse, I took one last look toward the house. I was surprised to see my lord Potiphar watching from between the pillars. I never knew what he really believed about his wife and me. He looked old, bowed down, and defeated on that last morning. Even in my own pain, I felt sorrow for the man who had been a good and kind master. Dala had betrayed him even more than she had betrayed me.

In the days, weeks, and months that followed, I had plenty of time to ponder my lord Potiphar's thoughts. Why had he had me imprisoned rather than executed? Could it be that he really knew the lady Dala better than we all thought? What had he meant by the grieved statement that I could have been like a son to him? Did Potiphar really believe his lady wife or me? Was he aware that I spoke lies to shield him from the truth?

My final conversation with Nukor that morning on the road shed little light on the solution to these questions. When we were well out of sight of the house, Nukor reined his horse under a group of palm trees. I was glad for the rest and sank to the ground as soon as we stopped. My beaten back continued to send fiery stabs of pain through my body. Scrapes and bruises on my knees throbbed from the times I had stumbled and fallen along the road. And my arms ached from being pulled ever forward by the horse's motion. I heard Nukor's footsteps but didn't even look up until a cup of water was pressed to my lips. Greedily, I gulped at the water, the taste reminding me that I had been given nothing to drink for a day.

"Slowly," Nukor removed the water. "When you are very thirsty, you must drink slowly."

Then I felt the cool water being poured over the lash marks on my back. Gently, the Nubian washed the blood off.

I broke the silence with one hoarsely croaked word. "Why?"

"After my troops were beaten and I was a captive and slave of my lord Potiphar, he took me into his tent. There, he cleansed my wounds. I was a bitter young man, angry at being defeated. However, his actions showed me the humanity of the man. I promised myself that sometime I would have the chance to pass on the kindness."

"No, why am I alive?" My voice was clearer now as I drank more of the water he held to my lips.

"Hebiru, I do not know. My lord Potiphar was greatly grieved by the lady Dala's story. I know that both Clep and Phu were closely questioned before he sent for you. The bearers, too, and even her ladies had to answer to my lord. I only know what the lady said because she greeted my lord Potiphar at the door with her hysterical tale."

"Does he not see what she is?" I asked the question that nagged at me from the first time I saw the lady.

"Perhaps he chooses not to see. If he sees what she is, he has to take action. As Pharaoh's niece, she could beg royal protection. The whole thing could be very sordid and ugly."

"Also," Nukor continued after a moment. "I think he truly loves the lady. But, when an incident is brought to his attention, my lord must take action. As long as the lady is circumspect, my lord Potiphar can look the other way and pretend he does not see."

Nukor left me to get more water from the canal. It felt good running down my back, cooling and cleansing the lash cuts.

"I will tell you that the lady was not pleased with your sentence. She hates you, lad, and would prefer you dead or in the galleys."

"Why does she hate me so?" I could not understand how a lowly slave like myself could cause such feelings of malice in a highborn lady.

"Are you still so innocent that you don't understand?" Nukor was surprised at my question. "You refused her! The lady has never been turned down before. The fact that you put loyalty to my lord Potiphar over lust put her at a disadvantage. She went to great lengths to get your attention. And even greater lengths to get you alone."

"What do you mean?" My head shot up in surprise.

"The cracked axle. Clep told me that it had been tampered with." The words lay between us. We both understood that I could have been the one to tamper with the wagon. I shook my head, feeling a chill that had nothing to do with the soft breeze from the river.

"Then I fell into her trap." My actions seemed even more foolish.

"It could be." Nukor offered me a chunk of bread. Clumsily, I raised it to my mouth, the ropes reminding me that I was a prisoner on my way to jail with no reprieve in sight.

Nukor stood up. "It is only a couple more miles to the guard post. There I turn you over to Pharaoh's men. They will transport you to the king's prison near Memphis. Few come out of there. But, who knows, your God has preserved your life even now. You may be one that comes out of the jail."

"I thought this was a life sentence." I barely had energy to question anything.

"Unless Pharaoh himself pardons you, it is. Stranger things have happened," he reminded me. "You have led an interesting life – prince made slave turned honored scribe and now prisoner. Who can see what the gods or your God may have in store for you? I have learned to accept the changes that the gods hand out and look for the good. For this life continues after death if your heart is weighed and found pure and light."

With a glance at the sun, Nukor said, "I have to be back tonight, so we must be going. Hebiru, I will hate to turn you over to Pharaoh's guards. Do not become bitter, keep your faith. If Clep or I see an opening we will speak to my lord Potiphar on your behalf."

He helped me to my feet and we embraced as brothers. I saw tears brimming in his eyes and my own were full.

The last couple of miles to the outpost went too swiftly. Refreshed by the water and bread, I was able to walk without stumbling.

Nukor saluted the commander at the post. "This prisoner, one Canaanite slave known as Hebiru, is remanded to your custody for transport to the Pharaoh's prison at Memphis. The crime is attempted rape for which the lashes have been administered. The prisoner will now be placed in custody in the King's jail." Nukor formally read the crime and punishment before handing over the scroll. Each word seemed to pound into my mind like a nail into the prison wall.

"Attempted rape by a slave. He's lucky to be alive." The commander commented.

"My lord Potiphar was inclined to be lenient." Nukor shrugged as though he had no thoughts on the subject.

"So it would seem, but not too lenient." The man caught sight of my back as Nukor handed over the rope.

"Also, Commander, you may find it useful to know that the boy is an accomplished scribe."

"Really," one eyebrow raised in interest, as the soldier looked me up and down. "Perhaps he can be useful before the wagons come through. Reports are not something I enjoy writing."

An order was barked and I was marched away to the locked room in the rear of the building. Despite the fact that the one window was too small for any but a small boy to squeeze through and too high up for that to be a possibility, my hands were left bound and the rope was attached to a post anchored in the wall. With a slap on my beaten back that sent knives of pain, the soldier spoke, "Enjoy your lodgings," followed by a laugh and then the soldier left.

I sat down on the thin mat in the corner. This, I surmised, was my bed. The small amount of light let in by the tiny window vanished too soon, leaving me alone in the dark with my thoughts. Time seemed to roll backward as I remembered the last time I was beaten and put in a dark pit. The beating and betrayal by my brothers had ultimately brought me to this second jail. Once again betrayed and lied about, I sat beaten and alone. The dreams of the youngster were lost in the pain and desolation of the young man sitting in the darkness. Exhaustion finally claimed me and left me with troubled dreams.

My brothers joined with the lady Dala in mocking me. They swirled around me in a mad dance asking, "Whose god won?" "Where are your dreams?" "Who do you think you are?" "Prince?" "Prisoner?" "Refuse me?" "Be greater than us?"

I was glad when the crashing open of the door awakened me. For a moment, I was disoriented. Then the rope on my wrists and the stiffening of the lash wounds reminded me that I was Pharaoh's prisoner from now on.

The soldier held a plate of food with some unappetizing looking mush on it. "Eat up, the Commander wants to see you."

He stood in the door as I ate, watching me struggle to swallow the mess that tasted pretty much like mud. Then he took my rope and led me like a dog to the front of the building. The morning sun made me blink after the darkness in my cell.

The Commander was seated at a table strewn with scrolls. He looked up as the soldier shoved me into the room. I landed on my knees and bit my lip to keep from crying out in pain. "You may go," the officer instructed my guard. With a brief salute, he turned away. "Get up." The words were impatient.

Awkwardly, I levered myself to my feet.

"Nukor, the lord Potiphar's personal guard who brought you here, tells me that you are a scribe. Is that true?"

"Yes, lord Commander," I replied wondering what difference it made.

"Commander will do. I am not of the rank to be called 'lord'." The words were brief and tinged with bitterness.

"Sit here by me and I will tell you what to write. I will see what kind of scribe you are."

Squatting on the floor, I awkwardly took the scroll he handed me. My bound wrists made it difficult for me to get a good grip on the roll of papyrus and I could not imagine how I was expected to write.

"I can read and write myself, so do not try to change what I say," he warned.

"No, Commander." I struggled to figure out a way to hold the scroll open and use the reed. The man finally noticed and shouted for the soldier standing at the door.

"Bring a new binding cord," he ordered. Without even acknowledging the salute, he drew his dagger and cut the rope. I gasped as blood flowed freely into my hands, unhindered by the knots. My wrists were chaffed where the rope had bit into them as it dried and tightened. I massaged them gently and gradually the pain quit throbbing with every heartbeat. The Commander took the new rope that was brought. Instead of binding my wrists, he used it around my elbows and waist, leaving slack so that I had use of my hands, but not enough to allow complete use of my arms.

"Now we will begin." With military precision, he unrolled one of the scrolls on the table. I could see that it was covered with strikethroughs and corrections. "I need a clean copy of this report," he ordered.

"Yes, Commander." I bent to the task. After watching me for a few minutes, the officer appeared satisfied and moved to the door. Restlessly, he returned to take the scroll and compare it to the original.

"Good," was all he said as he handed them back, "finish this one. Then I have several more that need completed before the prison wagons come."

I wanted to ask when that would be. Instead, I dipped the reed and continued the writing. When I completed the first scroll, the commander provided me with another to transcribe. In this way, the day passed. When the light started fading, the commander returned to the room. My guard from the morning was with him. He carried two plates. The one for the officer made my mouth water. It held beef and flat bread and fresh vegetables. The one the soldier slapped in front of me was an improvement over the morning meal. The piece of flat bread was spread with a bean curd mixture that I savored happily. I could have eaten another, but none was available.

"You will finish these tomorrow." The commander gestured vaguely at the table covered with scrolls.

"Yes, Commander." I stood and bowed, aware that I was being dismissed to my cell for the night.

The guard took up the trailing end of the binding rope and bound my hands together roughly. With a jerk, he led me out into the cool night air. Obviously under orders, the man led me in a brief exercise walk to the nearby canal, and without a word, escorted me back to the outpost. The stars were brilliant and the night sounds of the water and evening animals tried to soothe me, but the memory of the dark cell awaiting me kept me from any enjoyment. A shove on my back sent me into the cell and the door clicked shut. I dozed off eventually, despite the renewed pain in the lash marks that the soldier's hand had ripped open. It was hard to find a comfortable place to sleep. I could not lie on my back comfortably and with my elbows pinned to my sides by the rope, any other position was equally awkward.

After a meal of the same plain flat bread I was taken from the cell to the office in the early morning.

The commander was impatient and urged me to work faster. By evening, there was only a couple of scrolls left to rewrite.

"Bring a torch." He ordered. "You must finish these tonight."

My stomach growled in protest and I thought that the rush must mean that the prison wagons would be arriving on the morrow. By the flickering light of the torch, I struggled to decipher the report. My shoulders, head, and hand ached from sitting hunched over the scrolls for hours. The commander refused to allow a rest. If I so much as paused to stretch my neck, his voice, sharp as a whip, cracked across the room.

"Don't waste time."

Every little while, he came to check my progress, sometimes cuffing my head and urging greater effort. Finally, I was done and the man was satisfied. As he shoved me into the darkness of my cell, the commander mentioned, "I shall make a note that you are an amenable prisoner and a passable scribe. Perhaps that will be of some use to you in Pharaoh's jail."

I had barely fallen asleep when a racket of shouting voices and creaking wagon wheels jerked me up. The door entered and the soldier entered to drag me to my feet. I knew it was the prison wagon, but exhaustion, hunger, and pain kept me from feeling dread. Forced into an already crowded wagon, my wrists were tied firmly to the side of the vehicle. I stood next to a short, pugilistic looking man who had obviously been in a recent fight. One eye was swollen shut and he sported several other bruises and cuts on his face, arms, and chest. The look he gave me was anything but welcoming, as he grudgingly moved over when the wagon guard prodded him with a whip handle. A second full wagon stood on the road waiting until the drivers finished talking to the Commander. The guards stood at ease, visiting with the sentries at the outpost. News was eagerly exchanged. The prison wagons traveled up and down Egypt, so their attendants brought news from far away.

The sun rose higher in the sky as they talked in the shade. The prisoners stood in the wagons, bearing the heat of the sun. Each man stared apathetically at nothing, lost in thoughts of the past or dreams of escape. Sweat began trickling down my back, burning into the lash cuts. Finally, with salutes all around, the wagons started on their way. Another outpost was reached in late afternoon and two more men were crammed into the loaded wagon. Camp was made as the sun started to set in the west. Ordinarily, I would have enjoyed watching the colors changing as Ra finished his daily journey. This night, all I wanted was the water the guards were doling out, as the wagons were unloaded. We eagerly waited while the first wagon was emptied of its human cargo. Prisoners were bound together in pairs and given a gourd of water and a piece of the flat bread that seemed to be standard prison food.

I was paired and bound to my wagon neighbor. Stiffly we walked together to receive our meal. Greedily I drank and then ripped into the bread.

"One meal a day," my partner grumbled when the last crumb was gone. "You would think Pharaoh could feed his prisoners more."

"Have you been in jail long?" I ventured to ask.

"They can't keep me locked up." He nodded toward the guards and boastfully stuck out his chest. "That is why I am being moved to Pharaoh's prison. Broke out five times already, I have."

I mumbled some vague response but he continued.

"Your first time, then, experiencing Pharaoh hospitality?" His words held a bitter irony for me. I was indeed going to be experiencing a new part of Pharaoh's hospitality from that which I enjoyed with my lord Potiphar in the palace at Memphis.

I nodded, not wanting to go into any details about myself.

"Noticed your back." His words were a statement of fact as well as a question. "Somebody gave you a good beating."

Not wanting to discuss my crime and punishment, I asked. "And your bruises?"

He was easily diverted back to himself. Proudly he stated, "Took four guards to bring me down and one of them is lamed up pretty well now."

"Silence!" The guard's order was accompanied by a blow to the side of my head with his whip butt. My partner angrily raised his hands to fight but was felled by the same whip expertly wielded under his chin. He wilted without a sound, dragging me to the ground with him. A final kick in my ribs reminded me of my current status as did the words "enjoy your last sight of the stars. Where you are going stars don't shine."

I lay awake with the hard ground gouging my aching back. My mind sought solace in the habit of prayer. "God of my Fathers, where is your plan? God of Abraham, Isaac and Jacob let me know you are there. Who am I? I am no longer Joseph bar Jacob nor even Hebiru, servant to Potiphar. Lord God, if You have abandoned me I am indeed alone." My heart's cry winged into the night but only the blinking stars answered. Their light seemed to mock the promise given to Abraham. If I was the son of the promise as my father always said, why was I abandoned to die in jail in a foreign land? Sleep refused to come as I stared at the stars and appealed to God for an answer that never came.

A gourd of water was given to us as we were herded into the prison wagons. Bound again to the wagon, we set out on the last leg of the journey.

The prison was a huge edifice set back from the road and so distant from the river that it backed against the desert hills of the east. No graceful lotus topped columns, no paintings or engravings of valiant deeds by gods and men broke the façade, only a huge door in the center where the road ended. At the arrival of the wagons, a score of Pharaoh's guards poured out of the door to stand at attention. The Captain Warden of the prison marched out to receive the report and quota of prisoners. One by one we were unloaded and marched through the door. Each name and crime sounded like a knell, read as it was while we walked through the line of guards. I wondered if any of the soldiers stationed at the prison were men I might have met while traveling with my lord Potiphar. I doubted it, remembering that my master mentioned that the prison guards were not part of his jurisdiction.

I heard my name as from a great distance. "Hebiru, slave of Potiphar, Captain General of Pharaoh's Guard, attempted rape."

The blackness of the prison seemed to reach out and drag me in. Rough hands took my arms. My long walk was down stairs and through corridors, past rows of closed doors. I heard an occasional curse, moan or shout; but mostly, the prison was eerily silent. We stopped at last. I felt the cold metal as the guard cut my binding rope from elbows and wrists. Shoved into a dark cell, I fumbled forward until I found the wall and bed mat. Gradually, my eyes adjusted to the darkness and I noticed a water jug in the corner. But, it was empty. Dropping down on the mat, I allowed myself to fall into despair and anger.

Chapter 8

Alone in the dark, I marked the days by the opening of the door to bring the daily ration of food and water. The tiny slit far up in the wall did not allow enough light to let me know the time of day, only that it was light or dark. I spent days angrily cursing my brothers, my lord Potiphar, the lady Dala, even God. Many hours were spent planning horrible retribution on my brothers and Dala. I wept for Jacob and for Potiphar, both betrayed by unfaithful and dishonest family members. In anguish of spirit, I paced the confined space demanding an answer from God. "Lord God of my Fathers – if you exist – how is it that you let me, Joseph, son of Jacob, be brought to this prison? You are the God who spoke face to face with my great-grandfather Abraham and the God who renamed my father Jacob. You called him Israel, the 'one who strives with God', and renewed the promise of greatness to him. I, the son of that promise, the son of the barren Rachel, You have deserted. You leave me here to rot in this dungeon. God, how can You let my brothers prosper in their plans? Perhaps You are no more real than the statues of Ra and Nute and Isis. Or can it be that those same gods are the powerful ones? The lady Dala trusted her gods, and even though I was loyal to my master, I am the one in jail. Why are they – the betrayers and liars – free, while I am shut away from light and family and friends and even You? Why am I of all men most cursed?"

Eventually, my raging subsided to a dull ache of desolation and emptiness of spirit. With nothing else to do, I began to think back over my life and childhood. Vague memories of my grandfather Laban came to me. I remembered the stories my father told of the deals he made with Laban to marry my mother, Rachel. By the time I was born, I had ten older brothers born to Leah and the two slave girls that were also Jacob's wives. My father always called Rachel his first wife and first love. He often referred to the Egyptian concept that the son of the Chief Wife was the heir no matter how many older brothers he had. It was an idea he had heard from his grandfather, Abraham, who learned it when he visited Egypt years before. Because I was, in Jacob's eyes, the heir, I received the privileges due the first-born. I got tutors and learned to read and write. I was the one kept by Father's side and introduced first to visitors. It was not for me the drudgery of tending the flocks from field to field. I was trained to be a prince. To me was given the promise of a trip to Haran for a bride. Sitting in prison, I began to see my brothers' point of view. Not only did Jacob shower me with special favors, but also, I liked to brag about how remarkable I was. In the lonely darkness of the prison cell I remembered the often-forced smiles, for my father's benefit, with which they greeted each new honor. "The next caravan to Haran, I get to go." I bragged one morning just before my seventeenth birthday. "My mother's relatives will help me get established. When all is ready, I'll send for you to visit." My attitude had been condescending to say the least. Then to add insult to injured pride, I shared my dreams. Of course, the wonderful long sleeved, embroidered coat that Jacob presented to me on my birthday was too much to bear. Reflecting back while sitting in the dark cell, I even doubted that my interpretation of the dreams was right. It had seemed so real and sure at the time. The sheaves and stars bowing to me could only mean that I would be powerful, famous, and rich. But, through the lens of the reality of a life sentence in Pharaoh's prison, I could see no way for those long ago dreams to be anything but a mirage. My brothers had never believed that the dreams would be a reality and they mocked my plans of grandeur in Haran. I remembered their words: "So, you think to lord it over us." Reuben, my oldest brother, made a contemptuous movement with his hand after I expounded the dreams to my gathered family.

"You'll find Haran isn't all that easy to be rich and famous in." Judah told me. "You'll be crawling back here in a year, begging us for work.'

"Pampered pup, why do you think I would bow to you?" Levi sneered.

Even my father reprimanded me after he caught me strutting and bragging in front of Benjamin.

"My son, it is not fitting for you to boast of things that have yet to happen. Your dreams may be sent by God as a promise. But, such a covenant comes with responsibility on your part, too. You will have to work toward the fulfillment yourself. It will not be easy."

At the time I had argued with him, I had the bravado and assurance of a youth against the knowledge and wisdom of age. Now, looking around my narrow walls and gnawing the daily ration of bread, I remembered his final words to me when he sent me to see my brothers with the flock at Shechem and to make my peace with them.

"Do not scorn your brothers, my son. Even if the God of my Fathers has assured you of great things, the family must remain the most important thing in your life after your relationship with the One God."

I had no chance to be reconciled to my brothers. Even if I had planned to attempt pacification, they had struck first, throwing me into the cistern and selling me to slavery. I bowed my head and wept, for the first time understanding how much I lost by my conceit and egotism.

"God of Abraham, Isaac and Jacob, hear me I beg. I was a foolish boy. Dreams of grandeur that were fed by misguided pampering made me a pompous fool. My father tried to warn me, but I did not listen; therefore, I am brought here to atone for the foolishness of youth. Lord God, am I to have no chance of reconciliation with my brothers? Have You totally forsaken me?"

My soul cried out night after night for respite. Sometimes I paced my cell like a caged animal. I thought long in the lonely silence of the endless days and nights. My dreams, when they came, were troubled with images from my youth. I remembered the days in Haran and Hebron when my brothers really had loved and cared for me, before I became proud. The anger and pain of the betrayal of my brothers came crashing against the bleakness and misery I clutched. Each day my heart crept closer to the knowledge that I needed and indeed missed my brothers. I could feel their distress as they watched Jacob lavish special favors on me. My conceit had only fed their grief and animosity. As a slave and prisoner, I understood the inferiority they experienced watching me grow haughty. I wept for the love I squandered in my arrogance and cried out for pardon even though I knew that I would never have the chance to be reconciled to my brothers. Suddenly, one morning I awakened not troubled, but with a sense of peace. I knew, somehow, that the One God was real and that there was a plan for my life. On my knees, I offered myself to God.

"God of Abraham, Isaac and Jacob, I know You have a mighty plan. I see that I needed to learn humility and dependence on Your power alone. God of Abraham, who You brought from Ur and promised descendants as the stars of the night, let me follow You as he did. God of Isaac, saved from sacrifice by the ram of God and made heir to the promise, may my life be a sacrifice to You. God of my father Jacob, wrestling with You and named Israel, I see that I, too, have wrestled against You. My God, Ruler of the Universe, You have kept me alive in the pit, in slavery, and in prison. You are still with me. Whatever Your plan is, here I am. Use me as You will. I will no longer seek my way, but your will."

Then I cried tears of healing and cleansing for my soul. The rage was gone, replaced by peace. Fear and despair were swallowed up in a deep serenity of spirit. When the guard brought my daily ration, I greeted him with a kind word. The man looked surprised, but did not respond. I did not care. I would wait for God's plan, whatever it brought. That night God sent a dream. The same dream came many nights. When I fell asleep I dreamed of grain being ground to flour and formed into a mountain of bread. I pondered on the dream, knowing that God was grinding me to form a fine grain for his use.

Chapter 9

My situation did not change. I remained in my cell with a daily visit from a guard who brought my meal and a jug of water. What had changed was my attitude. I no longer snarled or ignored the man who came each day. Although I rarely received any response, I always made some general comment to the soldier.

Not long after, a new Commander was assigned to the prison. Each prisoner was brought before him for a review of the charges. It was the first time I had been out of my cell. My hair and beard had grown long and matted. I had long since given up being concerned about the dirt that covered me.

It was a pleasant surprise to be ordered from my cell by two guards. Hands bound and led through the hall, I looked around as we the climbed stairs that led to the ground level. Shoved into a room with narrow windows all around the top of the wall, I blinked in the unaccustomed light.

"Into the water! The new Commander will see each prisoner only after they are cleaned up."

"Stupid waste of water," commented the second guard.

The first shrugged and gave me a shove forward into the murky water. Obviously, I was not the first to bathe, but it didn't matter. The water felt wonderful! Ordered out before I really had time to enjoy the sensation, I found myself marched into an adjoining room. Here three barbers were shaving off beards and cutting prisoner hair into the normal Egyptian look.

From conversation between the guards, I gathered that the new warden had an odd quirk about how prisoners should be treated.

"Clean and shaved, how long does he think that will last?" One guard sneered.

Another scoffed, "Everyone knows that prisoners don't have feelings. They are like animals, enjoying the filth they live in."

"Did you hear that he wants the prisoners exercised too?" Another soldier inserted.

"Complete waste of time," snarled the man holding my rope. "The only reason they are here instead of the galleys is that they are too dangerous or evil to be allowed out. Come along, you." His irritation was evident in the way he jerked me forward.

I was most curious to meet this humane soldier and wondered where he got such ideas. When my turn came, I was marched to the Commander's office. It reminded me of the office at the guard outpost with scrolls everywhere. A leather helmet sat on the corner of one table. In the room beyond, I caught a glimpse of living quarters. A breastplate and shield stood on a stand just inside the door. Through the window that opened to the west I caught a glimpse of the Nile steadily flowing north beyond the levee road. A man was seated with his back to the window, the light behind him meant that I could not see his face.

An aide read my name, charge, and sentence. I was led forward and shoved to my knees before I had a chance to kneel.

"I know you." The voice was familiar and I raised my head only to receive a cuff on the cheek from my guard.

"No!" The commander was stern. "I want to see his face."

Looking up, I recognized the officer from the two days at the guard outpost.

"It is you, the scribe from the Captain General's house." He voice was surprised and almost glad.

"Yes, Commander." I inclined my head.

"It has been four years since you were in my custody. Did you have any idea of the time?"

"No, Commander." Indeed I was amazed that so many years had passed.

"Guard, this prisoner will be of use to me. Aide, see that he is moved to a cell on this level." Turning from me, he gave the order.

Both men saluted. Roughly pulled to my feet, I was led from the room. I was immediately taken to a cell at the end of the hall. It was no larger than my previous home but there were narrow windows along one wall. Through them I could see the Nile and beyond the river, in the distance, the temples and outbuildings of Memphis. The sight of the evening stars served as a reminder that once again God was giving me a sign of His presence.

"God of my Fathers, again You raise me from the pit to see Your promise in the night sky. I trust You to fulfill in me what You will. Thank you." The humble prayer came from my heart as I stared at the night sentinels. The same stars looked down on the tents of my father in Canaan, and I felt a link with my family for the first time in many years. There were more surprises in store. The Commander sent for me the next morning. As before, he set me to transcribing reports. Working together, I learned that he had once been a prisoner himself. Falsely accused of murder, he had spent two years in this very prison before being exonerated and given back his commission. During that time, he learned the degradation of prison life and vowed to make changes if he was ever in the position to do so. He worked his way up from guard to aide to post commander and now, at last, Pharaoh rewarded him with the position of Commander and Warden of Pharaoh's Prison. Days passed into months while I kept the prison records for Commander Atra. A little at a time, he gave me more and more responsibility. Given license to roam the prison, I made it a habit to visit with each prisoner at least once a week.

Finally, after nearly two years, he put me in charge of all new prisoners. Each new man was logged onto the scroll by name, date, crime, and sentence. It was my responsibility to assign each new prisoner to his cell. On separate scrolls, records were kept of the prisoners that were scheduled to be released. These were much shorter scrolls. As Nukor had told me many years before, few came out alive from Pharaoh's prison.

A few months after my new assignment, two of Pharaoh's own men were sentenced to prison. The chief baker and Pharaoh's personal butler were charged with conspiring to poison the King with stale bread. They were two more frightened men I had never seen. Nearly unable to walk from terror, the men were dragged out of the wagon by Pharaoh's own household guards. Roughly marched into the office, they sank to their knees begging for mercy.

I restrained a smile, looking at them, because they were so obviously a baker and a butler. The baker was a short man with a belly that made him almost as wide as tall. His hair stuck out in all directions and being white looked as though he had dipped his head into a flour barrel. On the other hand, the butler was tall and thin with long nervous fingers that never stopped twining themselves around one another. With his amazingly long nose, I could imagine him staring down an importunate visitor or slave. With pity, I assigned them to a cell together.

"It's the young Pharaoh, you know," confided the baker to me the next day. "He gets with his friends and they party after the hunt. The least little thing sets him off. My bread wasn't stale at all," he insisted, "and you can't poison a person with stale bread.

What am I to do? My wife, my children, they don't even know what has become of me." He moaned in agony and grabbed my arm.

The butler shook him by the shoulder. "Come, man, don't act like that. Look at me, lost my position over a stupid joke. It wasn't even the bread I served that the Great Pharaoh said was stale. Someone brought him some other bread that I didn't even see.

I've lost more than you! My family has been butler to Pharaoh's house for generations. The shame, it is too much to bear!" In misery, he sank down on the mat, twisting his hands together.

I left them to their distress and went on, pondering the fact that a young King now sat on the throne of Egypt. What had happened to the Pharaoh I knew? From Atra I learned that the old Pharaoh had died, not long after I came to the prison. The heir died mysteriously soon after and the old King's brother had ascended the throne. A chariot accident ended his short career. Now his son, nephew of the old Pharaoh, was reigning King of the Black Land, Lord of the Upper and Lower Nile and Son of the Gods.

"A young man, learning how to rule as he goes on," was Atra's assessment. "I think he will be a wise king once he finds prudent counselors."

"May God grant him such men." I agreed wondering how my case would ever come before a man who had never heard of me.

My duties prevented me from visiting Pharaoh's servants for a few days. When I again saw them, both men seemed resigned to prison life. They were curious about my duties.

"How is it that you, a foreigner and a slave, are allowed to move freely about the prison?" The question came from the butler. It was the same question that came from every prisoner in one form or another.

"The Commander finds me useful in working with the prisoners. Although a prisoner myself, my God has given me skills of use to the Commander of the Prison and indirectly of use to Pharaoh."

"Really?" The baker was incredulous. "What skills can you use here to help Pharaoh?"

"The Commander uses my skill as a scribe to transcribe the reports to the Mighty King." I responded shortly, the thought crossing my mind that Atra could be reprimanded for using a prisoner to keep the scrolls.

"Is it Ptah, god of scribes and wisdom that you pray to for such skill and honor?" The butler asked, obviously not concerned about the political implications of a slave and prisoner producing records for the kingdom. "I would pray to the god who causes a prisoner to become aide to the Commander of Pharaoh's Prison."

"It is not Ptah but the God of my Fathers, the One True God who has given me the skills for this time."

"The One true God?" The baker was confused. "Which is that?"

The butler clarified, haughtily displaying his knowledge, "The man is a foreigner and speaks of the god of his people. The Hebrews from the Land of Canaan all insist that there is only one god. I have heard emissaries from that place speak of it. They believe that this god has given them all the land and will preserve them no matter what. Is that true?"

With a smile, I agreed, "Yes, we have been promised the land from the Euphrates to the Great Sea. Also, our God has promised us descendants as the stars. Such was the covenant with my great grandfather, Abraham."

"Yet you are a people with no cities. Nomads. How can you claim such a promise?" The butler appeared sincere in his question. I lifted my hands and shrugged in the universal gesture of not understanding.

"God will in His time bring to fulfillment His plan. And He will fulfill the dreams he gave me as a youth." It was the first time I had referred to my dreams since I had been in Egypt.

"You know dreams?" the baker was interested. "The priests claim to interpret dreams, but not a single one of their interpretations has ever come true for me."

"My God has given me the ability to interpret some dreams," I replied as I left the men to continue my visits and to report to Atra that all was well.

Atra, as Commander, had made many changes in the prison. All except the most violent were allowed a period of exercise outside the walls once a week. We were allowed the luxury of bathing monthly and the food was better. It was still served only once a day, but vegetables were added weekly and occasionally meat was supplied. Even the guards had ceased grumbling about the changes when they saw the result was more manageable inmates. Together we worked to draft enlargements and improvements to the prison. I found that my gift for numbers stood me in good stead when calculating the new additions like the exercise yard where prisoners would be allowed to walk unbound and unaccompanied by a guard at the end of the rope. I enjoyed making the drawings for presentation to Pharaoh's council.

Barely a week passed before I again saw the butler and baker. From the look on each face, I knew something was wrong.

"What is the problem? Poor food?" I asked noticing that the daily meal was untouched for two days.

"No." It was the butler who spoke at last. "We have each dreamed and we are troubled because we don't understand the dreams."

"Did I not tell you dreams are from God and so is the interpretation?" I asked, wondering why the words came from my mouth. I had never actually interpreted any dreams but my own.

The two men looked at each other in silent communion. Then the butler spoke again. "I will tell you my dream. Perhaps your god will tell you what it means."

I nodded and leaned against the wall to listen, winging a quick prayer to God for guidance.

"In my dream," the man started slowly and then with more momentum continued, "there was a wonderful grapevine. More lush and green than any I have ever seen in all the Black Land. Then huge clusters of grapes – rich purple ones – appeared on the vine. These were lovely, tender grapes, full and round, bursting with juice.

I stretched out my hand and gathered handfuls of the grapes. The best ones were selected and I crushed them into Pharaoh's golden goblet. It is his favorite cup, the one encircled with the ostrich hunt. I did this three times and the cup was full. As the juice came out of the grapes, it turned into a splendid wine, sparkling in the goblet. Then I put the cup on a golden tray and carried it to Pharaoh as he sat on his throne. He reached out his hand and took the cup. But I woke up before he drank." He finished the story and looked at me. "I don't know if he liked the wine or not." When he stopped speaking, the butler came to stand in front of me. "Can you tell me what my dream means?"

I closed my eyes and clearly into my mind came the answer. "Give God the glory. For He has told me that the meaning of your dream is this." Standing straight I looked him in the eye. "The green vine and plump grapes are a promise. The three times you pressed the grapes to wine are three days. Pharaoh took the cup from you, therefore, in three days you will be restored to your position."

The joy started in his eyes and traveled to his mouth. Grasping my hand he repeated over and over. "Thank you, thank you. What can I do to repay you?"

I gripped his arm. "When you are restored to your place, do not forget me. I was falsely accused and imprisoned by the lies of a woman. Only Pharaoh can pardon and free me."

"Of course, of course," he promised, relief making him less stiff than his usual demeanor.

Then the baker stepped forward. His white hair was more in disarray than usual as though he had been tearing at it in his agony.

"I, too, will tell you my dream." He spoke softly as if still unsure of the wisdom of the action.

"Yes, do," his friend urged.

"I pray the interpretation will be as good." After a little more hesitation, he finally plunged in, staring at the floor rather than at me.

"This is what I dreamed. I made three wonderful loaves of bread for Pharaoh's table. Then, I placed them in a basket on my head. I set out to take them to the palace. But, I had not gone far when huge birds came down all around me. They landed on the basket and started eating the delicious bread I made especially for the King. I tried everything to get them to leave, but the birds would not be frightened away. When I woke up I was exhausted from trying to chase them away." He stopped and looked up from the floor. His eyes were pleading.

Again the rush of understanding came into my head. This time I felt the cold chill of danger. I took his hand in mine and looked into his eyes. "My friend, I fear the interpretation of your dream is not so good." I tried to make the words gentle. But they hung in the air as his eyes darted from mine to the butler's. Still holding his hand, I continued. "The three loaves of bread are also three days. The birds that came down and devoured the bread," I paused searching for words to ease the blow. "The birds mean that you will never again bake bread for Pharaoh. In three days you will be executed."

The poor man gave a cry of despair and sank down to the floor. He rocked back and forth sobbing. "My family, my children, no, no."

I left the butler holding himself like a child and went to complete the reports due on Pharaoh's birthday. Walking down the hall, weighted down by the news I had just imparted, I remembered that the birthday was just three days away. Atra greeted me with the statement that on his birthday, Pharaoh had decided to review the sentences of all royal prisoners. Immediately, a list was to be compiled of all the inmates put in jail by order of Pharaoh. This was also to include all royal prisoners from his uncle and father. Sure enough, three days later, as part of the celebration, Pharaoh announced pardon to some and death to others on the list of royal prisoners. Of the score of prisoners under Pharaoh's edict, only seven were freed. The rest, including the baker, were executed.

I wondered if the butler would remember his promise. As the days turned into months, I knew he had forgotten. Again, I sought solace in prayer. "God of my Fathers, I thought that the butler was sent as a way to Pharaoh's ear. My God, am I wrong to seek to leave this prison? How can Your promise be fulfilled in such a place?"

That night I dreamed of my brothers. We were all lost in a sandstorm. I was seeking them, but the sand obscured my sight, and I was left alone when the storm cleared. The next night the same dream came, except that when the storm stopped I found my brothers buried in the sand. Now I had more questions than ever. Was I to save my brothers somehow? But how? Atra left me little time to ponder. New prisoners meant new reports. My days returned to the normal routine. I resigned myself to life as a prison scribe.

Chapter 10

God was at work. His plan was about to include me. The first hint I got was the slamming open of my cell door that woke me. Atra stood in the torch light. It was still pitch black outside. Even in the flickering light, I could see concern on his face.

"Hebiru, get up!" His voice was gruff. "Is it true that you can interpret dreams?" A second face appeared in the dancing light. By the look of the helmet, I could tell that the face belonged to one of Pharaoh's personal guards.

Somewhat groggily I stood up and stepped forward, saying, "I cannot, but God gives the interpretation."

The answer did not please him, but Atra ordered, "Hurry, you must bathe and shave, for Pharaoh has summoned you!" At the urgency in his tone, I moved out into the hall. Two of the prison guards escorted me to the bathing room. By the light of the torches they held, I rapidly bathed and shaved. The water was almost cold in the darkness of the predawn, so I did not linger. A clean loincloth of the coarse linen used by slaves and prisoners was provided. I dragged a comb through my short cut hair wondering why Pharaoh had sent for me in the middle of the night and what dreams had to do with it.

Seeing that I was done, one of the guards took my arm and we marched back to the commander's office. Pharaoh's officer was pacing agitatedly. Atra looked up with relief when I entered the room.

"Pharaoh is troubled, and all Egypt with him," I was told. "He has dreamed and none of the priests can interpret the dream."

When I made no reply, the officer continued. "The Great King of the Upper and Lower Nile has heard that in prison there is a man who can explain dreams. It is an honor such as has never been heard of before that a man should be brought from jail to interpret for the king." He leaned very close to me. "See that you do not fail."

Despite the veiled warning, I did not feel fear but anticipation. I did not even mind that Atra bound my elbows and wrists before we hurried out the main door. It was the first time I had been outside the prison walls since the door closed behind me when I was twenty-two. That was eight years ago, I realized in amazement.

When I saw the royal chariot and prancing team of bays, I knew that indeed this was an urgent errand. No slow creaking wagons or balking donkeys or even foot travel for this royal commission.

Pharaoh's guard leapt into the chariot. I was hustled in, followed by Atra. The boy holding the horses sprang up behind as the chariot whirled forward. Straight to the boat landing, the well-trained horses didn't pause, but trotted steadily across the plank onto the boat deck. The boatmen immediately cast off and poled out into the water. Oars were plied to the rapid beat of the drummer. The sun was barely starting to turn the sky to gray in the pre-dawn when the boat bumped against the palace dock at Memphis. No time was wasted in securing the plank and the chariot rolled onto dry land again. Up the incline the horses trotted to pull up by the pillared porch in the front of the palace. I remembered the hundreds of lotus-topped columns that lined the porch. Now, I could only see a couple in each direction because of the dim light. I had no time to look around because Atra took my arm. We followed the officer into the palace.

Torches lined the walls inside the palace. I noticed that the murals now depicted massive hunting scenes rather than the war victories that had adorned them before. As we rapidly walked past many doors and groups of people, I saw many curious stares. Surely, I thought, it is unusual to see a prisoner bound between two of Pharaoh's officers being escorted through the main hall of the palace. There was an air of tension in the place, too. I felt it as soon as we entered the hall. Dignitaries gathered in small groups, talking in hushed voices. The slaves went about their morning tasks, pausing to whisper to each other and glance out any window they passed. I suddenly realized what their concern was. Pharaoh, as the god king, had to perform the morning ritual in order for all of Egypt to begin another day with the gods blessing.

In a short time, we reached the royal apartments. Pharaoh's officer stopped to speak to a guard in the hall who trotted forward and entered a room. This must be the King's private chamber I decided, looking at the doors. Taller than three men, they were made of ebony wood with the falcon god Horus in gold with wings outstretched in protection on each door. One door swung open and we were ushered in. The King sat on a low chair, which had the claw feet and again the protective wings rising behind him in reminder that as Pharaoh, the man before me was also the god incarnate. Various animal skins on the floor and walls were evidence of the king's prowess as a hunter. More murals depicted the glorious hunting exploits of the current ruler. Although these were his private chambers, the King was attended by a large number of slaves and priests. Beside him stood the man I remembered from prison while slaves plied fans behind the chair. Priests hovered near, dressed in their elaborate headdresses or draped in the skin of the animal representation of the god they served. Concern was plainly written on each face. Pharaoh himself was striking the flail, emblem of judgment for the land, on his hand in an irritated fashion. The crook, symbolic of the fact that the King was Egypt's shepherd, lay in his lap.

I saw all this even as I fell to my face before Pharaoh, Lord of the Black Land, Ruler of Upper and Lower Egypt.

"Is this the man?" The question broke the silence.

A pair of sandals appeared in front of my face. A hand tilted my head and I looked into familiar eyes.

"Yes, my Great Lord Pharaoh," the butler replied. "This is indeed the man who interpreted my dream and the old baker's correctly."

"Come forward, then," Pharaoh spoke again. Atra and the butler helped me to my feet. "You guards can wait outside."

"My Lord King!" The officer was aghast. "I cannot leave you alone with a prisoner."

"Does it look like we are alone?" The young man gestured at all the attendants and priests in the room. "Are we ever alone? This man does not look to be a desperate criminal. Also, from what we are told," here Pharaoh looked at Atra, "this prisoner is actually of some use to our prison commander."

Bowing low, Atra managed to reply, "Yes, my Lord Pharaoh, I am sure he will be of great help to you, oh Mighty One."

"Then go!" With a wave of his hand, the king dismissed my guards. The slaves also left the room at a sign from the butler. Only the priests and my friend from prison remained.

Rising, Pharaoh began to pace back and forth.

"Our butler here has told me that you can interpret dreams." He stopped to stare down at me as I knelt by his vacated chair.

I nodded and replied, "Great Pharaoh, the interpretation of all dreams is from the One who sends the dreams."

"Bah!" He dismissed my words with an angry gesture. "The priests of Nute, goddess of night, were of no help."

"Let not my Lord Pharaoh be displeased, but dreams are sent by the One God and he gives the interpretation." The words were out before I thought and I marveled at my boldness.

"What talk is this?" Rounding on the butler, Pharaoh scowled.

"My Lord, Mighty Pharaoh, let the Great King remember I did tell you that this man is a foreigner and believes in this strange One God." The man bowed in supplication.

"So you did." Mollified, his gaze returned to me. "Then your god will tell you what our dream means?"

"Great One, all dreams have interpretation," I replied, praying that God would indeed grant an explanation of whatever dream was troubling the King of Egypt.

"Listen to my dream and provide the answer we seek." He gave the command as he sat down again. "We have been troubled this night because none of these wise men or priests can tell us what the dream can mean."

With an angry scowl at the group on the side of the room, Pharaoh turned his attention to me.

"I am in your hands, oh Mighty Pharaoh." I responded, bowing my forehead to the floor.

Gazing out the window toward the river that was just becoming visible in the early morning light, the king began. "As I slept, I dreamed that I was walking the River, the Great Nile, life blood of Egypt. It was lovely; I could almost smell the evening air. As I paused by the river, I saw seven healthy, prime looking cows rise up out of the center of the river. They waded to shore and walked past me, lowing softly. I could have reached out and touched them. All of them started to graze in the field. I have never seen such fine animals in all the land."

After a short pause, he turned to look at me and continued. "Now the strange part comes. As I still stood watching the fat, sleek beasts feed, I saw seven more cows rise out of the river. These cattle could not have been worse off. Their bones showed and even the hides were patchy where hair had fallen out. Really, they barely looked like cows at all, but skeletons. Up out of the water they came. They walked right past me, too. I drew back in fear of the sickly looking creatures. Straight up to the good strong cows they went." Pharaoh stood up to take a restless turn around the room. The priests mumbled among themselves. I could feel their eyes boring into my back. The king returned and sat down. He leaned forward, his eyes fearful as they stared into mine.

"Great One, tell me the rest." I urged.

"You would have thought that the weak and sickly cows would start to graze once they reached the rich field of grass, wouldn't you?"

I nodded when he seemed to be waiting for a response.

"But they didn't." He put his hands on each side of his head as though the memory was too much for him.

"Yes, Lord Pharaoh." Gently I probed. "What happened?"

"The scrawny cows *ate* the fat cows! They ate every scrap. Nothing was left of the good herd — not a hoof nor horn." He shook his head. "But the bad cows were no better than when they came out of the Nile. They were no fatter. They were not healthier. And then I awoke." The King of the Upper and Lower Nile stared into my eyes, beseeching an answer.

Somehow I knew that there was more to tell. I returned his gaze and pressed him to tell the rest. "Let not the Mighty Lord of Egypt be angry, but there is more, isn't there?"

A buzz of whispers erupted from the corner where the priests conferred. Pharaoh nodded slowly, a look of astonishment on his face.

"How did you know?" Then without waiting for an answer, he continued the story. "Finally, I drifted to sleep to dream again. The second dream was similar. All my wise men and priest could tell me was that the two dreams are one." He tossed an irritated glance in their direction.

"God will give you the interpretation you seek." I stated, causing a louder murmur from the priests.

"You believe that?" The man looked intently at me.

Calmly I returned his gaze, "Yes, Great One, I do."

"In my second dream," the man continued, "I was walking in a fine field of grain. There in the middle of the field was a wonderful stand of seven strong stalks. There was so much grain on each head that I couldn't understand why the stalks didn't bend and break. As I stood admiring the rich harvest a south wind came up. Then I saw that there were seven puny plants growing next to the heavily loaded plants. These plants were withered and brown. When the wind blew, the seven dying plants engulfed and demolished the wonderful stalks of grain." He paused to shake his head. "I never saw anything like it. One plant *ate* up the other! Again, the blighted plants didn't thrive, even after they consumed the strong. They fell to the ground and rotted. Now tell me, if you can, what these dreams mean."

I bowed to the floor again, touching my head to the ground just in front of Pharaoh's foot. When I lifted my head, I knew the interpretation. I sat back on my heels.

"Lord King of all Egypt, Ruler of the Land from the Cataracts to the Great Sea, you are most blessed for God has shown you what He plans to do in Egypt and the world. The two dreams are indeed one. By this, Great One, know that not only is it determined but will soon come to pass."

"And ..." Pharaoh rose to stand at the window. The sun stood on the rim of the Eastern Desert. Ra was ready to start his daily journey. Priests and slaves alike feared the consequences should that journey start without Pharaoh performing the daily offering.

Against all the proprieties, I stood and followed the king to stand at his right side.

"Behold the Nile, mother of all life in Egypt." I pointed to the steadily flowing river. What I was going to say seemed impossible, but I knew I was right. "For seven years there will be great bounty in all the land. So much grain, so many animals, so great a harvest each year that it cannot all be eaten."

"Then this is a good dream?" With great hope, Pharaoh turned to me.

"Mighty King, God has shown you that after the coming seven years of plenty will come seven hard years of famine. A famine so deep that nothing will grow."

"Do you tell us this to mock?" Angrily, he raised a hand to strike me.

I was never sure why, but I stood still. Rather than grovel, I looked straight into his eyes. "God has shown you all this before it happens. He has done this so that you can prepare and so that Egypt will not be destroyed by the famine. Take heed, for if you do not, the Black Land will be consumed as surely as the thin cows ate the fat ones and like the blighted grain destroyed the good grain." When he made no response, I continued. "You should appoint some wise councilor to oversee a collection of a fifth of the harvest throughout the land in each of the seven years of abundance. This must be stored in safety against the seven years of famine. When the drought and lack begin, you, Mighty One, will provide food to save the people."

"My Lord Pharaoh," the butler burst out, coming to stand behind his master, "you will indeed be as the gods, giving food when there is none."

My service complete, I bowed and stepped back. I quietly went to squat by the wall near the door. I refused to acknowledge the amazed, but hostile, stares directed my way from the priests. From the words that drifted to my ears I knew that they were discussing who would be appointed the vizier to oversee the project I outlined.

After a long period of silence, Pharaoh spoke in response to the butler's observation. "Indeed, that could be so. We would be greater than a warrior to provide food for the people. What better legacy to carve on our tomb?" He turned from the window, looking around the room, his eyes rested on me for a long considering minute. Then Pharaoh faced his priests. "As you could not explain our troublesome dream," Pharaoh took his seat. The priests hurried forward with many a bow and salaam. "We employed a foreigner, this Hebrew prisoner from Canaan. He has been able to do what you could not."

General protestations sprang from every man.

"Silence." The King was enjoying himself. "We now need your expert advice. You have heard the interpretation. For seven years, the Nile gods will give more bounty than the land and people can use. After that, the gods will turn away for seven long years. There will be such a famine that nothing will grow.

So, my advisors, what shall we do?"

The men were thrown into a panic by his question. One of the older priests spoke up finally. "My Lord, Mighty King, what can we do against famine?"

"We grow impatient." Pharaoh had resumed tapping the flail against his hand. "Not only are you unable to decipher a simple dream, you cannot find a solution to a small dilemma."

"Small – Great Lord – seven years of famine! That is hardly a small dilemma!" exclaimed a pudgy priest. I suspected he already felt a pang or two of hunger at the mere thought of a famine.

Pharaoh held up his hand. His next sentence took me completely by surprise. "Fortunately, a solution has been provided with the dream interpretation. Let the prisoner step forward." Everyone turned as I scrambled to my feet and came forward to lie on my face before the man again. Placing his hand on my head, the king told the assembled men. "You heard this man state the answer, yet your pride kept you from repeating it just now. You let your prejudice against this man, a foreign slave and prisoner, prevent you from seeing that his solution is the thing that will save Egypt." His severe look quelled the murmurs before they started. "A governor shall be appointed over Egypt, second only to the Throne. This man will be charged with collecting a portion of the crops into the storehouses during the years of plenty. When the famine comes, he will provide, on our behalf, food for the people."

I sensed rather than saw the preening behind me as each man envisioned himself as the new official. Everyone suddenly had something to say.

"But, of course, my Lord Pharaoh."

"So simple, so effective."

"Mighty One, you will be as a god."

"Such a wise King."

"The perfect solution."

When he stood, the talk ceased. His hand had remained on my head but now he grasped my binding rope and raised me to my feet. Drawing me to his right side, he announced. "We have decided. This man will be our new second in command."

My knees buckled and I knelt to kiss the royal ring. Dimly I heard the appalled gasps and exclamations of dashed dreams. In my heart, a paean of praise to God sang out. "Glory to You, Lord God of Abraham, Isaac and Jacob. You alone can set the captive free."

"Arise. You will now be called Zaphenath-Paneah, Interpreter to the King and Preserver of the Land. We will have you always by our side. Your home will be here in our palace." He turned to the butler. "Have our Prison Commander Atra and our Chief of the Household Guard come in."

The man opened the door and ushered in the two soldiers. Both stopped in amazement just inside the massive door. The sight of their prisoner standing next to Pharaoh and his arm over my shoulder was a sight they did not expect.

I saw his smile as he ordered. "Commander Atra, remove these ropes from our new governor."

"My Lord Pharaoh?" The words were part question, part exclamation.

"You shall have to find another scribe. Egypt has greater need of his services. We have granted a royal pardon for any crimes he may stand accused of."

"Yes, Great One." My friend bowed low.

"Ctah," the King addressed his butler, "go with Zaphenath-Paneah and the Commander. See that his bonds are removed and provide him with appropriate clothing. Our new governor will live in the Eastern apartments. Tomorrow we will introduce you to the court."

Again, I bowed low and kissed the royal ring.

"My Lord Pharaoh, Mighty and Wise King of All Egypt, my life is fulfilled in your service."

With Atra on one side and Ctah on the other, I walked past the priests who were still stunned with the turn of events. In their eyes I recognized the jealous anger I last saw around a morning meal in Canaan. I prayed that I would have the wisdom to deal with their resentfulness and mistrust before it reached the boiling point.

As soon as the door closed behind us, Atra turned to me. "What magic did you perform? From slave and prisoner to governor in one meeting with Pharaoh! Such a thing has never been heard of in all Egypt!"

Ctah answered for me. "He gave my Lord Pharaoh the solution to a problem that has been vexing my Lord, the King." I caught his warning look and understood that the true nature of the conversation would be confidential.

Still shaking his head, Atra followed the butler down the hall. We walked through a private garden between tall, white pillars to another building set slightly apart from the palace. I saw windows looking out on the garden on each side of a wide entryway. It reminded me of my lord Potiphar's home with its view of the fields and river. Ctah opened the door and, to my surprise, bowed to me. "My lord governor," he said.

As though suddenly remembering, Atra took my bound hands. With his dagger he cut the binding rope. Then he, too, bowed to me. "May your service to my Lord Pharaoh prosper Egypt as you have helped me."

When he turned to go, I reached out to stop him. "Commander."

He turned to me and I was touched to see the hint of a tear in his eyes. "Hebiru, I shall miss you sorely. Not just your work but also who you are. This must be farewell. Commanders, even of Pharaoh's prison, have little converse with the Governor of Egypt." Atra gripped my arm as a brother. I watched him leave, striding briskly back between the pillars to the palace. He was right, it was not likely that we would meet again and we would never be on equal ground.

"Farewell." I saluted his departure with a lump in my throat feeling I had lost another friend. After a moment, I turned to Ctah. He motioned me to enter my new apartments. In awe, I looked around. The entry hall was wide and airy with the view of the gardens. I followed the butler as he showed me each room. Graceful carved furniture, chairs, tables, and beds were found in each room. Animal skin rugs were arranged artfully on the walls and floors. The murals on the walls represented Ra in his daily travels, the story of Isis in her search for Osiris and the birth of Horus.

Ctah understood my curiosity and explained. "These apartments were built, but never occupied. At one time, my Lord Pharaoh thought to install a priest of Ra here, but was dissuaded by certain of his councilors, who thought it would cause great jealousy among the other priests."

I nodded, my mind turning back to the angry looks I saw on the faces in Pharaoh's chambers.

"You can, of course, do what you want with these rooms. Slaves will be sent to you and you will want to purchase some of your own."

Shaking my head, I sat down on one of the chairs.

"My lord," the butler seemed unsure how to proceed.

"Yes," I looked at him, thinking how much I owed him. "I need to thank you, my friend, for remembering me to Pharaoh."

"It must have been your god that recalled you to my mind." He glanced at me guiltily. "I had forgotten you as soon as I was free of the prison and safely reinstalled in my position."

After a pause, he blurted. "Do you really believe that your god gave you the interpretation of Pharaoh's dreams?"

"I did not know the answer on my own. It was just like when you and the baker told me your dreams. The interpretation came to me from outside my mind. I asked the God of my Fathers for help and I knew."

"Yes, my lord." Ctah seemed satisfied with the explanation. Looking around and remembering his duties, the man bowed. "My lord, I will leave you now. I will return with slaves and clothing fitting to your station."

So, I was left alone with my thoughts. In wonder, I thought back over the morning. "Lord God of Israel, Your works are wonderful. You have taken me from my home and brought me through slavery and prison to be Governor of Egypt. My God, give me the wisdom and discernment needed to serve both You and Pharaoh. I pray that You will grant me reconciliation with my brothers in Your time. Glory to You, Ruler of the Universe."

Chapter 11

A feeling of unreality clung to me. The butler returned with a crew of slaves to see to the running of the house and to help with my bath and clothing.

When I protested, Ctah insisted that it was necessary. "A man in your position will have many slaves." He indicated the man standing behind him. "This one, Set, is a gift from my Lord Pharaoh to be your steward. If you would like, I will be happy to go with you to the market and select others."

Humbly, I agreed. "I would like that. I must say that I feel very strange and off balance," I confided.

Nodding, the man smiled. "I know the feeling. Two years ago, when your prediction of my release came true, I walked around in a daze for weeks. You will adjust Lord Governor Zaphenath-Paneah." He bowed in honor.

"That too, I will have to learn," I said. "This is the third name I have had in my life. First, Joseph, son of Jacob which means 'God adds'. Then, in Potiphar's house, I was called 'Hebiru' for my race. Now, my name is Zaphenath-Paneah. What does that mean?"

" 'Gifted by the gods to know their thoughts', " Ctah answered.

He brought new garments. My rough slave loincloth was replaced by the fine linen tunic of the rich and powerful. I fingered the cloth, amazed that the same process of spinning and weaving could produce both the rough slave cloth and the delicate, almost transparent cloth I now wore.

It felt very odd to sleep on the bed. For the first time in my life, I was not lying on the floor or ground with only a mat or pile of skins for comfort. Finally, I fell into a restless sleep. All I remembered from my dreams when I awoke was that Pharaoh, the priests, and even my brothers had been in them.

My new steward, Set, came to tell me that Pharaoh would see me in the audience chamber as soon as I bathed and dressed. Ctah came to escort me through the palace.

"Last time I was here, I was a slave and scribe to Potiphar," I mused, pausing by the tall door into the council chamber. Ctah, however, led the way into one of the side chambers. I was to learn that this room adjoining the royal library was Pharaoh's favorite place. It was easy to see why. Tall windows shaded by a long pillared portico looked out past a verdant garden onto the tranquil Nile. One could see the boats plying up and down the water. Out of sight were the busy docks where cargo was loaded and unloaded. Further south was the private pier where Pharaoh's barge lay.

With a bow, Ctah announced my new name and title as he ushered me into the room. "Mighty Pharaoh, at your command, here is the Lord Governor, Zaphenath-Paneah, Interpreter to the King and Preserver of the Land."

"Come in, come in. We have much to do!" The King seemed eager.

Bowing low I moved forward to kneel at his knee. But he indicated the chair next to him.

"Sit here. You are our governor and we have much to discuss. In private, we will not stand on ceremony."

"Yes, Great One." In amazement, I took the seat, wondering what further surprises were in store. Few men were given the right to sit in Pharaoh's presence.

"Your apartments are satisfactory?" His question took me by surprise.

"Yes, Lord Pharaoh, more than satisfactory. I am but a simple man. The slave, Set, was a pleasant surprise."

A complacent smile appeared and the King asked, "He will be useful then?"

"Yes, Mighty One, I am honored by your care of me." I bowed my head to him.

"Good, good." Waving his hand, the man turned to other issues.

"Now tell me, how much time do we have to prepare for the seven years of plenty as promised?"

"Great Lord King," I spread my hands wide in a gesture of surrender, "I am a humble dream interpreter, not a prophet. But," I continued as he frowned, "the dreams were doubled which indicates that God proposes to act soon. It is now fall. I believe that with the Inundation will come the beginning of the seven years."

"Then we have six turnings of the moon before planting time comes." Pharaoh counted on his fingers. "That is eight before the first crops are harvested. Show me your plans for storing the surplus."

The rest of the morning was spent making sketches and doing sums. Pharaoh added many useful suggestions as we went along. I came to admire the man beneath the crown during that first morning. He gave me a short piece of advice when the growling of our stomachs called a halt to the mornings work.

"I didn't know the first thing about being a king, but I have learned who to trust and how to play factions against each other. As Governor, you too, must guard your thoughts. Keep your council from all but the very few people who have proven themselves trustworthy. Most diplomats are like a nest of vipers, as ready to bite the hand that feeds them as each other."

"I will remember, Great King, your council is wise." My head bowed in homage.

"Even brothers will turn against brother to obtain advancement."

"That I know," I murmured, turning my head away to hide the sudden sting of tears.

"Really?" The word was not so much a question as a command to explain myself.

"I was sold into slavery by my brothers because they were jealous of my father's attentions to me as son of the favorite wife." The statement was without expression.

"And you came to Egypt," Pharaoh filled in. "Perhaps this one god of yours brought you here to prepare for the coming time of famine."

He clapped me on the shoulder. "Enough. Let us eat. This afternoon you must visit the slave market. A man in your position must have many slaves."

"Yes, my Lord Pharaoh," I smiled. "So Ctah tells me. If you could spare his services, Great One, he has offered to accompany me to the market."

"That is a good idea. He will get you a fair price and keep you from being cheated."

I knelt to kiss his ring. "Mighty Lord, you are most gracious."

The afternoon spent in the slave market was an experience I never willingly repeated. Too vivid were memories of my time as a slave boy with the Ishmaelite caravan. The resignation and desperation on the faces of the men, women, and children in the market was heart wrenching. I remembered, even as Ctah found the perfect house and personal slaves, how much fear and anger I felt at each stop on the trade route. Even though Borz had determined early on to bring me to Egypt and Potiphar, the slave market stench still hung in my mind. Some of the men were tightly bound, some with a pole behind their backs.

At my question, Ctah said, "Probably troublemakers. You don't want to buy any of them. Your life would not be safe. Men like that are good only for the galleys or the mines."

"Or the army?" A plan tickled the back of my mind.

We were standing in front of a young man, heavily muscled and bound not only with the back pole but also by the neck to a stake. The slave master flicked his shoulder with the whip when he saw my interest. The man turned in anger to be brought up short by the rope around his neck. "Find out where he is from."

With a shrug, Ctah asked the trader.

"From far Syria." The trader responded with a low bow, a look of greed appearing in his eyes. "Leader of a band of renegades, he was finally captured with those of his followers who weren't killed. The wise master will see, just here, the lovely women also taken."

The slaver moved to the opposite side of his booth to draw back a curtain. Three women stood clinging to one another in fright and embarrassment. Clad only in a single thin linen tunic, they sought to cover themselves with their hair.

The young man strained against his bonds, anguish for the women visible on his face. I turned back to him and addressed him in Hebrew. The words sounded alien to me after half a lifetime in Egypt. "Man, do you understand my words?"

His head turned toward me in astonishment. Slowly, grudgingly he nodded.

"Good. Then answer. The women, are they your wives or sisters?"

He didn't answer immediately, so I continued.

"Answer truly, not as Abraham did."

For a long minute, he stared into my eyes. Ctah stepped forward to speak, but I held up my hand.

"My wives," the Syrian said, his voice rasping from suppressed emotion. "Except the youngest. She is my niece, daughter of my murdered brother."

The slave trader grew impatient with the conversation and moved restlessly. He was not used to Egyptian nobility discussing family history in Hebrew with the merchandise.

"Ctah," I drew the butler aside and ordered him, "purchase the entire group for me at a fair price."

"My lord Governor," he remonstrated, "the man is vicious. The women, now," he licked his lips and glanced toward the cowering group, "I can understand your desire."

"They are his wives. I will not have the family ripped apart. Buy them all, Ctah!" My words were sharp.

"Pharaoh will not be pleased." The butler warned, twisting his hands nervously.

"I will bear his displeasure. The man will be of use, but not without his family." I responded shortly.

Shrugging with resignation, Ctah turned to bargain with the trader.

A thought crossed my mind and I interrupted the negotiations to ask, "Were there any others in the group? Children perhaps?"

The trader and Ctah both gave me an odd look.

"The children are too young to be of any use. They have been a nuisance for the entire journey," the trader growled in disgust. "I don't know why I even kept them alive."

"Ctah, the children too," I insisted, turning away from the accusatory look in the man's eyes. Unable to stand still, I roamed restlessly around the marketplace. My hands itched to jerk the ropes off of every man and woman standing in despair in each booth. The butler and trader were deep in discussing the transaction and did not even notice that I left and returned several times. At last the deal was done. The trader smiled smugly. He was satisfied with his profit.

As we started to walk away, Ctah told me that he was not happy with the purchase. "I got you a bargain price, although I fear you will regret the deal."

Shaking my head at him, I turned to the Syrian. I addressed him in Hebrew.

"Man, you and your whole family, wives and children, have been bought. You will all serve me as I order. Remember this kindness and all will be well."

Something like hope flashed across the man's face.

"Yes, mighty lord." He responded with a bow of his head, as far as the rope would allow.

Ctah gave instructions for delivery to the palace and we moved on.

"Lord Governor, do not think me bold." He spoke after we walked in silence out of the market.

"Speak up, my friend." I felt more relaxed now that the sights and smells and noise of the awful place were behind us.

"The man, is he of your tribe?" Curiosity forced the butler to exceed the bounds of his normal reticence.

"No," I shook my head. "But he will be of use." I could not begin to explain the depth of reasons I had for the purchase. There was only a vague idea in my mind that the man would make a powerful guard, which I might need.

"And the wives and children are insurance for his good behavior." Ctah decided with a nod of commendation. "Perhaps my Lord Pharaoh will be pleased after all."

I let him think what he wanted about my purchase of the women and children. It was true that I purchased loyalty with them, but I also was compelled to rescue the man and his family from the slave mart.

I was impressed by the order already established in my apartments when we reached home. Set had each new slave assigned to a task.

"Lord Governor," my butler greeted me with a low bow. Just in time I stopped myself from bowing in response. "Your pardon, my lord, I do not know how to assign the latest arrivals. And my lord, please forgive my shortcomings, but I cannot speak their language." With a wave of his hand, he indicated the Syrian family. The man stood protectively in front of the women who huddled in a corner. I saw one or two small faces peering out to be snatched back by a mother's hand.

"The man is not a household slave." I instructed. "His skills will be invaluable to me. He is to be housed separately until I can deal with his training." The plan fell into place as I spoke. I would indeed drill the man to be my personal guard. The lessons of Nukor would be useful. The problem solved in my mind, I started to leave the room.

"The women?" Set looked helplessly at Ctah who shrugged.

"They are his wives." I stated.

"But, my Lord Governor," Ctah spoke up in support of his fellow butler. "They will need a separate room. All your other slaves are men."

"Yes," I agreed, "see to it. They can be set to weaving some rugs for my floors and walls."

"Rugs?"

"Squares made of wool woven in colorful patterns," I explained, recalling that I had not seen carpets in Potiphar's house. The floors had animal skins just as the palace did.

Ctah shrugged at Set. "A room will be prepared, my lord. Please enlighten your poor servant as to what is needed."

"Later." I was suddenly exhausted by the changes in my life. I wanted to be alone to sort out the myriad of emotions brought to the surface by the visit to the slave sales.

Again I started to leave, only to turn back to the Syrian. "What is your name?"

"Adam, great lord." The answer came as he fell to the floor at my feet, kissing the ground in homage.

"Then, Adam, your strength and race have saved you from the galleys or mines or worse. My compassion saved your wife and children. They will have a room away from the other slaves. I would have some rugs woven for my chambers. Set will show you where to go. Also, you must learn Egyptian for now you are in an Egyptian household."

The man raised his hands in reverence to me. "My lord, I beg you, let me serve at your side. Let me protect you from any enemies."

His words seemed a sign from God that my plan was good. All I said was, "I will think on it. Go now"

Ctah voiced his amazement when Adam and his family left the room behind Set. "My lord, you transformed the man from an animal to your abject slave. What magic do you possess?"

"I used no magic, just compassion."

The butler was still shaking his head in astonishment when I sought my room.

Chapter 12

I lay awake long into the night, pondering the changes wrought in less than a week. From lowly prisoner to lord governor, second only to Pharaoh himself. Looking at the stars visible through my window, I considered how the God-given interpretation of Pharaoh's dream led to my change in status.

Then, my mind roamed on to the many things necessary for completion before the next harvest. Pharaoh and I had discussed these things each morning for the past three days. Granaries and wagons, and new laws and officials throughout the land to collect the crops were just a few of the steps to be taken to preserve the nation. In the morning, Pharaoh said a full council would be convened and the plans presented.

Gradually, I drifted off to sleep only to be wakened at dawn by my new body servant, a young black man, chosen in the market because of his resemblance to my friend Nukor. His name, I learned, was Kevak. He was eager to impress me in his new position. My clothes were laid out and my private bath waited. After shaving and trimming my hair, the young slave helped me into the tunic. I was grateful for his assistance in draping the dress. Although I had seen Potiphar and other important people wearing the garment, I had never needed more than the kilted loincloth of slave and scribe. The fineness of the cloth and the gold thread woven around the edge identified me as a person of importance. His curious glance wandered over the scars on my back as he assisted me with the clothing. I was grateful that my back was covered. There would be enough questions buzzing around without the sight of an obviously beaten back to add to the rumors.

I allowed Kevak to adjust the wig of black hair on my head. Although I hated it, Ctah and even Pharaoh had impressed upon me the need for the wig.

"It is not seemly for one of your station to not wear a wig. You will find that you become accustomed to it and will not want to be without it." The butler had patted his own wig as he spoke.

"As a slave, it did not matter that your hair was not black and straight, but as our governor, you must not be different than all the other officials." Pharaoh had been stern.

I sat still with my eyes closed as Kevak prepared to apply the kohl to my eyelids. It was difficult not to fidget as I wondered how the council would take Pharaoh's announcement. The priests, I knew, were still antagonistic. Kevak told me what some of the other slaves heard. "The priests of Ra and Nute say that they would have interpreted the dream if they only had a little more time to consult the omens. They plan to protest your appointment, my lord."

"I am not surprised, but I thank you for the warning." My thoughts turned from plans for the nation to trying to figure out how to placate the priests before they became greater enemies. I was still turning the problem over in my mind when I followed the steward into the antechamber that opened onto the throne room.

"Wait here until the proper time," he instructed me. "I will come for you."

Slightly nervous, I paced the floor as I heard the council arriving. By parting the curtains slightly, I was able to see the men taking their places. Pharaoh was seated on the alabaster throne. Behind him, the great bronze figures of Osiris and Isis and Horus towered on the wall. The falcon wings of

Horus protected the throne. Slaves stood on each side of the throne, fanning gently. It was not a warm day, but I was sure that beneath the heavy crown and regalia, the King was hot. He wore the double crown, signifying that he was acting for both Upper and Lower Egypt. On his chin was the gold beard and the wide gold and jeweled collar forming again the wings of Horus rested on his chest. In his hands were the crook and flail, emblem of his care both as guardian and lawmaker of the land. It was the first time I had seen the man in full royal grandeur.

However, I had come to know the man beneath the ceremony. He was only a year or two older than me and was facing a crisis to his nation unknown in the history of the country. I felt sympathy and forgetting my personal concerns, prayed. "God of my Fathers, let my words be full of Your wisdom. Your ways, oh God of Abraham, Isaac and Jacob, are not clear, but You sent me here for this time. I am Your servant."

Pharaoh rose to speak. He stood still and silent until the talk in the room ceased.

"Noble counselors, the gods have shown to us, as their fellow god, what is in store for the future of Egypt."

I smiled as he continued to declaim. "By dreams and omens we have learned that the great Nile god will pour out great bounty for the next seven years. There will be such bounty that new storehouses will need to be built." Cheers greeted this announcement. Then the King raised his hand. Silence fell and he continued. "The gods must keep all in balance. Therefore, the seven good years, as foretold by the gods and omens, will be followed by seven years of famine. The mighty Nile will withhold the yearly Inundation for seven years."

"Mighty Pharaoh, intercede for us with the gods."

"Who can survive such a famine?"

"Woe is coming to Egypt!"

Chaos reigned until Pharaoh raised both his hands, extending the crook and flail toward the council.

"Your king has indeed found a solution. We are shepherd and judge of the people of the Black Land. The gods have been gracious to provide relief."

He pointed toward my curtained alcove. The steward drew open the curtains. As though on cue, I stepped through and knelt before the king, my forehead pressed to the floor.

"Behold the intervention from the gods – Zaphenath-Paneah," Pharaoh proclaimed.

I heard surprised murmurs and saw out of the corner of my eye one of the priests step forward to speak. He didn't get a chance because the king continued his announcement.

"This man will be second only to me in the land. As my royal governor, known henceforth as "The Lord Governor, Zaphenath-Paneah, Interpreter to the King and Preserver of the Land" he will be in charge of all the plans we have made for the nation. New storehouses will be built. You will each be responsible for collecting a fifth of the produce from your provinces during each year of the bounty. This will be stored until the famine. The country will then come to me and to our governor Zaphenath-Paneah for relief." Grumbling started at the mention of a tax of a fifth of the harvest. Pharaoh silenced them when he continued. "As our council, you will be allowed certain credit toward the purchase of food in the famine. Allowances will be made for you to retain your own harvest against the years of shortage."

Nods of agreement were now seen. The men saw gain for themselves in the collection. I marveled that our carefully discussed plans had easily won over the nobility of Egypt. The king continued to explain. "These concessions will be based on your participation and assistance during the preparation. Plans have been drawn up for the storehouses.

Work crews will be assessed from your provinces to build them. Also, for the workers, a food ration will be collected over and above the fifth tax for the famine."

"Mighty Lord Pharaoh," an elderly counselor raised his voice. "How will our credit be calculated?"

"Old Zokor, your eagerness does you credit." The king smiled, knowing full well that it was not eagerness, but greed, that motivated the speaker. "To your southern province is given the honor of providing the first quota for building."

"Thank you, Great King." The old man subsided and no one else dared speak.

"Now, Zaphenath-Paneah." Pharaoh raised me from my knees to stand next to him. "As my governor, we give you this royal signet ring. Only in matters of legal judgment will you be below us. All men will know that you are as we are. Wear this collar bearing our royal name and the sign of our brother god, Horus. Take this staff of office and the headpiece of our governor." He continued by placing a gold circlet on my head and pressing a staff topped with the royal cartouche into my hand.

As one, the council bowed to me.

"Hail to the Lord Governor, Zaphenath-Paneah, Interpreter to the King and Preserver of the Land, favored of the gods and of Pharaoh!" they shouted.

Pharaoh also placed thick gold bracelets on my arms and declared, "A chariot will be prepared and a herald will go before you to announce that the Lord Governor, Zaphenath-Paneah, Interpreter to the King and Preserver of the Land, is approaching."

The council again cheered. Pharaoh looked pleased. Slaves brought an ornately carved chair and placed it beside the throne. Together we sat.

With a wink, the king said, "I have one more surprise for you, Lord Governor. It is not right for a man to be alone. Behold your bride."

Everyone turned to look when the door opened to reveal a priest. I recognized him as Potiphera, priest of the temple of Ra at On. He escorted a heavily veiled woman into the room.

"Asaneth!" I heard the name whispered around the room. The name was familiar. I searched my memory. She was the only daughter of Potiphera. I remembered that Phu had explained her presence in the temple. She was then a little girl of five or six standing next to the Chief Priest.

"That is the High Priest's youngest child. She will be a royal prize. Her mother is sister to the King and only Pharaoh can give her as bride. The man who weds Asaneth will be made part of the royal household and, of course, be blessed of Ra."

Pharaoh stood up and took the girl's hand from her father. He placed it in mine.

"Asaneth, only daughter of Potiphera, priest of Ra at On, has consented to be your bride. We present her to you."

With a flourish, he drew off the veils to reveal a young woman, poised and beautiful, whose eyes gave no indication of whether she was delighted or angered with her new husband.

I bowed low to Pharaoh and raised her soft hand to my cheek.

"My Lord Pharaoh, you, in your generosity, have again overwhelmed me with the gracious bounty of a mighty king. The lady Asaneth is lovely, Great One. I will honor her with my life just as I will serve you will all my loyalty."

Her father removed a scarf from her wrist and bound it to mine.

"So are the two joined." He intoned. His eyes remained downcast, so I was not able to determine if he was gratified by the marriage.

Looking immensely pleased, Pharaoh said, "Take your lady wife and go. Tomorrow, Lord Governor Zaphenath-Paneah, we will begin the real work of preparing Egypt. The gods have given us the blessing of time to prepare. We must not waste their favor."

Hand in hand, Asaneth and I bowed to the King of All Egypt. I led her from the throne room.

Chapter 13

Walking together toward my apartments, I felt her hand trembling in mine. Beneath the calm exterior, she must be as nervous as I was about the turn of events. My only experience with women had been the lady Dala, hardly a reassuring memory. I tried to assure her that she would be comfortable.

"You will have your own chamber and if you have special slaves, I will have them sent for. If you want anything, just ask."

"Yes, my Lord Husband," was her only reply. Her voice was soft and sweet, but expressionless.

When we reached my rooms, Set was waiting.

"The Lady Asaneth, my bride." I explained briefly.

The man bowed low in welcome.

"Have the Syrian woman, sister to Adam, brought to serve my bride until her women can arrive," I told him.

Bowing, he hurried to obey.

"I bought a strong, young Syrian slave yesterday. His two wives and sister were part of the deal. The sister shall be yours, my wife," I explained as my lady stood silently staring around the room. It was barren of ornamentation, except for the skins on the floor, the few pieces of furniture and the murals of the gods on the walls.

"You will want to add your own touches to this house," I stated, hoping for some response.

Before she could respond, Set returned with the young Syrian woman.

"What is your name?" I asked, first in Hebrew and then in Egyptian.

Looking up from where she knelt before us, I was surprised when the girl responded slowly in Egyptian.

"Sarah, if it please you, Mighty Lord. I do know some Egyptian."

Although her accent was strange, the words were understandable.

Slowly and clearly, I told her, "This is my bride, the lady Asaneth. You are hers. Anything she needs, it will be your duty to supply."

Turning to the lady, Sarah placed her hand on forehead, then heart in the tribal flourish of honor and submission.

"Most lovely Lady, I am yours to command," she said, touching her head to the floor.

For the first time, I saw the hint of a smile on my bride's lips.

"A kind gift, my lord," she said. "Have you had much experience in favors to a lady?" She tilted her head to look at me. "You have such sweet words and presents. Surely, you will know how to see to all my needs."

I felt my face flood with color, at the memory of similar words from Potiphar's wife that led to my imprisonment.

"No, my lady," the statement was stammered.

"May I retire?" With a curious look, she took pity on my embarrassment. "The journey was long and unexpected."

Relieved, I nodded and pressed my lips to her palm in salute. "Rest well, my Lady. Set will show you to your chambers."

"Yes, Lord Governor. This way, my Lady." Set escorted Asaneth from the room. Sarah gathered up the discarded veils and followed.

After they left, I stood staring out at the garden. I remembered the other part of the ceremony and removed the circlet to stare at it in wonder. The scarab ring bearing Pharaoh's imprint and the staff surmounted by the royal name were symbols of my new position. I pondered the change in my status. Zaphenath-Paneah, Lord Governor of Egypt, I turned the name and title over in my mind. Joseph son of Jacob seemed further away than ever. If the man, Joseph, was in danger of disappearing as slave to Potiphar, how much more would I be unable to retain that identity as second in command to the King of Egypt? "Lord God, You brought me to this place. Let me not forget who I am and let me remember that You are the Mighty One." I murmured the prayer, turning as a knock sounded.

Set bustled past to open the door. It was Ctah.

"My Lord Pharaoh asks the attendance of the Lord Governor, if he is not occupied." His eyes darted around, alighting on me.

"The lady has retired," I told him with a smile. "I will come now."

Pharaoh was waiting in his personal chambers. This time he was alone except for the fan bearers and personal slaves quietly moving around the room at their duties.

"Is my Lord Governor pleased?" were his first words.

"Mighty Lord Pharaoh, your graciousness is exceeded only by your wisdom." I told him bowing to the floor.

"We are private, Zaphenath-Paneah. I do not need empty words from you."

"My lord, the lady is lovely and shy. I have given her the Syrian's sister for her own."

"Your wisdom is exceeded only by your bounty, Lord Governor." He mimicked my words. "I heard of your purchase of the Syrian and his women. To be honest, I thought you had other motives for their purchase."

"My lord, with them I purchased the Syrian's loyalty," I explained simply, shrugging.

The King nodded and returned to the subject of my bride. Without explanation, he stated, "Asaneth shall have women of her own choosing. Her women will not be joining her. Have Set and Ctah see to it."

"Yes, Lord Pharaoh."

Even though I asked no question, the man elaborated. "To have the women from Potiphera's house would be to introduce outside eyes and ears. Even though he is Priest of On, it was only the bride price that purchased his alliance to the plans we have set in motion. The priests are not entirely convinced of the validity of your interpretation."

"I remember." Indeed I did. The memory of many pairs of jealous eyes haunted my thoughts.

"It is because of such men that I wanted to meet with you." His emphasis on the personal pronoun caused me to look up in surprise. He leaned forward with concern in his eyes that were more than from a King for a useful official. I saw genuine care and friendship in them. "Find a strong man who you trust to be your personal guard. We can assign one of the royal guards."

When he reverted to the royal plural, I replied, "I understand, Wise Lord. The thought had occurred to me also."

"Then we are satisfied." He sat back with a nod of dismissal. "Return to your bride. I believe her to be an amenable girl and not swayed by her father's anger and viewpoint."

Bowing from the room, I walked back to my own. I had indeed thought of the need for a personal guard, but had not thought to require one so soon. Remembering Nukor's loyalty to my lord Potiphar, my thoughts turned again to the Syrian. Certainly, he was strong enough. But what of his fighting skills? I determined to test him and reviewed in my mind the skills and tricks Nukor had taught me so many years earlier. I realized that I should resharpen my own proficiency, too.

Then, my thoughts turned to my unexpected bride. I knew that the priests were not happy with the promotion of a foreign prison slave to Lord Governor of the land. The fact that Pharaoh had bought the loyalty of the Chief Priest of Ra at On with the bride price for his daughter was not surprising. What troubled me was if she knew of my history and what her father's instructions might have been. Determined to find out and be honest with Asaneth, I quickened my steps. My first action was to ask Set which rooms she was housed in.

Sarah opened the door when I knocked.

My lady was having her hair brushed and I was struck anew by her loveliness.

"Asaneth, my wife, I would talk to you." Standing just inside the door I waited for her reaction.

She nodded with composure and turned to face me. Sarah retired to the corner of the room to continue unpacking the trunk. Asaneth folded her hands quietly in her lap and looked up at me quietly and steadily. I remembered the same poise and unnatural self-possession on the face of the girl at the temple twelve years before. It occurred to me that my wife had never been a child and that she had always been expected to be on display. How difficult it must have been to measure up to being niece of the incarnation of Ra in Pharaoh and daughter of Ra's priest.

Seated, she waited calmly while I stood by the door undecided how to begin. I picked up a stool and set it in front of her.

Sitting down, I took her hands. They were cold and now that I was close, I could see uncertainty deep in her eyes and even a glimmer of fear. "My lady," I started, then paused to start again. "Lovely bride, Pharaoh has been most generous and gracious to me. Not only has he given me the most beautiful lady wife in the entire land, he has also raised me to great honor above many others. Did your father tell you any of this?"

"No." The word was soft but her eyes were wide with curiosity at my words.

"Then I will tell you my story." I swallowed past the lump of apprehension in my throat and began. Still holding her hands, I looked past her and saw in my mind again the fields of Canaan.

"I was not born Egyptian, but the eleventh son of the richest sheik in Canaan. My brothers became jealous because of certain dreams that the One God, the God of my Fathers sent me. They sold me to a trader bound for Egypt soon after my seventeenth birthday." I had to stop and take a deep breath as the old feelings of desolation swooped down and threatened to choke me. "The trader sold me to the Captain General of Pharaoh's Army. You may remember Potiphar; his house is near On. I saw you once when you stood next to your father at some ceremony the slaves were allowed to attend at the temple." With a smile, I looked at her. My eyes searched her face for some response. She was watching me intently but didn't return my smile.

"My lord Potiphar was a good master. Because of my skills as a scribe, I became his chief aide, honored above others in the house, although still a slave. However, my master's wife lied to him. I was falsely imprisoned for attempted rape. The darkest hours of my life were spent in that prison cell until I realized that despite all that had happened to me, the God of my Fathers was preserving and preparing me. When I understood that somewhere there was a plan for my life and quit fighting against God, He raised me from the darkness.

The new prison commander used my skills as scribe to assist with reports and prisoners."

I ventured a glance at my wife to see how she responded to the news that her husband was not only a former slave but also a former prisoner. There was no revulsion in her attitude. Instead, she seemed to be leaning toward me with what I hoped was sympathy in her eyes.

"A couple of years ago," I continued, "Pharaoh sent two of his servants to prison. One was Ctah his butler; the other was his chief baker. They both had dreams that I was able to interpret. The butler was reinstated and the baker was executed. When Pharaoh needed someone to interpret a troublesome dream, Ctah remembered me. Because my God gave me the interpretation, the Mighty King pardoned my sentence, freed me from prison, and made me his Governor with the new name of Zaphenath-Paneah. And, he gave me the lovely Asaneth as bride." At last I released her hands, which I had been gripping throughout the story. I didn't dare look at the woman until her hand touched my cheek. Tears stood in her eyes.

"And my father was angry because he could not interpret and gain more eminence!" Her vehemence surprised me. "I remember when he came home a week ago, to tell me I would be wed. He was livid and kept saying 'it is heresy and the *maat*, the Universal Order will be destroyed'. Why, I did not know and he didn't explain. Then, my father told me he loved me and would find a way to make it all right! But he told me to watch and listen." She paused to take a ragged breath. Rising suddenly, she began to pace around. "Suddenly I was useful to him. This was the man who only tolerated me because I was of the royal line, the priest who berated and beat my mother because she never bore a son to carry on the line, the royal appointee who used his power to intimidate and not help …"

Her voice died out on a sob. The anger and vehemence surprised me, coming from the woman I thought so meek and quiet. My first thought was to comfort her pain and I gathered her shaking body into my arms. Tears slid down her cheeks to soak my tunic. "My father didn't love me. He thought to use me to spy. To betray my Lord Pharaoh and my husband for his advancement." I understood her bitterness and betrayal, but all I could do was stroke her hair and let her cry. When the torrent finally eased, I drew her onto my lap.

"You need have no fear," I assured her. "If you don't want to visit your father, you will not have to. You can start a new life here and forget the old." Even as I said it, I knew that the scars would remain forever. Despite coming to terms with my brothers betrayal and the lady Dala's lies, the pangs of the memories still had the power to hurt.

"Also, my sweet Asaneth, Pharaoh has promised that you may buy all new slave women of your own choosing. Ctah and Set will go with you."

"Really!" Like a child promised a treat, she clasped her hands together. "I have never been allowed to have a say in my serving women."

Involuntarily, I glanced toward Sarah. Asaneth saw and smiled. Her dark eyes lighted up and her lips parted in the first real laugh I heard from her. She took my face between her hands.

"No, my husband, she is a sweet and gentle soul. I already love the girl you so thoughtfully gave me. You are a kind man, Zaphenath-Paneah, favored of Pharaoh. I do not understand you."

With a trusting and endearing movement she nestled into my arms with her head resting on my shoulder. I was enchanted by her trust and gently pressed a kiss to the top of her head. "My lady wife, I should leave you to your toilette."

She pressed closer and I was reminded of the thinness of her dress and my tunic.

"Is your business more important then me? Am I not your bride?"

"Asaneth, you are lovely and my sweet bride. I do not want to frighten you or force you into something you are fearful of."

"And you are my handsome and wise husband. Why would I be afraid?" She tilted her head back and looked up at me through half closed eyes. Her slightly parted lips invited me to kiss her.

As our lips met, I vaguely heard the door close as Sarah left. Then I was lost in the wonder of my bride. Her shyness was offset by her willingness. I explored her body as she pressed against me. Burying my hands in her hair, I searched her mouth. Drawing her close, we moved to the bed. There we discovered each other before uniting in an explosion of joy. Sated, we lay in each other's arms. Dozing, we awoke with kisses. Thus, the night passed like a dream. As the moon set in the west and the morning sun lightened the eastern sky, I left my bride. In my chambers, Kevak was waiting to assist me with my morning ablutions.

I sent for Adam while I dressed. When he arrived, I questioned him. "The slave trader said that you were a fighter. Tell me about that."

He rose from his knees to stand, pride in his face as he spoke. "Let my lord the Governor know I was a peaceable man. I only took to fighting as a last resort. My village was visited too often by slavers from the east on their way to this place." Rancor was in his voice as he continued. "Egypt is insatiable in her appetite for slaves. Anyone standing in her way is killed or 'annexed'." The young man's lips curled in a bitter sneer. "My father was one of the first to be murdered. He tried to stop a caravan from carrying off the best young men and girls from their homes. He was struck down without a qualm – a sword slash across his neck. I took to the hills with my wives and sister as well as the few able bodied men that were left."

"And how were you spared?" I understood his anguish as he replied, head bent and tears standing in his eyes.

"I was away from the village on a sheep buying trip to Haran. If I had been there, my father might still be alive."

"Or you would both be dead," I pointed out. "How long were you in the hills?"

"We had been living in the hills, attacking caravans and freeing prisoners for nearly three years before the traders managed to place a spy in our midst. One of the men we freed was really a slaver. We didn't learn that until too late." The despair was etched on his face as he concluded the story. "He betrayed our location. We were surrounded and slaughtered or beaten and bound. I saw my brother, Sarah's husband, disemboweled. The women and children were herded like sheep and kept in line with whips. We surviving men were tied hand and foot to each other. We had to walk ahead of the women and any supposed infraction on our part resulted in the lash. But not to us, rather, to the women."

The Syrian gazed into space. My own thoughts recalled a slave boy's journey from Canaan. I could only guess the despondency, anger, and anxiety Adam must have felt hearing the cries of his wives and the other women. Before I could muster my voice, he turned to me. Falling to his knees he bent his head to the floor. "Only luck left my wives, children, and sister in the hands of the same trader who took me to sell. I do not know the reason you picked me, Great Lord. Know this, I would give my life for you. You are the man who saved my women from degradation."

"Adam, the God of my Fathers urged me to buy you. I did not know the reason, thinking it was only compassion. I, too, have walked the slave trail bound behind a camel."

In surprise, the man threw his head up to stare at me. Ignoring the question plainly written on his face, I remarked, "However, my bride tells me that Sarah is a great help. I find that I have need of a loyal personal guard. Your survival and scars speak of your skill. Today I will test you, myself. For now, Set will see you outfitted for this position."

"Great Lord, I will serve you to the death!" Again he bowed his head to the floor.

"I sincerely hope it will not come to that," I murmured, mostly to myself. Calling Set, I gave him instructions for my new guard. A short time later, Adam returned, appropriately dressed in the unfamiliar clothes of an Egyptian guard. He fingered the cloth, so different from the wool he was used to and rubbed his arms against the unusual feel of no covering. With a smile of remembrance, I assured him that he would get used to it. Privately, I acknowledged that with his long hair and beard, rippling muscles and proud air, he made an impressive looking escort. Followed by my new attendant, I proceeded to the throne room.

Pharaoh was seated in state hearing various petitions. He looked up at my entrance. Although quickly hidden, I saw the look of astonishment that crossed his face. Crossing the floor, I felt many eyes on me and heard the whispers.

"Look, it's the new Lord Governor."

"Hand picked by Pharaoh."

"I heard he was a political prisoner."

"No, son of a rich potentate who bought his position."

"Didn't you hear, he's the illegitimate son of Potiphera."

"That's why Asaneth was allowed to marry him."

I tried not to smile at the rumors and speculation I heard swirling around the room. Some comments were aimed at

Adam, who marched proudly behind me, his eyes watchful. I knew he was awed by the magnificence of the room, just as I had been years earlier. Bowing to the King, I pressed my forehead to the floor in homage. Adam prostrated himself behind me.

"Rise, The Lord Governor, Zaphenath-Paneah, Interpreter to the King and Preserver of the Land. Sit here at my side." With a regal wave of his hand, he indicated the seat beside him. Adam took his place behind me, taking his duties very seriously I was happy to notice. "We will talk after our audience is done," the King remarked in an aside.

"Yes, Great Lord of the Two Lands." I inclined my head in response.

He only heard a few more appeals before rising, thus signaling that he was done for the day. Everyone bowed as he stepped off the dais. A nod of his head indicated that I should follow. Adam and I fell into line as part of the retinue that trooped through the tall ebony doors. We walked down the pillared hall to the library. Pharaoh waved off his attendants at the door. Two guards took up positions by the entrance. With my hand, I motioned to Adam to wait before following the king into the quiet room.

Inside, the man laid aside crown and regalia to sink into a chair with a sigh. He leaned back with eyes closed for a minute. Patiently, I stood awaiting his pleasure.

"Now, Zaphenath-Paneah, our Governor, let us proceed."

The morning passed swiftly as we reviewed plans for the storehouses and looked at the map to determine the best locations.

"Tomorrow the Master Builder, Servant of the Gods, will meet with us. He will be in charge, under your direction, of the building of these storehouses." Pharaoh stood up and stretched.

"Do you attend the lady Asaneth to the slave market this afternoon?"

"With my Lord's permission," I responded to his change of subject.

"Yes, go. See that her choices are as wise as your own. We see that you have made use of the Syrian. We approve. Any man would be foolish to challenge him."

"Thank you, Great One." I bowed in acknowledgment of his compliment then trailed him from the room. Adam leapt to his feet and took his place at my back after bowing to Pharaoh.

The afternoon in the slave market was no more comfortable than my previous visit. Ctah again accompanied us, as did Set. Asaneth was attended by Sarah, who hovered close to the lady's litter, partly from loyalty and partly from fear. Adam carried himself proudly, but I sensed smoldering anger beneath the surface.

Before long, my lady called me to her side. "I don't know how to decide. Never have I seen so many slaves together. How do you know which to buy?"

"Let your heart decide," I suggested. "Ctah and Set are here to help, too."

Finally she agreed to purchase twins from Crete advertised as skilled in hairdressing. A girl from Nubia was obtained for her bath. Others were bought for cosmetics and for room attendants. The final purchase of the day was a young boy and girl who, when prodded by the slave trader, played the lyre and sang sweetly.

"I must have those!" Asaneth exclaimed, we had started to leave the market when she saw them. Set had gone ahead with the purchases so Ctah was left to conclude the deal.

"Are you satisfied and happy, my bride?" I asked at the palace door. Lifting her from the litter, I held her light form in my arms and looked into her eyes.

Her smile and soft kiss was answer and payment enough for the agony I endured in the market. When I bent to kiss her again, she wrapped her arms around my neck and responded warmly. I willingly would have followed her to her rooms, but she danced up the steps saying, "I can hardly wait to see how those girls from Crete can do my hair. I want to surprise you."

"My love, nothing can make you more beautiful."

Her laugh answered me. I watched her slender figure until she was lost from sight between the pillars.

Feeling disoriented by my feelings, I saw Adam.

"Come, let us see what fighting skills you have."

I was surprised to see Atra in the guardhouse. Happily, I greeted him and then asked if he could test Adam's skills.

"Gladly, Heb, uh, Lord Governor." He stumbled in his greeting, a little unsure how to relate to me.

Adam proved to be an effective, if not subtle fighter. After watching them spar, I suggested, "Atra, let me see if I still remember my training." I took the weapon from Adam. The short curved sword felt odd in my hand after so long, but after a few fumbles, the moves that Nukor taught me began to return. I felt the old thrill when, with the sudden wrist twist, I sent Atra's weapon flying.

"Quite a trick! Where did you learn to fight like that?" The man was amazed. Adam, too, was watching with surprise.

"A friend taught me," I replied. Together we walked back to the building.

"Your man will do quite well with a little practice. I would suggest that Tarka, Chief Guard here, could help with the training."

So my days settled into an agreeable routine. Mornings were spent with Pharaoh and the Master Builder to receive reports on progress and discuss what was needed. The early afternoon was spent resting from the heat in the coolness of my apartments. Slaves stood ever ready to wave the elaborate ostrich fans should Asaneth or I grow warm. Sometimes my bride and I joined the King and his Chief Wife for a game of foxes and hounds. I suspected that he knew I let him win, although nothing was ever said. When the evening breezes came off the river, Adam and I went to the sparring yard. Tarka proved a competent teacher, increasing both my skills and Adam's. The nights were my favorite time. Alone, Asaneth and I learned to love and understand each other.

Half my age, she possessed a mind eager to learn all that had been denied her in the sheltered life as the daughter of a domineering priest. I taught her to write and then to read. From her, I learned more of the Egyptian ways. She helped me understand why each carving and painting had to be done in the exact and precise way it was. The *ka,* she explained, needed the perfection of the picture so it would know where to reside. Without the *ka* a person or living thing was nothing. That was why so much care was taken to preserve the appearance of a person even after they died. Asaneth stressed that the *ka* of the Pharaoh was especially important because his *ka* became one with Ra when he traveled West in death.

To her I told the stories of my family's history – the travels of Abraham from Ur that occurred because he believed that the One God called him out. She listened eagerly to Jacob's adventures in Haran with my grandfather. Laughter greeted my recital of how he encouraged his sheep to breed striped or spotted depending on what Laban said he could keep as wages. Her sympathetic hand held mine when I told her of my carefree childhood and the wonderful coat gift from my father that brought it all to an end. Only to Asaneth did I tell the dreams I had long ago in Canaan where my father and brothers bowed to my sheaf and star.

"You are a man of power now," my wife told me, angry on my behalf. "Surely Pharaoh would allow you to send and find your family so that you could punish your brothers as they deserve!"

"My love, in prison I left the desire for vengeance behind. My God showed me that He would bring His plans and dreams to completion when He wants to. Just like He has prepared Egypt by the dreams He sent to Pharaoh." I knew she wasn't happy with my answer. That night as I lay beside her, knowing I needed to return to my rooms, but unwilling to leave the haven of my love's arms, I saw a shooting star through the window.

The next day I approached Pharaoh. "Mighty King of the Black Land, last night I saw an omen in the stars. My God has reminded me that the people must be reassured and prepared for the collection of the harvest. Great Pharaoh, I beg your permission to go from the cataracts to the Great Sea. Let me carry your royal proclamation and ease the fears of your people. I will bring you a report of the progress of the building."

Slowly he nodded. "You are right. We dare not leave this only to my councilors. It would be easy for someone to use this quota to raise rebellion. The people must know that the gods have given us the solution and that all will be well."

"My Lord, the King is wise."

"Let us write out the proclamation and we will send trumpeters with you to announce your importance and royal sanction."

It was late morning by the time Pharaoh was satisfied with the wording of the scroll. The royal scribes were set to copying the document while Pharaoh walked with me toward the private apartments of the palace.

"Zaphenath-Paneah, we will miss you at our side." His hand gripped my arm. "Dine with us tonight in our chamber.

Let Asaneth come also. She will miss you, as well. It has not escaped our attention that you enjoy your bride greatly." He added with a grin.

"Great One, the lady Asaneth is the best gift I have received from your gracious generosity," I replied with emotion as we parted.

Set received my instructions with a bow. "Kevak and Adam will accompany me. You I trust here with my lady and her needs," I told him after explaining that I would be leaving in the morning.

"My lord does me honor," the man responded with a low bow.

Asaneth wept and begged to go with me.

"I wish you could, my beloved, but I serve on Pharaoh's commission this time. Sometime I will take you to see all the land."

With that she was reconciled, but she clung to me in the morning. Dressed in my official robes and headdress, I took leave of Pharaoh in the throne room. He was wearing the great joined crown of Upper and Lower Egypt surmounted by the falcon and cobra heads. Dramatically, he raised his hand for silence. Standing, he motioned me forward. Kneeling at his feet I heard him proclaim, "Let it be known that The Lord Governor, Zaphenath-Paneah, Interpreter to the King and Preserver of the Land, now goes out to console the land and review the progress on our royal storehouses. The first harvest comes soon and a share will be gathered into safe storage for the years that the gods have shown are coming. Go then! Let all men bow before you as to us. Inscribed on this scroll are the words of Pharaoh, Son of Horus, Shepherd and Judge of the Two Lands. They are our presence to the people. Read and see that they are heeded by all the people from highest official to lowest slave."

After bowing to the floor, I accepted the scroll from the King's hand. Formally, he embraced me. "May the gods favor you, my friend, Zaphenath-Paneah." He spoke for my ears only. The words brought a tear to my eyes so that I saw the court only through a haze as I left the throne room.

The trumpets sounded and I left the palace. A gilded chariot drawn by a matched team of sleek blacks was waiting to carry me to the royal barge. The charioteer assisted me into the vehicle. Adam jumped in after me. Kevak and my baggage had gone ahead to the boat. Another flourish of trumpets and we rolled down the road. The honor guard of palace soldiers that Pharaoh provided marched in formation behind. Along with the many servants, they would be with me for the whole trip.

Chapter 14

From the capital, we headed south. The regular Nile breezes carried us steadily up the river. The pole men and rowers kept the movement going even when the wind died down. In less than a week, we were at the southernmost outpost of the land.

With interest, I looked around, remembering my one visit with Potiphar and Nukor. Not much had changed. The mines still produced gold for the coffers and tombs of kings and nobles. The black skinned natives worshipped the gods of Egypt and their local deities as they had done for generations. Overseers from further north maintained a benevolent alliance with the regional chiefs. Adam and I traveled the last few miles in the chariot. In my unaccustomed headpiece and cape, I was sweating in the intense heat. The Syrian looked uncomfortable and hot in the leather armor and helmet, although he stood stoically behind me. Not for the first time I wondered what had become of my old master and his faithful guard. I hoped to see or hear something of them on this journey.

Trumpeters announced my arrival. Worried elders hurried from their homes. Standing in my chariot, I faced the gathered crowd. The herald announced my name and title. As one, the people fell to the ground with a collective gasp of awe not unmixed with fear. The representative of the god king did not visit their area often.

"I bring you the words of Pharaoh, Benevolent Ruler of the Two Lands who seeks to reassure all that order will be preserved. Hear the words of the Mighty, Wise, Comforting King." With a flourish I held up the scroll and took it from the leather covering that protected it from moisture. I could almost hear the collective breath being released when I unrolled and began to read the words:

"Pharaoh who Looks upon All Egypt as a Father, Pharaoh who Protects the Two Lands as the Cobra, Pharaoh who Provides for the Black Land as the Falcon, To all Our People, Greeting. Pharaoh, the Great One who Shepherds and Judges from the Cataracts to the Great Sea, takes this opportunity to reassure and comfort all. Let it be known to each person that the gods have given to Pharaoh as to their peer, a vision of the future. Great and wondrous and terrible things will come to pass. This has been shown to Pharaoh, the Mighty Son of Horus, inheritor of Ra. Our wish is for peace of heart to all within the royal kingdom of Egypt. For the god and Pharaoh have together provided for the sustenance of our people that none shall know want. Behold, the gods promise each farm will produce great bounty for seven years."

A gasp of delight followed this announcement. I continued to read:

"For the good of all, for the maintenance of order, a special collection will be made at each harvest. It is our wish that the Lord Governor, Zaphenath-Paneah, Interpreter to the King and Preserver of the Land, who sits at our right hand, who you see before you, will place the god's surplus in storage until the time of the Nile's famine."

Murmurs at the word 'famine' were hushed quickly. With a deep breath, I finished reading the scroll:

"As the Falcon provides for his young, our bounty will be distributed to the Two Lands and no one will grow faint during the time the Nile withholds bounty.

To the Lord Governor Zaphenath-Paneah, it is our will that you extend such hospitality as you would to our royal self for he indeed sits at our right hand and acts on our bidding. When the time of harvest comes, our wagons will come to collect the fifth part of each harvest. The gods have graciously shown to our royal self, their Brother and Heir, that there will be no want or need left unmet in the land if this is done.

Sealed by our royal cartouche as you can plainly see. We are Pharaoh, King of Egypt."

I held up the scroll for all to the see the unmistakable royal symbol on the scroll. Looking out at the crowd, I saw fear and awe on each face. The elders came forward with much bowing to beg me to accept their humble hospitality. A goat was roasted and a great feast prepared while I sat at leisure answering questions from the village leaders. Finally reassured and convinced that their village would not starve, the elders relaxed and the evening was spent enjoying the evening meal and the dancing girls' performances.

In every town the same scenario played out. In the larger cities, home to Pharaoh's counselors, the welcome was more elaborate but the response was always the same. Initial fear and trepidation for the welfare of the town followed by the gradual acceptance of the royal edict. At every stop, I was careful to include all the officials and priests in the planning of the best way to accomplish the collection of the fifth of the harvest.

In some places, rumors had been running rampant as the quota of storehouse workers returned from a distant location. Relieved to understand the purpose for the unusual conscription, the people turned from angry to amenable. As one elder told me, "we usually work on Pharaoh's temples and monuments during the Inundation. To have to send an additional quota during the Going Down when all laborers need to be in the fields had seemed unreasonable. No one understood that the Mighty One had a message from the gods."

At Thebes, city of priests, I learned that few of the counselors and priests had done anything except order men to leave their farms and work on Pharaoh's projects. Angrily, I confronted one of the priests. He had been present the morning when I interpreted the dreams for Pharaoh.

"They are only peasants and slaves. Why should I concern myself with explaining Pharaoh's will to them? It is their duty to serve the Crown in any way they are ordered to. It is the only way to preserve the *maat* – the Order of All Things as ordained by the gods. I have more urgent matters to attend to than the feelings of farmers."

Gritting my teeth against an angry response, I replied, "Pharaoh himself wants the people told."

"And the Great One, Son of the gods, has sent his lap dog to do that job." The mocking reply grated on my ears.

Silently, I turned away, not daring to reply, knowing that my exasperation at his hostility would explode.

But the scornful voice continued, "Poor prison slave, can you think of nothing to say?"

"Perhaps time spent in a prison would give you a new perspective on the situation." I replied, calm settling on me, as I exercised the royal authority. "See that this man is locked up for reviling the words of the King."

Realizing too late that his envy and animosity had trapped him into saying too much, the man tried to bargain. "Mighty Lord Governor, you misunderstood." I turned my back and with a motion of my hand signaled two guards forward. "Wait, you must know I meant no harm, no disrespect. Please, I am truly loyal to Pharaoh. He is the Morning and Evening Star of the Land. My lord, Zaphenath-Paneah, please believe me."

"Take him," I instructed. "Time in jail will give this man a chance to consider his words more carefully."

Immediately, I called a meeting with the rest of the priests and leaders of Thebes. Once again, I read Pharaoh's edict and requested their ideas on how to best accomplish the collection. "You are among the few in Egypt who know that it was in his dreams that the Mighty One received knowledge of the impending famine," I reminded them. "With that knowledge comes responsibility for leadership and guidance of the people in your care. In order for *maat* to be maintained and the promise of God fulfilled, all must work together for each other. The King has granted you and the other royal appointees in the Black Land the chance to be exempt from purchasing the food during the time of shortage. The Lord of the Two Lands expects your administration of his edict to be fair and thorough."

I stood silent awaiting the response. Small groups formed to discuss my words. Finally, the priest of Ptah stepped forward. A short man, the tail on his leopard skin tunic dragged behind him. However, I knew he was a man of importance among his peers.

"Lord Governor, your words are sensible. In our envy, we have forgotten that Pharaoh indeed possesses the wisdom of the gods. You are generous to remind us of this." He paused as though he would continue, but did not.

The priest of the river god Hapi, spoke up. "We will work with you to accomplish what the Royal Son of Horus desires of his people."

"Indeed that is all my Lord Pharaoh, King of Egypt would desire." I accepted the indirect apology with a nod to the assembled men. We spent the evening and the next day outlining procedures for the area of Thebes; additionally, they gave me many ideas to implement throughout the land.

In my daily report to Pharaoh, I included a brief line saying that for disrespect to the Crown, I had imprisoned the priest of Sobek and awaited his pleasure. I also reported that the storehouses were nearing completion and the plans were being carried out in every detail, including the special dividers and airflow to prevent spoilage. In closing, I told him of the support of the priests at Thebes and listed some of their ideas.

Days stretched into weeks as I traveled north through Egypt. Word of my prompt response and jailing of one of their own preceded me. Whatever their personal feelings, other councilors and priests were careful to keep quiet and were embarrassingly ardent with patriotic fervor upon my arrival.

Although I rejoiced in my freedom, I also found myself missing Asaneth. I wrote her long scrolls telling of my travels and received in return laboriously penned missives full of palace gossip. Pharaoh occasionally sent a personal greeting, but most of our correspondence was official. I was able to report that the fields were full and rich as harvest drew near.

With mixed feelings, I stared at the landscape as the royal barge drew closer to On. Memories of Potiphar and my life in his house came to me. A grand reception was prepared to honor my visit. I saw Potiphera, my father-in-law, in the group of dignitaries that greeted the boat. Scanning the crowd, I was disappointed to see that the Captain General was not present. After my usual reading of Pharaoh's proclamation and the extravagant evening entertainment, I walked out along the levee toward my first home in Egypt. Adam silently followed me. He was used to these evening excursions, for I often walked out in the cool to look at the crops and to be alone, away from fawning officials. What I could see in the flickering starlight concerned me.

Early in the morning, I announced my plan to tour the nearby holdings. The chariot was prepared. Accompanied by Adakra, the local counselor, we set out. My trumpeter was left behind but the ever-present troop of royal guards marched behind. Purposefully, I directed the charioteer down the well-remembered road leading to Potiphar's house.

With great agitation, the local official took my arm. Pointing on down the levee road, he urged us to continue straight ahead. "My Lord Governor, surely you do not mean to visit every estate in the area. Just a little further on this main road is my own land. I would be honored if you would..."

"Who is in charge of these fields?" I interrupted. We had driven far enough along the road that I could see in the daylight what I had thought I saw in moonlight. The land lay fallow. Nothing had been planted. No one was in the fields working and only weeds sprouted here and there. The canals had not been cleaned and rebuilt after the Inundation. "Was not the landowner told of Pharaoh's edict?"

In an agony of fear, the man replied, "Please, let not the Great Governor, Second only to the King of the Two Lands, hold this poor plot against my record. Indeed all the area was told the order of Wise and Divine Pharaoh. Let me explain." His pleading died down and his hands twisted together in desperation. The chariot rolled inexorably forward. Adakra spoke again.

"There is only a woman in charge here."

"And how is that?" In surprise, I turned to face the man. My shock and anger made him fall to his knees in the vehicle.

"Please, Great Governor, the woman is the widow of Lord Potiphar. You may have heard of him. Captain General of all Pharaoh's troops under the old King. Soon after Pharaoh joined the gods, my lord Potiphar was found dead. There were rumors that he was poisoned. They were started, I believe, by the old man's steward and personal guard."

"Why would they risk starting such a rumor?" My heart was saddened to hear that my good master was dead, possibly murdered.

"They had nothing to loose, for the widow, the lady Dala, cast them out of the house upon his death. She has installed her own guards and lives as she pleases in the house."

"Tell me, why does she feel herself above Pharaoh's orders?" My look was stern and the counselor quailed.

"Let not Your Lordship be angry. But the lady was niece to the old King. I fear she has never been held to account for anything." He added the last in a whisper.

"And the old retainers? What became of them?"

"My Lord, I took them in and gave them a small house on my land. It was the least I could do for they served my lord Potiphar well and long. We could visit them and you could ask them yourself what happened." He looked at me with hope, but I stared ahead at the house now drawing close. The whole area had a look of decadence and decay.

My companion became even more nervous when he perceived that I planned to continue on to the house. He laid his hand on my arm.

"Lord Zaphenath-Paneah, hear me I beg. It is not seemly that you go to this house."

With an arched eyebrow I questioned his presumption.

"Let not my Lord be angry, I do not know how to say this. The lady, that is, she has, I mean, the house ..." The words faltered to a stop.

"Well?" I prompted.

"The place is a brothel," he blurted out and looked away.

"Indeed? And you allow the widow that leeway, but do not require her to tend the lands. This situation shall be remedied." I spoke sternly to cover the revulsion the woman always caused in me.

"Yes, my lord." Meekly the man followed me from the chariot. Adam pounded on the heavy wood door. I was transported back to a moment half a lifetime earlier when I stood in the same place. Then I was an angry, prideful youth, sold into slavery. Now, I reminded myself, I was Lord Governor, Zaphenath-Paneah, Interpreter to the King and Preserver of the Land with the authority of the throne behind me.

A slovenly man opened the door as Adam continued to pound. His eyes boggled at the gilded chariot and troop of soldiers at his door.

"The Lord Governor, Zaphenath-Paneah, Second only to Pharaoh," Adam announced. The butler continued to stare, his gaze now shifting to me. His mind finally recognized authority and he fell to the floor in obeisance.

"We would see the lady Dala," interjected Adakra with a nervous glance at me.

Calling up all my reserves, I stepped over the prostrate servant into the hall. I looked haughtily around, hiding my sorrow at the destruction of the beauty that had graced the house. The butler scuttled away in confusion to summon his mistress.

"The lady will see you in her chambers." He reported on his return.

"No!" My response was immediate and brusque. "I will see her here. Immediately! Pharaoh's business will not wait. See to it!" He fled at my order only to creep back into the hall with much bowing.

"The lady asks your pardon, but she has not made her morning toilette. Would my Lord care for a drink while waiting?"

"I do not care to drink, nor do I care to wait." I stated, mimicking all the self-important dignitaries I had ever met. "Perhaps she would find in prison time enough to complete her beauty treatments."

"Yes, Lord Governor." Miserably, the man shuffled from the room. I felt sympathy but did not dare show it.

The apparition that swept into the hall a few minutes later was a sad travesty of the regal lady Dala I remembered.

"Who dares *demand* my presence?" she raged. "What right have you, Adakra, to come unannounced?" She did not see me standing in the shadow. I wondered briefly if she would recognize me.

"The Lord Governor, Zaphenath-Paneah, Interpreter to the King and Preserver of the Land." He introduced me with a bow in my direction.

Whirling toward me, the lady stormed across the floor. Memory of a previous attack flashed over me. It was all I could do not to retreat. But I stood still, staring at the woman with all the scorn I never dared show before.

She faltered in her charge and stopped. Gathering herself together and pinning a beguiling smile on her lips, she spoke: "What can such a handsome Lord Governor want in my humble home?" The seduction was back in her voice and the well-remembered perfume hit my nostrils.

"Pharaoh's business. Your fields lie fallow. You have, I am sure, heard of the fifth portion to be collected from each plot of land this harvest."

She moved closer. "But my lord, I am only a poor widow with no one to tend my fields."

"Then this year's fifth will be taken from your house and the land will be given to a worthy landowner."

"You would not dare!" Gone was the woman of seduction. In her place was the tiger of vengeance.

"The King of the Black Land will not be balked. The gods have given him the vision to save the country. One woman will not be allowed to stand in the way."

"I will apply to Pharaoh himself," she spat.

"Perhaps when you do that, you can explain the rumors concerning the Captain General Potiphar's death. I am sure he would be interested. He held the man in high esteem." It was a random shot, but I read the guilt on her face.

"Would you beggar me then?" Back was the pleading, seductive charmer. "As a woman, I have no resources to give you the fifth you request."

"As a woman, you have the estate you inherited from my lord Potiphar and the bridal portion from the King that the Captain General never touched." Her angry eyes greeted my response.

"How did you know that?" she hissed.

"When I return from the Delta, I expect payment." Implacably I turned from her. The butler scurried to open the door. Her animal scream was all the warning I had. Adam moved simultaneously and the dagger buried itself in his shield rather than my back. His spear pinned the woman to the far wall.

"By the gods, I never expected that!" Adakra was clearly shaken; he wiped his forehead with a shaking hand. "Your man is amazing." He stared at Adam in awe.

"Good man." I told the Syrian with a grasp of his arm. The touch of his solid muscle reassured me that I was still alive. A gleam of pleasure lit his eyes but he only bowed in response and crossed the room to retrieve his spear.

"So is justice done by the gods." My companion still stared at the crumpled form on the floor. The butler stood stunned in the far doorway. I heard the clatter of gathering servants. I, too, felt judgment had been accomplished. The lady Dala had finally received the just result of her actions.

"This house and land is confiscate to Pharaoh." I announced. "I will see the lord Potiphar's servants and put them in charge until a new owner can be found."

The royal guards supervised the dispersal of the women and house slaves while I sat on the portico. I didn't want to go inside the house, for Dala's cloying presence lingered even though her body and women were gone. Looking across the barren estate lands I was sad to see it so neglected. My old master had taken pride in his estate and even loved the woman who had betrayed and possibly murdered him. In my lap lay the scroll I had just completed for Pharaoh detailing my meeting with the lady Dala. I would complete it after talking to Clep and Nukor.

Adam stood by my side, but he was not on guard. Rather, he leaned at leisure on his spear, gazing toward the river but I knew he was alert.

"I was a slave in this house." My words broke the silence and took Adam by surprise.

"My lord?" He turned to me.

"I was a young man of seventeen sold into slavery by my brothers. The slave trader sold me to the master here as a scribe. It was another lifetime." Indeed there was a sense of unreality to sitting in the very chair Potiphar used when negotiating with Borz for the slave boy.

"Look, my lord," Adam pointed up the road. My two old friends were warily approaching. I had given instructions that Clep and Nukor were to report to the new master. I wondered if they would recognize me. The two men looked older than I remembered until I reminded myself that over eight years had passed since I was bound to prison. Reaching the stairs, both servants threw themselves to the ground.

"Rise and approach." My voice choked with emotion and I wanted to embrace them both.

"My lord," Clep stood slowly and bowed again as he came forward. "I am Clep, former steward of this house. This is Nukor, personal guard to the master of this house. You sent for us?"

"Yes, I did. You served the Captain General well." It was a statement, not a question.

"Yes, Mighty Lord," he agreed.

I could not stand the distance that time and position had placed between us. Standing up I stepped out of the shadow of the porch.

"Do you know who I am?"

"No, my lord." Neither man looked at me, each keeping his head bowed.

"Look at me." The command was rough with emotion.

Surprised, Nukor was the first to look up. I stood only a cubit away from the two men. The Nubian stared in disbelief.

"It cannot be," he murmured, leaning forward. "The eyes and the nose, but ..."

Clep too was stunned. "Hebiru, could it ... I mean, my lord." He stopped and bowed low.

"It is I, the slave you knew as Hebiru." My hands reached out to grip first Nukor and then Clep to prevent them from bowing again. "By the provision of my God, I have been pardoned from prison to serve as Pharaoh's Governor during this time foretold in Pharaoh's dreams."

The two men stared at me and at then each other in amazement. When I opened my arms, they embraced me joyfully.

"And now you are here again." Clep shook his head, still bemused by the turn of events."

"I don't understand." For the first time since I knew him, Nukor seemed confused and ill at ease.

"Nukor, truly it is Hebiru, your student at arms. Just as you said, the God of my Fathers had a plan for my life. Through slavery, imprisonment, and now in service to the King of the Two Lands, I have learned that the One God will not be thwarted. All things He uses for His purposes."

Still the big man shook his head, comprehension and belief coming slowly.

"Now, the reason I sent for you." I turned the conversation back to mundane things, understanding that my friends would need time to understand how a slave could become a prince in the land.

"The lady Dala is dead." The simple statement caused both men to stare at me. Through their eyes raced the thought that I must have used my power and position to have her killed.

"How?" Clep ventured the question, almost fearfully.

Stepping back onto the porch, I sat down before answering. "The lady has let the land lie fallow against Pharaoh's order that all the land of Egypt is to be tilled to produce the bounty promised by the gods. She refused to pay the fifth portion to Pharaoh and tried to stab me in the back. Fortunately, Adam here," I indicated the faithful man at my side, "was more swift and intercepted the dagger. His spear pinned her to the wall." The retelling left me more shaken than the actual event. I truly realized how close I had come to death at the woman's hand.

"So, the gods provide justice," Nukor said.

"And *maat* is preserved." Clep nodded with satisfaction.

Continuing, I told them, "Clep, you and Nukor will be in charge of the house and land until Pharaoh provides a new master. The land must be sown with whatever crops will give a harvest even at this late date. See that the house is cleaned and whitewashed. Only, do not harm the murals. Hire servants, as you know best. Here is a purse. I will stop by when I return from the Delta."

Standing, I ended the interview. The two men watched me in awe and then prostrated themselves at my feet.

"It will be as you order, great lord," Clep replied.

"Do not grovel at my feet," I begged, feeling the gulf widen between us again.

"You are the Lord Governor," Nukor reminded me, unnecessarily, from his prone position.

"And you are my friends," I said the words to myself, knowing that I could not bridge the gap.

The royal guard formed and I stepped into the chariot to return to my lodgings in On.

"Farewell, then!" I saluted the men. Through a cloud of tears, I stared at the passing landscape. The past was gone and I was again left with the question of who this man called Joseph, Hebiru and Zaphenath-Paneah was. No longer a Hebrew shepherd or foreign slave, I was still not comfortable with the trappings, property, and power associated with being Lord Governor. Even the title felt uncomfortable.

"Lord God, help me to be who You want me to be. God of my Fathers, help me to figure out who I am." I prayed as the chariot rolled down the road.

Chapter 15

The trip to the Delta had to be postponed for a day while I met with the priests and officials at On. The counselor explained over and over what had occurred until finally the men were satisfied.

"Then *maat* is restored. Evil has again been defeated by the power of Ra," was the pronouncement of the priests led by my father-in-law, Potiphera. Throughout the proceedings he had stared at me. I knew he would have liked nothing more than to prove me guilty of something and so rid the country of my influence.

He waited for me after the other officials left. "Lord Governor Zaphenath-Paneah, I want to ask you about my daughter. Is she well? Is she happy? I have not heard from her since you were wed."

I inclined my head graciously. "Asaneth is well. I received a scroll from her just yesterday."

"She knows how to write?" The man was astonished.

Hiding a small smile of triumph, I replied, "Yes, I taught her. She enjoys forming the words and drawing little pictures for my eyes only."

"Why does she not write me?" I was surprised to see hurt in his eyes. Asaneth was so sure that her father did not care that this evidence of his concern was unexpected.

"Perhaps she believes you would not care to hear from her." The words were out before I could think.

The father was silent. When he spoke it was not in anger as I expected. "Zaphenath-Paneah, does she hate me? I know I was not a kind father. Like most men, I thought I wanted a son. By the time I realized what a treasure I had in my daughter, it was too late. She and her mother had moved into their own house. After her mother died, I brought Asaneth back to the temple, but she was always wary of me. I could not break through the reserve. For too long, I did not want to and then I did not know how."

My heart swelled with sorrow for the man standing in front of me. His rash actions had left him bereft of the only child he would ever have. I laid my hand on his shoulder. "I do not know if my bride hates you, but she does fear your anger." I spoke the words slowly, not wanting to add to his pain. Even so, I felt him flinch.

"Tell me how to heal this estrangement." His voice was ragged with suppressed tears. "I sent her away at Pharaoh's request. I did not even tell her that I loved her. All I did was ask her to be my eyes and ears at court, for I did not trust you."

"I know," I told him as his eyes lowered in shame, "she told me."

"Then you must despise me." The father sank heavily into a nearby chair. "Then I have truly lost the chance to reconcile with my daughter."

I stared at the man, no longer the priest, but a man seeking to make amends for past mistakes. My heart wanted to trust his conversion and believe his words.

"My father," I said the name without thinking. The surprised hope in his eyes was reward enough.

"My father, I will talk to Asaneth. I will tell her of this conversation. The answer will be up to her."

"It is more than I dared hope for. You are wiser than your years, Zaphenath-Paneah. Pharaoh is fortunate to have you to guide him."

His words left me speechless. I never thought to hear from Potiphera, priest of On, that he approved of my service to Pharaoh. We parted more in harmony than I expected.

The trip to the northernmost lands of Goshen and the Delta was swift. Mostly grazing land and watered by the sea breezes, this area would be little affected by the Nile famine. Also, I was anxious to return to the capital. My heart yearned for Asaneth, for her gentle voice and soft touch. My heart ached for Potiphera and I hoped I could help my bride see that her father did want to be reconciled. Pharaoh too, was impatient to meet with me and hear from my lips a report of all I had seen and done. I knew he wanted a full report on the loyalty of his priests and counselors. He knew that I had not put everything down on the scrolls.

A short stop at Potiphar's house confirmed that Clep and Nukor were the right pair for the job. Already the fields showed a hint of green as the baby plants pushed through the soil. The house was cleaned inside and out. Servants and slaves worked efficiently applying whitewash and restoring the gardens to their former beauty.

With no further delay, the boat headed upriver to the royal landing. The palace gleamed white in the afternoon sun. I was glad to be back. We left just after the Inundation ended and now it was harvest time. Four full turnings of the moon had passed. The closer we got, the more I wanted to see Asaneth.

Pharaoh's door steward greeted me with the welcoming cup of wine and then escorted me to the throne room saying, "My Lord Pharaoh has wanted to see you as soon as you arrived."

"I am travel stained and dusty," I remonstrated.

"Come," was all he said, flinging open the doors and announced with a flourish, "The Lord Governor Zaphenath-Paneah, Interpreter to the King and Preserver of the Land."

The court parted to allow me access to the King. I hurried forward to kneel and touch my forehead to the steps leading up to the throne.

"Great Pharaoh, I am at your service. Mighty One, I beg you forgive the travel stains, but I came to you as soon as I arrived."

"Lord Governor, we are pleased with your reports and will talk more in the morning. We are glad to receive you back safely, thanks to the gods and the services of your good man." He nodded kindly at Adam who knelt behind me.

"Now we will send you to your wife." A small secret smile caught the corner of his mouth and a low murmur of laughter rippled around the room.

I looked at him with a question forming, but he waved a hand in dismissal. "Go, now." Again I touched my forehead to the stairs and retreated from the royal presence.

Curious and a little concerned, I hurried to my chambers. Set was waiting. "Where is my lady wife?" I asked.

"In her rooms." Again something almost like a smile nearly slipped past his façade.

"Adam, take a well deserved rest," I instructed before splashing water on my face and hands. Quickly changing into a clean linen tunic, I hurried to my lady's apartment.

A slave woman I did not recognize answered my knock. Beyond her I could see many women going about their tasks. Musicians played softly in one corner. Primly, she attempted to deny my entrance.

"My lady is resting and cannot be disturbed," She repeated, seeming to not believe that I was Asaneth's husband.

Sarah hurried across the room to intervene before I lost my temper. "Maka," she said, "my lord the governor wishes to see his wife."

The woman's terror was evident as she fell to the floor at my feet.

"Sarah, who is it?" I heard Asaneth voice from the far room. Ignoring the prostrate slave, I hurried to the inner room.

"It is I, my love," I exclaimed, rushing to her side. She stood up to greet me and I understood the smiles and suppressed laughter. My slim wife cradled her belly with her hands and glanced up at me with a shy smile.

"Asaneth, my wife!" I staggered back to sit in a convenient chair. "What is this you have kept from me?"

I gathered her into my arms and lap. With wonder, I touched her blossoming belly.

"Are you pleased, my lord husband?" she asked, running a finger down my cheek and looking into my eyes.

I answered her with a kiss.

"Most pleasantly surprised," was my response. My hand rested gently on her and I felt the child stir within her.

"I was not sure when you left," she told me shyly. "So I didn't say anything."

"But you never wrote me of this miracle," I chided.

"No." She punctuated each word with a tiny kiss. "It – was – my – surprise – for – you."

I chuckled and hugged her closer. "But the whole court knows, don't they?"

She nodded, smiling happily and laying her cheek on mine. I briefly regretted not taking time to shave but she didn't seem to mind the stubble as she nuzzled and stroked my face.

"My Lord Pharaoh and his lady wife agreed that I could be the one to tell you. I was so anxious for you to return," she finished.

The next little while was spent most pleasurably in the arms of my wife and mother of my unborn child. When I left the room, the moon hung high in the sky. The slave woman still lay by the door where she had collapsed. Her moan of fear at my approach caused me a moment's qualm.

"Get up, woman. I will be generous in my joy. See that you know me in the future."

Sobbing her gratitude, she gabbled her thanks while kissing my feet.

"Enough," I ordered and left her kneeling, still thanking me.

"Is all well?" Set asked when I entered the room. Adam too, was waiting with an eager expression on his face.

"So everyone knew but me?" My voice was edged with laughter.

"No, my lord, I just learned from my wife," Adam replied while Set grinned his answer.

Too excited to sleep, I called for Kevak to help me with my bath and dressing in preparation for the morning meeting with Pharaoh. Luxuriating in the water and attendance of the man, I marveled at the goodness of God. "Thank you, Lord God of my Fathers, for even here far from my kindred, You have given me a family. In Your bounty, I have a wife and will have a child. So it is that You never leave Your people but give them good things." The prayer rose from the depths of my heart as I allowed Kevak to smooth the scented oil over my body.

The King greeted me with a wink as he asked, "Is all well?"

"Yes, Great Lord of the Two Lands." My smile told him what he wanted to know.

At his signal, I took my place next to him. After the morning audience, we walked to the familiar library. Here I gave him the report from my travels. Carefully, we reviewed each scroll I had sent. I learned that the priest remained in prison for his comments about Pharaoh's plan. The King commended my immediate response and applauded the support of the remainder of priests and nobles in the land. "We are glad to have such a report of loyalty in all Egypt," he commented before asking about the storehouses. I was glad to report that all were complete, awaiting the first shipment. The network of supervisors I set up along the Nile was already at work gathering the quota for storage.

Satisfied at last with the results of the months of planning, Pharaoh picked up the last two scrolls. "Here we have a report from Adakra, my counselor in On." He said. "It is of concern that anyone was able to attempt harm to you as our Lord Governor. We seem to recall that this same woman was the cause of your imprisonment."

"Great Pharaoh, it is true that nothing escapes your wisdom." I bowed, speaking past a sudden lump of fear in my throat.

"Then it was the same lady Dala who was wife to my uncle's Captain General?" The King already knew the answer, but I nodded anyway.

"Yes, Mighty Lord," I responded. Then, curious to see how much the counselor had told, I asked, "Does Adakra also mention that there were uninvestigated rumors that the lady poisoned my lor– er, Captain General Potiphar after your uncle, the King died? Does he confess that by his own admission to me the house was a brothel with the women not in the service of any god?"

Pharaoh allowed a small smile to break the severity of his features. "He did mention that the lady was not a lady. But then she never was, from all we hear." I made no response, and he continued with a frown. "However, there is no mention made of rumors of murder."

"It was something that slipped out in his efforts to dissuade me from visiting the house. The accusations were from Lord Potiphar's steward, Clep, and his personal guard, Nukor. Both good, honest men but ignored because they were only servants. Adakra installed them on his property to keep them from spreading such stories."

"These same men, you have now put in charge of the house, I see from your report of the 'incident'." The King glanced at the roll in his hand.

"Yes, may you know, Mighty Ruler, that these are faithful and trustworthy men. Clep chose to become Potiphar's steward rather than serve under another man in the Army. Nukor was defeated by the Captain General in a battle, but I have never seen more loyalty to a master."

"You don't need to defend your choice, Zaphenath-Paneah," he told me. "We know of these men."

Returning to his real concern, he asked, "Do you think the woman recognized you?"

"No, my Lord King," I reassured him. "She was angered at my insistence on her compliance with the royal edict. Because she had no crops, I demanded a fifth of her wealth. She became enraged, but I did not anticipate the dagger. Adam indeed saved my life with his instantaneous response."

Pharaoh nodded, pleased at being reminded of the Syrian's action. "We are indeed grateful to him for that service. The reflex that ended the woman's life has also saved us from the need of further investigation into the Captain General's death. Also, not least, his action saved for us our faithful Lord Governor." He sat silent, tapping the scroll on his hand in the characteristic gesture the man used when thinking deeply. "Zaphenath-Paneah," he said finally, "I ask you, as a friend, for your honesty."

"Yes, Lord King, I have always been honest with you."

"The house and land cannot remain tended by two servants, no matter how honest."

I nodded, not sure where the conversation was going.

"The house no doubt holds certain memories for you," again he paused.

"Most are surprisingly good," I replied after some consideration. "Even as a slave, my lord Potiphar gave me certain special freedom as a scribe. I even accompanied him to the palace to meet with your uncle."

"Oh, yes, the ill-fated 'Alliance.' I had no concern for political things then." Pharaoh looked slightly wistful remembering a carefree youth before the weight of crown and nation were placed on his shoulders. I was reminded that we were of a similar age. Both of us seemed to be in the grip of a power beyond our control that was directing our lives. "Then, Lord Governor, we will honor your work tomorrow with the presentation to you, of the Captain General's holdings. It will give you a place of retreat from the palace, too."

"Great Lord Pharaoh, you are too generous to your humble servant." Indeed as I knelt to his knee, I was overwhelmed by a mixture of emotions.

"You can take your lady wife north and your son will have a place to play and grow away from the court. Perhaps, we will join you for a time, too."

With a clasp of my shoulder, the king stood. I rose to follow, saying, "My Lord King, you are welcome in my home at any time."

I was still in a state of grateful surprise when Pharaoh announced to the court that he was giving to his Lord Governor the house and land recently owned by Captain General Potiphar.

Asaneth was excited when I told her that she would have a real house of her own. "As soon as the baby comes, I want to go." She reminded me of a little girl waiting for her birthday. I promised her that when she was able, we would indeed travel north. Remembering my talk with her father, I broached the subject carefully.

"My love, we will be living near On. Your father spoke to me while I was there." Her expression did not give me much hope for immediate reconciliation, but I tried anyway. "Sweet wife, I believe he would like to try again to be a good father. He seemed truly repentant about his neglect of you and of your mother."

"And you believed him." Her voice was touched with scorn and she drew back from me. "I would think that you of all people would understand that betrayal by a member of the family is unforgivable."

Feeling the sting of her words, I bent my head.

Immediately remorseful, Asaneth grabbed my hand. "Dearest husband, I am sorry."

"I also know the bleakness of being separated from all family for a long time." Taking her soft hands in mine, I caressed them. "God has given me your love and the coming child in place of the brothers and father that I have lost. I would not harm or cause you any pain. You do not have to meet your father until you are ready."

A tear fell onto my hand.

"Do not cry, beloved, I should not have brought up the subject." Contritely, I drew her close.

"I will give it some thought." The lady told me as she dried her tears on my tunic.

Stroking her soft hair, I wondered what I would do if confronted with my brothers. It was easy to forgive from the distance of miles and in the darkness of the prison cell. Would I be able to acquit and welcome them in person? Deciding that the chance was not likely to occur, I pressed my lips to the head nestled against me. Here was my family and my treasure. Nothing would be allowed to harm Asaneth and the baby.

Chapter 16

The late harvest was safely gathered in. By making many short excursions, I was able to both check on the storehouses and also be with Asaneth as her time drew near. The time for the Inundation was drawing near and Pharaoh often asked if I believed it would be as high as the previous year. I continued to assure him that if God promised something, it was fulfilled.

Sarah came for me early one gray morning. "My lady wants you."

"Is it time?" I hurriedly rubbed the sleep from my eyes and followed her torch down the hall.

The midwife frowned at my entrance, but Asaneth held out her hand.

"Jo-seph," she called. As always I was touched by her use of my birth name rather than the official name given me by Pharaoh.

"Here I am, my love." Kneeling by the bed, I was surprised by the strength in her hand as she gripped mine when a pain shot through her.

"It is our son," she said, trying to smile, releasing my hand.

"Do not talk, my lady. Save your energy." The midwife snapped.

"A man here, what next?" I heard her mutter. My concern was for my wife.

Finally, although it seemed hours later, the sun was barely rising when the midwife told her. "It is time. Bear down with the next pain."

"I cannot." She sounded so lost and exhausted that I didn't know what to do. Stroking her hair and holding her hand didn't seem like enough.

"Yes, love. Use my strength. Hold me." I babbled on, wanting so much to ease the pain. A part of me feared for her life. I remembered my mother's struggle to birth Benjamin. Too clearly, I saw in my mind her death and burial. I understood now my father's devastation and prayed desperately for Asaneth to be safely delivered.

Asaneth gave a wrenching cry. The midwife exclaimed, "Good!"

The sound of a baby's wail broke the morning air. Dimly, I heard the women and musicians behind the curtain in the adjoining room burst into the welcoming song for a newborn.

"You have a son," the midwife announced. "A fine boy," she repeated.

Kissing my wife's flushed forehead I murmured, "You are so lovely." Truly I found her, even exhausted from the birth, to be more beautiful than ever.

Sarah brought the baby to us. Asaneth looked down at him with a gentle smile. Then her eyes rose to mine. "Your son."

"He shall be called Manassah, for that means God has made me forget." I told her. "My God has indeed made me forget all my hardships and loneliness. He has given me a new family." I sealed my words with a kiss on the forehead, first of my wife then of my son.

The midwife bustled up to assist with getting the child, my son, to suckle. I stepped back to marvel at how gracious indeed the God of Abraham, Isaac and Jacob was to me.

Pharaoh sent congratulations and even visited later in the day to see mother and son.

"We are pleased. You have a fine healthy son." He told me with a broad smile. "Mother and child are resting, but you look done in. Days of traveling do not wear you down as much as the birth of one small boy, eh Zaphenath-Paneah?" The man continued with a slap on the back. "I know how it is. Because of that, I rarely attend the birth – that is for the women."

I laughed half embarrassed that my weakness should be so obvious.

"Come, we will drink to the health of your son. We will not require your presence for the next couple of days," the King told me magnanimously when he left my chambers hours later. "Enjoy your wife and child."

"Thank you, Mighty One," I knelt to kiss his ring in gratitude but he raised me with a hug. "I only hope I will be as strong when the Queen's time comes."

"Lord King, that is wonderful news!" I knew that although many of the harem wives had born sons and daughters, the Queen, his Chief Wife, had not been able to conceive.

"No one is to know for a while," he cautioned. "She doesn't want to be coddled."

"Yes, Great Pharaoh," I replied, thinking of the secret the whole court had kept from me for months.

I spent the next week reveling in my wife and son. In memory of Abraham's covenant, I circumcised my son on the seventh day, despite Asaneth's protests that the priests should do the job when the boy was older.

"It is the least I can do to honor the covenant the One God gave my grandfather. Surely God has protected me and blessed me as He promised. So, I will keep the covenant."

Too soon, however, I had to resume the visits to various parts of Egypt. The round of duties resumed. As scheduled, the Nile god rose in richness and bounty. All the land was flooded. Every year, during this time, work crews converged on the monuments Pharaoh was erecting at Thebes and further up the Nile. He sent me to supervise progress and I was astonished at the amount of work done. Great blocks of limestone and granite were floated down the flooded river and put in place. Obelisks topped with gold, massive Sphinx, and elaborate temples were all in the process of construction. I reported back that all was in order.

Asaneth did not let me forget my promise to take her to her new home. When Manassah was only a month old, she declared that she was ready to travel. With Pharaoh's permission and aboard the royal barge, we floated swiftly down to the dock at On. I was gratified by her reaction upon seeing the house.

Clep and Nukor had outdone themselves. The walls gleamed white in the sun. Flowers and vines that I did not remember covered the south side of the house. The formal garden could be glimpsed on the north side and the scent of the flowers wafted to greet us. A row of neatly dressed servants stood in line to greet the new master and mistress.

With a smile, I lifted her out of the litter. A flourish of my hand encouraged her to move toward the house on my arm. With each step, she gained confidence. Clep introduced her to each servant and they welcomed her with elaborate bows.

Asaneth blossomed as she worked with Clep to create a real home. Wisely, she retained the Egyptian style animal skin rugs in the main hall and guest chambers. But, for me, she placed the Syrian rugs and hangings in our private rooms, the vibrant hues contrasting with the stark white of the walls. For my birthday, she surprised me with a mural of my own in the long hallway, depicting the building of the storehouses and collection of the surplus.

I saw Potiphera often, but Asaneth remained firm in her resolve to have nothing to do with her father. My heart ached for his sorrow but my words had no effect on her decision. I prayed that she could someday be reconciled to the man I now held in esteem and friendship.

The years slipped by with the Nile's flow. Season followed season, unchanging as it had been since the beginning of time. The river god sent the flood, then as it receded fields were tilled and planted. Canals were reopened and brought the river water into the fields. Then came the harvest, rich and full each year. The storehouses filled up as planned. I spent much time traveling up and down the land. Part of each year was spent at court, for Pharaoh always wanted to review my reports in person.

As promised, the King and his queen came each year to On. While the women visited and the boys played together, I took the Lord of the Two Lands on a tour of the storehouses. We often stopped at temples of the gods and he always wanted to check on the construction of his own mortuary temple.

The sameness of the cycle lulled my thoughts until I barely remembered that a famine was coming. My son's fifth birthday reminded me that time was slipping by. I realized that my son was old enough to start learning of the God of our Fathers.

Asaneth whispered special news to me before we rose from our beds on the morning of the birthday. "Before the fall harvest, there will be another child." Her eyes danced at my delighted expression.

"You are sure?" Scooping her into my arms I kissed her face, lips, eyes, and ears.

Laughing she nodded. "And my lord husband is pleased?"

My only reply was more kissing.

Later in the afternoon, we shared the news with Pharaoh and the Queen. After hearty congratulations, we men walked out to look at the flooded fields.

"One more year of the promised plenty," I reminded the King.

"There is no sign of a coming disaster. We keep asking the priests to search the omens."

"Do you doubt your dreams? My Lord, that was your sign and your promise from the One God."

"But all is going smoothly and the Nile continues to flood and nourish the land," he argued, waving his hand over the wide expanse of water stretching from our feet to the far horizon.

"And so it will for one more year. Then we must be prepared to respond to the people's fears and needs," I replied, seeing in my mind a Nile far below the normal level. "I will spend much time this year teaching the supervisors at each storehouse how to make the distribution honest and equitable all across the land. As we have discussed, it shall be one measure of grain per person in a household each month."

"We leave that to you, Zaphenath-Paneah. You have our complete confidence."

"Have you given consideration to the royal response when emissaries from other countries come for grain?" Again in my mind, I saw drought in the surrounding lands also and caravans crossing to Egypt for grain. I remembered how dependent my father was on the rain in Canaan. It was eagerly awaited each year. Without the torrential rains, the pastures did not green up and the flocks went hungry. Even in Egypt, the power of the storms was known. We called it the "Nile from the Sky" for the deluge filled all the low places and wadis with nourishing water.

"Is that possible?" The thought had never entered his mind.

"Great Lord, your dream did not say how widespread this time of famine will be. Other countries may be affected and in need."

"Hmmm," he pondered tapping his staff on the palm of his hand. "We will be charging the people of Egypt for their supplies?" he confirmed.

"A modest fee, Great One, meant to cover the time and personnel required during the whole fourteen years."

"But, will be have enough for Egypt if the world comes to us?" A frown furrowed the royal brow.

"The bounty of the One God is such that the more you share, the more you have," I stated.

"I cannot understand this One God of yours," Pharaoh complained.

"Yes, My Lord King, it is difficult to understand. I don't know how it is, either. One must simply trust and believe." With a shrug I answered him.

"If you believe that your God will provide from our stores enough for the world, should it come, then make allowance and distribution as you see fit. Only the charge will be five times that of Egypt."

I bowed in agreement.

"Any foreign delegations will be directed to you by the border guards."

"Yes, Mighty One."

After the royal party left, I started taking Manassah outside each evening. Under the stars I told him the stories of the life of Israel, his grandfather. I told him of the promise the One God made to Abraham. "You are part of that promise," I told the boy. I explained that God keeps all his promises, just like a father keeps his word to his son.

One night when I returned from a tour of the northern lands, we three sat together. Asaneth, heavy with child, sat beside me. Manassah, my first-born, played in the cool of the evening. His unexpected question made me examine what I held as truth about my faith in the God of Abraham, Isaac and Jacob.

"Papa, how do you know that the One God keeps his promises? Aren't the gods of Egypt the same?"

"Come here, my son." I gathered him onto my lap.

"I know that the God of my Fathers does not fail and does not change his mind like the gods of Egypt. The gods of Egypt are man-made shadows that try to explain all the aspects of the One God." I sought for words to explain my beliefs to the not quite six-year-old boy.

"But," he insisted, "I can see and touch and name all the gods of Egypt. No one has ever seen your God."

"My son, do you know that I love you even when I am not here?"

"Of course, Papa." His little arms went around my neck for hug.

"I know the One God is real because I know he loves me and you." Pressing his body close to mine, I prayed for inspiration.

"For Mama, too?" The boy glanced at Asaneth, smiling in the lengthening shadows.

"Yes, for Mama, too."

"But, if you can't see him or touch him, how do you know he loves you?" The child persisted in trying to understand.

My mind reviewed the times in my life when I too had doubted not only God's truth and love, but even his reality. I turned my son so I could look into his face. "Manassah, I am going to tell you why I know God loves me." I took a deep breath. "A long time ago, I lived with my father and eleven brothers. Then my brothers got mad at me. They got really mad at me, for a lot of reasons, and would you believe, they sold me to a slave trader?" I smiled to lighten the words.

His eyes got very wide and he exclaimed, "They were bad men!"

"No, just angry and frightened," I said with a reassuring hug. I felt Asaneth touch my shoulder in support and love.

"But the important thing," I continued, "is that God was with me. I found out that even in all the bad things that happened, God had a plan for me. He kept me safe. Then Pharaoh set me free to serve him. I know God cares for me because he kept his promise to me. After all the bad things, I have you and your mother and soon we will have a new baby, too."

"Papa, I love you and I'm glad God loves you too." His little arms again went around my neck. Soon he was sleeping.

Softly I said, kissing his tousled curls, "I am glad God loves you and me and Mama, too." My arm reached out to include my wife in the embrace. "May God be with you, my son."

Less than a week later, Asaneth was brought to bed to give birth. As before, I sat with her as she labored. Before the sun was high, a second son was born.

Holding him in awe, I said, "His name will be Ephraim, for God has made me fruitful here."

Gently, I carried him to Asaneth.

"Jo-seph, is he not beautiful?" she asked, brushing her hand across the dark cap of hair.

"Not so lovely as my bride," I told her with a kiss.

"Will you bring Manassah to meet his brother?" Looking down at her suckling son, she wanted to include his brother in the joy.

He was amazed to see the tiny new addition. Tentatively, he touched Ephraim's cheek. "So soft." Looking up at me, he added, "he's really little, Papa."

"Like you were once, my son." I took his hand to leave the room.

He looked back at his baby brother.

"He will grow just like you did." My voice held a smile as I assured the boy. "Before long, you will be able to play with him. Come, Mama needs to rest now and so does your baby brother. His name is Ephraim," I told Manassah as we left the room.

The quiet family time was interrupted too soon when Pharaoh sent for me to report to the council.

"The counselors and priests have requested assurance that all is in order. Like me, they cannot believe that famine is indeed coming," the King told me before we entered the throne room. Squaring my shoulders, I followed the Lord of the Black Lands into the vast room to face the crowd of concerned men.

"The fall harvest is collected," I reported in conclusion. "Everything is in order for the coming famine time."

"Do you really think that there will be seven years of famine?" a skeptical official asked.

"Great King," I addressed the answer to Pharaoh himself, "God sent you dreams to tell you what was coming. The promised seven years of plenty are accomplished. I do believe we are prepared for the coming seven years of famine."

He nodded in support.

"The people have food from this harvest until the spring," I continued. "The storehouses do not need to be opened yet. When it is time and the supplies are needed, they will be opened."

"Who will decide when there is need?" an old man challenged.

"Zaphenath-Paneah, our trusted Lord Governor," responded the King. "He has been up and down the country diligently preparing for the coming famine on our behalf, as you all know." The stern look encompassed the entire crowd. "We believe that he will know when it is necessary to open the storehouses and begin selling food to the people."

"Selling?" A young counselor rose angrily in the back. "This is the people's own grain."

A murmur of agreement ran around the room.

"Would you deny the Crown a fair profit for the work of collecting and storing the god's bounty?" Pharaoh's words forestalled further complaints with their warning edge.

The young man melted back into the group with a low bow. After a few more general questions, the King dismissed the meeting. I felt drained and a little defensive.

"That went well." The man seated on the throne nodded complacently.

"Yes, Great Lord." My bow was low.

"You are not pleased, Zaphenath-Paneah?" One eyebrow rose in question.

"Mighty One, King of the Two Lands, I am at your service. If I have displeased my Lord the Ruler of Egypt, I beg you forgive me." Again I bowed low.

"We are not displeased with our Lord Governor!" He rose and clapped me on the back. "It was necessary to stop the murmuring before it started. A full report was the only way."

"Pharaoh is ever wise." My bow was ignored as he signaled for me to follow him to the now familiar library. Today he stood staring out the window. I found that he was not as confident as he appeared during the audience.

"Do you never doubt the dream interpretation? It would take only a few words in the right ears to raise rebellion if the fifth quota we have collected is not needed."

"The people have not gone hungry because of their donation to the storehouses," I responded to the second part of the question. "There have been few complaints throughout the land."

"And dealt with swiftly," the King nodded in agreement. "But the dream?"

"Lord Pharaoh, seven years of incredible bounty have come just as the seven fat cows and seven good stalks of grain foretold. Why do you then doubt the second part of the dream?"

"Zaphenath-Paneah, does not seven years of famine seem like excessive punishment? What have we done? What atonement could we have made?" I understood his quandary.

"Good and gracious Lord, King of the Land from the Cataracts to the Sea," moving to his side, I tried to explain. "The famine is not a punishment on Egypt. Rather, because God has made provision to save her, this is a sign of the great providence of the total plan."

"What is the plan?" Eagerly, he turned to me.

With a smile, I answered, "My Lord, if I knew that, I would be more than a man. All I can say with assurance is that the One God of my Fathers has planned and prepared Egypt for this famine. Egypt will survive and become rich and strong through this famine time when other nations are not prepared."

"Then, even famine can be a good thing to this god of yours?" His attempt at a joke fell flat.

"It is the saving of lives that matters to the One God," I replied seriously.

"And to us," Pharaoh agreed. "Our people must not be in want."

"Nor shall they be, thanks to your plans and preparations, Great One." In all sincerity, I gripped his hand and bent to kiss his ring in homage.

"Perhaps, but thanks also to you, friend," he replied, drawing me up from my knees.

Late into the evening we reviewed the details of the food distribution. In the morning, I set out to visit each supervisor and each storehouse across the land. Nothing was to be left to chance. Each man had to know the procedure without question. The penalty for either accepting bribes or refusing need was death.

Chapter 17

Too soon the moon's turnings brought us to the time of Inundation. But the river god did not leave the banks. The water flowed placidly northward; no black and fertile water covered the land. The priests sacrificed and burned incense night and day trying to appease Hapi.

Runners brought me daily reports from all parts of the kingdom. I knew that the storehouses needed to be opened. Throughout the land, people were complaining of failing food supplies and entreating the gods and Pharaoh for help. I sent word to Pharaoh and the next day runners went north and south telling every supervisor to open the storehouses.

Leaving Asaneth and my two sons, I boarded my barge and visited each city. At every stop I observed orderly distribution and commended the overseers for their diligence. My final destination was the capital. Pharaoh, as always, welcomed my verbal report as confirmation of the scrolls that he received. After my official report before the court, he met me in the library.

"So, all is going well?" he questioned without preamble when he entered the room. "No riots or discontent?"

"Mighty King, all is proceeding just as you set in motion with your plans."

"Then Egypt owes you a great debt, The Lord Governor, Zaphenath-Paneah, Interpreter to the King and Preserver of the Land."

"My reward is your peace of mind, Great One." I bowed to him as he took his accustomed seat near the window.

"Nevertheless, we will find an appropriate honor."

"As you will, my Lord King."

"Have any foreign requests been made for the grain?" The man unexpectedly changed the subject.

"I have only just received the first tentative inquiries from the Libyan ambassador."

"And your response?" He turned to look at me.

"Is as we discussed, Wise Pharaoh. The cost is five times that of Egypt for the same ration. I think that the price will be paid, but not all the people will benefit from the purchase."

"The grain will be resold, you think?"

"Without a doubt." It saddened me to think that the poor of the land to the west would still be hungry while the rich filled themselves with Egyptian grain. But, there was nothing I could do short of not selling the grain at all.

"Egypt will not run short?" Again he sought assurance from me.

"No, the King of the Two Lands can be reassured that there is plenty and more for Egypt to share."

"Then proceed as we agreed."

After a little more discussion, I bowed from his presence to send for the Libyan delegation. Five camel loads of grain were sold and the price paid without demure, confirming my belief that the food would be resold for a high profit once across the border.

It did not take long for word to spread throughout the famine struck countries around the Great Sea. Soon envoys arrived from Syria and Haran. The price was paid, often with grumbling, but it was paid. Pharaoh's treasury grew fat and the storehouses were still full.

I was able to snatch an occasional week with Asaneth and my growing sons. Ephraim toddled around after his brother. Manassah was careful of his little shadow. Although we missed one another, both Asaneth and I knew that I needed to be at court. We agreed the boys should be kept away from the palace until the famine ended. Even though he stayed in Memphis, Pharaoh sent the Queen and his son to the quiet of On, away from the increasing intrigue in the government. Some of the councilors were trying to obtain special favors from the King in the form of an additional allotment of grain. When I heard of the plan, I spoke to Pharaoh. "Mighty Lord, let not the King of the Black Land be angry for your servant would speak."

"Continue, Zaphenath-Paneah, your counsel is wise. We value your words."

"Great One, Life of Egypt, I have heard that certain officials want additional grain for their use."

"We have heard their request." The King inclined his head.

"Wise Lord, word has come to me from my overseers that the reason for this additional allotment is to sell the grain privately to certain foreign princes who have slipped into the country and spoken secretly to these councilors."

Pharaoh stood up so suddenly that the chair tipped over. A slave hurried forward to set it up, cowering away from the anger in the man's face.

"How dare anyone seek to subvert the throne in such a way?" The roar of rage caused the scribes and slaves in the room to fall face down in fear.

"Mighty King," I faced him, "you are the Great One, Lord of the Two Lands. It is from ignorance that these men act."

"Ignorance!" He repeated the word with a furious turn around the room. I had never seen a man so enraged. "They shall die as a lesson to other upstart, rebellious officials."

His anger turned on me as I started to speak.

"Do you dare to plead their case? Are you in league with these traitors?"

Falling on my face, I replied, "Great Ruler, you know that I am loyal only to you as you are only devoted to Egypt."

Spent from the rage, he sank back into the chair. After a minute, he replied in a mollified tone, "Yes, Zaphenath-Paneah, that we do know. Our Lord Governor is faithful and honest. We will deal with the deceitful councilors."

A few days later, I sat with Asaneth and the Queen in the cool evening talking about our children. Pharaoh had sent me away from court to 'spend time with my family'. A runner came with the weekly report. Included was mention that three councilors had been arrested for insurrection and were awaiting trial in Pharaoh's jail. Early the next morning, a message came from court requesting my return.

I assumed that there was an embassy from a foreign king wanting grain, but there was no one waiting to see me. The King never referred to the men in prison, asking instead for news of my sons and his family.

Nearly a week passed without importunate ambassadors. I was planning to slip away to see Asaneth again when Set brought me word that a group of men awaited me in my audience chamber.

"Ambassadors?" I asked.

"No, my Lord Governor, they claim to be brothers, not representatives of any government. But they are asking for food and supplies."

"Very well." Sighing, I put aside my plans. Kevak appeared to assist me into the tunic and other official regalia. My eyes properly painted, wig in place and with the governor's staff in hand, I allowed Set to escort me to the room. Adam, as always, walked just behind me.

"With any luck, I will be able to overawe this group of peasants and be done with them in short order," I muttered to Adam. "We can still be on our way north to our wives."

"Yes, my lord," he smiled in agreement.

"The Lord Governor, Zaphenath-Paneah, Interpreter to the King and Preserver of the Land," Set proclaimed, flinging open the door.

Without even a glance at the group of men, I strode to my chair on the raised dais. Only then did I turn and give a haughty look at the delegation.

They all immediately fell flat on their faces in obeisance. But I knew them. Ten of my brothers lay prostrate at my feet. Thankful for the chair, I sat down, my heart thundering in my ears.

"Mighty Prince," Reuben raised his head to speak.

I looked at the man, affecting not to understand him. A brief word sent Set for an interpreter. With a motion of my hand, I indicated to Reuben that he should wait. The ten men cowered on the floor. I stared over their heads trying desperately to control my emotions. My hands gripped the carved arms of the chair, thoughts in turmoil. The twenty-one years that lay between us were as nothing. I wanted to rush to them and make myself known. But, I also still heard their laughter at my pleas as they counted the money collected for my life. Was my father still alive? Where was Benjamin? Could I forgive in person the men who caused my slavery and imprisonment? But, I was governor because of their actions. Part of my heart wanted to embrace the men but a little voice tickled my ear telling me that it was only right that my brothers should cringe at my feet.

Adam, sensing my anguish but not understanding the reason, took a step forward. I was grateful for his dependable presence. I knew he was curious about my request for an interpreter. He knew I spoke the language as well as he did.

Set's return with the interpreter forced me to focus on the ten men.

"What do you want?" I asked.

The interpreter carefully repeated, "The lord governor wants to know what you want from him."

Reuben again lifted his head and sat up to reply. The interpreter repeated each word for me. "Great Lord, I am the eldest of these ten brothers. We are all sons of one man, a great sheik in the land of Canaan. We come before you and ask your mercy on our wives and little ones. There is no food in Canaan. Our sheep are dying and our families beg us for food. We heard that there was grain to be had here in Egypt, so we have come, Mighty Prince." He ended by falling face down again.

"So," I spoke as though considering the merits of his request. "You are all of the family? Is your father still alive? Have you other brothers?"

"The Mighty Prince knows all. Our father, the great sheik, Jacob bar Isaac, is indeed alive. He is an old man and would not be able to travel with us easily. The youngest of our brothers stayed with him in our tents."

"Ah." I tapped my staff thoughtfully on the palm of my hand in unconscious imitation of Pharaoh. "Then, you would have me provide food not only for you ten but for an unseen father and brother also. Perhaps you have heard that the allotment is one measure per male per month here in Egypt, and invent other family to increase the amount you can buy."

"Great Governor, I beg you, our wives and little ones grow faint with no food." Reuben's pleas grew more desperate. The other nine now joined their voices to his. Their begging and groveling was almost amusing. It was gratifying to hear them pleading, even though they did not know that I was their betrayed brother. I stood up to make reply and the long buried memory of my own two dreams flooded over me.

Rather than answer, I walked across the dais to gaze out toward the East. Adam remained at my side.

"I dreamed," I whispered partly to Adam but mostly to myself, "my brothers and I were gathering grain into sheaves. My sheaf stood up tall and theirs bowed to mine. I dreamed again and saw my brothers' stars and the sun and moon offering obeisance to my star. I see that God has fulfilled these dreams in my sight."

Adam glanced at the men calling after me with desperate cries.

"Great Lord of Egypt, have pity!"

"Mighty One, we are at your mercy!"

"Lord of the land, we beg of you!"

Collecting myself with an effort, I whirled and strode back to the center of the room. "Stop!" I ordered. "I believe you are not all brothers, but clever spies come to see the land!"

The aghast expressions on ten faces when the interpreter repeated the words might have made me smile at another time. Now, I overrode their disclaimers by announcing, "No! You will be put in prison to consider your story. When I have time, I will hear your case and decide the truth! See to it!" My last order was to Adam who saluted and summoned the household guard. I stood blindly staring over the heads of my brothers as they were bound and led away to the cells below the guardrooms. Then I sought my own apartments and wept.

"God of my Fathers, God of Abraham, Isaac and Jacob! What am I to do? You send me my brothers who sold me into slavery. Is it that I can have vengeance on them for the thirteen years of slavery and prison? But Lord my God; you showed me your mercy and your plan for preservation of life in the famine. You kept me safe in the dungeon and made me prosper even in my adversity. My God, it was easy to forgive them from a distance. Can I forgive them now as they stand before me? My heart yearns for them, even though I remember the treachery. How could my dreams have come true in such a way? My brothers are indeed on their knees to me, begging for food at my feet!"

I spent the night and the next two days in agony of spirit, feeling more alone and desolate than I have been since the first darkest days of prison. I wished Asaneth were near. My desire for revenge struggled against the love I found I still held for my family. Finally, I threw myself to my knees in surrender. "Lord God, the Almighty Lord of all. I cannot fight Your will. I shall send food to Canaan. Let Your will be done."

A peace of heart and soul enveloped me. I knelt there for a long time as confidence in God's goodness returned and comforted me. I stood up, calm and assured that God was with me to give me words to tell my brothers.

When I opened the door, Adam leapt to his feet. It touched me to realize that he had kept vigil outside my room. Set, too, for he now hurried forward with concern on his face. "My lord, will you bathe or eat first?"

"Faithful ones, I thank you." Simply, I acknowledged their care. "Send for Kevak, I will bathe and dress before eating. Go yourselves and be refreshed. Also, Adam, I know your oldest boy is with you." I smiled as I revealed his secret.

"Yes, my lord, forgive me. I thought it was time for him to learn to serve."

His startled look and bow made me reach out and lay a hand on his shoulder. "I agree. Bring him to me after you have bathed and dressed."

The water and Kevak's ministrations soothed away some of the exhaustion of the sleepless nights. At my request, he robed me in the elaborate ceremonial tunic. He carefully completed the eye makeup and adjusted the wig and headpiece. I never ceased to be amazed at the transformation that occurred in the mirror as I watched. I sat down a Hebrew man dressed in Egyptian clothes and rose a royal official of the land, indistinguishable from the many other nobles at court except by the coronet and staff which Kevak now handed me.

Adam and his son awaited me in the antechamber.

"How old are you, lad?" I asked as we broke bread together. Adam ate hesitantly, but the boy eagerly stuffed his mouth. I realized that I was hungry and bit eagerly into the bread and meat smiling a little at the father and son.

Shyly, with a glance at his father, the boy said, "Thirteen, my Lord Governor, sir."

"I have something I need you to do. It is very important but very secret." I leaned toward him. His eyes lit up at the hint of intrigue. "You will be going to the storehouse with some men today. After their sacks are loaded, I want you to put something in each sack of grain and close it back up. This has to be done without anyone seeing. Can you do that?"

The boy stopped eating as he listened to my instructions. Bright eyes met mine as he replied, "Oh, yes, my lord." He grinned in anticipation. "I put bugs in my sisters' baskets and they never see me!" Suddenly he gave a guilty look toward his father and sidled closer to me.

I couldn't help but laugh.

"What is your name, boy? I remember doing the same thing when I was your age." A brief memory of slipping under the tent flap into the women's tent and putting a fistful of grasshoppers into the workbasket flashed through my mind. The punishment had fallen on Gad who happened to be standing outside when the insects were discovered.

"Seth, my Lord, if it please my Lord." After a frown from Adam, the lad had reverted to formality.

"Seth, I think you will do just fine." I patted him on the shoulder. "Wait here until I send for you. You may have the rest of the food if you want," I added, rising to my feet.

"Adam, you have a fine, bright son." I told the man once the door closed on the sight of the boy happily devouring the reminder of the food. He bowed and nodded with pride.

"Set, send for the prisoners." My order signaled a return to business.

"Yes, Lord Governor." He hurried away with a low bow.

In full regalia I stood silent beside my chair as the ten men were marched in. They fell to their knees and bowed their faces to touch the floor.

"Unbind them and leave," I commanded.

Hopeful faces were raised to mine.

"Great Lord," Reuben ventured to speak after the guards exited.

My raised hand stopped his words. "Do you still claim to be brothers?" The interpreter repeated the question. He had a hard time with the answer for all responded.

"Yes, Mighty Lord!"

"It is true!"

"Indeed, Lord Governor, we are brothers."

Again, I raised my hand. Reuben moved forward with a low bow to make a formal response.

"Great Lord Governor of all Egypt, it is as we told you. We are indeed sons of one father. Once there were twelve of us brothers in all."

"You claimed that there were eleven total," I challenged.

"Noble and Wise Lord, there are truly only eleven of us remaining. One son," he glanced at his brothers briefly before continuing, "one son, our father's favorite, was torn by wild beasts and is no more."

Thus, I learned the story my brothers had concocted to cover my sale into slavery.

After a long pause, I replied, "I fear God and would not have your wives and children suffer because of your lies."

Reuben started to speak in denial but I continued. "Therefore, I have decided," I paused to take a turn around the dais, "one of you will remain here in jail while the rest of you take food to your father and your little ones. When you return with the youngest brother you speak of, I will believe you are not spies and free the prisoner."

Wildly, the men looked at one another and at me. Gathering together, they discussed the offer as presented by the interpreter.

"It is punishment for our treatment of Joseph."

"We heard his pleas and ignored them. Now God has visited this on us."

"But we must have grain or die."

"What can we tell our father?"

"We have no choice."

"Why did we betray our brother?"

"You would not listen to me when I warned you."

Standing with my back to the men, I listened while staring unseeing out the window. They had no idea I understood all the conversation. I gripped the governor's staff in my hand until pain shot up my arm from the tension.

At last, Reuben stepped forward. "Mighty Lord," his voice was somber and humble.

Slowly, I turned from the window and returned to sit in solemn judgment.

"Wise Governor, Noble Prince, Great Lord, we are your servants. Do with us as you will. Only we pray you give us food for our families lest they perish."

"Very well! Adam, take that man and bind him." I pointed at Simeon.

My heart ached as I watched my nine brothers bid farewell to Simeon. The memory of the different send off they gave a seventeen year old youth hardened my resolve. Adam led him bound to me and brought him to his knees. Over his head, Adam looked at me with compassion. I had to look away from his sympathy. Sternly, I commanded the rest.

"See that you return with this younger brother you speak of or you will not see my face or your brother again. Give me the money for the grain." Hurriedly, they each presented a sack of silver. I weighed one in my hand and seemed satisfied. "Wait here for the slave lad to escort you to the storehouse. You will be given grain as you have purchased." Nine men fell to their faces as I stepped down and crossed the room. I did not dare look at them. Adam marched Simeon through the door after me.

"Hold this man secure in jail until you receive further orders from me." I told the captain of the guard by the door, knowing that nine pairs of eyes still watched my every movement. Watching my brother being led away, I felt no satisfaction but rather a deep emptiness.

"Come, we must send Seth as guide." Even hurrying rapidly down the hall and seeing the boys excited anticipation did not ease my heart.

"Take these bags of silver and put one in each of the filled sacks of grain." I repeated the instructions as I gave the lad the pouches of money. "Remember, no one can see you doing this."

"Yes, my lord." He seemed to pick up some responsibility along with the silver.

"See the men to their first night camp and then return and report to me what has happened. I will be waiting in On."

"Yes, my lord." The boy bowed with all the maturity he could muster. The ten money sacks he stored around his body. Adam took him by the hand and I heard fatherly instruction being given as the door closed.

Restless, I paced the room. When Adam returned to report that Seth had charmed the men with his eagerness, I suggested we ride out and observe from a distance.

"I want to see them on their way," I lied. More and more, I desired that my brothers would stay nearby. "You would like to see how Seth does, too," I guessed. "Then we can head north."

"Yes, my lord." Adam readily agreed.

From the overlook north of town, we were able to see the ten donkeys being loaded and then the men set out. Seth was an ever-present movement among and around both men and beasts. Their road led straight east. When they were mere dots, Adam and I hurried to the boat landing and soon we were floating north toward Asaneth's soothing arms.

Late the next day, Seth arrived to report that the men were safely on their way out of Egypt.

"What happened last night?" I wondered if anyone knew the money was returned.

"One of the brothers, I think it was Levi, opened his sack to feed the animals. He showed the pouch to all the others and they talked for a long time. But I couldn't hear what was said."

"Thank you lad. You may go. Your mother is waiting for you." Sketching a bow, the boy ran off to join his family. I leaned back wearily and closed my eyes. So they knew about the money, but they weren't going to risk returning to court. I wasn't sure if I was relieved or angry. In the depths of my soul, I had wanted to prove them honest men and be reunited with my brothers. Now they left Simeon in the Egyptian prison and returned to Canaan without trying to make restitution of the money they found. I wanted to be angry, but I felt only sorrow.

Asaneth softly came up and began to stroke my hair and face with soothing oils. Eventually, I forgot my brothers and let myself be comforted by her love.

Chapter 18

The famine brought with it new responsibilities. My regular visits to the towns and storehouses were fewer but each supervisor sent the distribution reports weekly and a report was compiled for Pharaoh. My apartments at the palace were expanded to include a larger audience chamber. Not nearly as grand as the royal throne room, it was still extravagant and overly imposing for my taste. The walls were painted with scenes of planting and harvesting. Representations of the storehouses and the Nile god, Hapi, occupied the wall behind the official chair. In keeping with the theme of the room, my governor's chair had alligator claw feet and alligator head arm rests. Pharaoh was pleased with his gift and like a boy showed me the wonderful features of each mural.

"Zaphenath-Paneah, here you can brief the counselors about the progress of the grain distribution. Even the doubters now believe that my dream and your interpretation are correct. The priests are making themselves ill fasting and pleading with the gods. Perhaps you can convince them that it is useless, for five more years remain."

"I will speak to them at your command, Great One," I replied. In my heart, I doubted that any words of mine would convince either officials or priests that the continuation of the drought was inevitable. In fact, everyone agreed that Egypt was weathering the famine better than anywhere else in the world. Once a week, I opened my doors to petitioners from other countries. But, no further traffic came from Canaan. I wondered about my father and brothers. Simeon was kept in a small chamber near the guardhouse. I saw him when Adam and I did our exercises in the yard. Early on, there were whispers about the spy imprisoned by the lord governor. Now everyone knew that he was not a spy, but a political hostage.

With all the activity at court, I had little time to be at home with my family. I missed Asaneth and my sons. She wrote me a long scroll each week telling me about Manassah and Ephraim. On one of my rare visits I found a tutor for Manassah, and soon he began adding small notes to his mother's correspondence. Seth was allowed to learn from the tutor also, in order to become of assistance to me as a scribe.

Gradually, the weather cooled from the heat of the dry summer. Asaneth suggested coming to the capital. I wrote her eagerly, urging her to come with all haste. Set was put to work preparing her chambers. Pharaoh and his queen prepared a lavish welcome feast. For the first time in months I felt at peace with the world.

"Jo-seph," she asked a few days later. "Is your brother still in prison?"

Lounging with my head in her lap, I nodded drowsily, "Yes, love."

"Could I meet him?" The question took me by surprise.

"Why?" I was suddenly wry. I avoided actually visiting my brother, preferring to observe him from a distance when Adam and I exercised.

"To see one of the men who sent you to me. To try and understand." She looked down at me with a pleading look while stroking the hair from my forehead.

"He is just a man," I hedged, "and a lady should not go the guard area."

"That is not fair!" Her response was said with a pout. "If you won't take me, I'll just go with my ladies and a fine scandal that will be."

"Why do you torment me so?" Then I caught a glimpse of the impish light in her eyes. "Come here! I'll take you tomorrow, but you will be disappointed with what you see."

Catching her up in my arms I carried her to the bed where thoughts of my brother were banished for both of us.

Asaneth was waiting when I returned from the morning meeting with Pharaoh. With an inward sigh, I took her hand. Her eyes were wide as we walked past the rows of spears and other weapons. Soldiers stared and stumbled to their feet with bows at her presence.

"My lady Asaneth would see the political prisoner, Simeon from Canaan." I told the captain. "Bring him out into the yard."

"Yes, my Lord Governor." He bent low with a curious look at my wife. She stood totally composed at my side.

The ropes on Simeon's wrists made me cringe inside. For the first time, I noticed the gray hair at his temples. He blinked a little in the sunlight reflecting off the whitewashed walls. He looked tired and old. Not at all like the young man, angry at his brother's outrageous dreams. I turned my head, steeling my emotions.

Asaneth touched my arm. "Are you still angry at him? At them? Surely too much time and experience has passed for you to still be bitter."

Looking into her concerned eyes, I replied, "No, I am no longer angry." Saying the words out loud made me realize that it was true. The anger had given way to pity and now my heart held only longing for reunion and reconciliation. I turned my head but Asaneth saw the tears in my eyes. "I want to go." My wife took my arm.

"That will be all." My voice was harsh with emotion. I let Asaneth lead me through the gate rather than back down the hallway past the soldiers. Neither of us had any words to say.

"Your brother, Simeon, is just a man as you said. Jo-seph, is my father just a man, too? Will you send for him? I think I could meet him now."

"Beloved, he will be so pleased. It is what he prays for." I left her with a kiss. A runner was sent to Potiphera at On with the news that Asaneth would speak to him.

He came as a man, not as a priest. Anxiously, he gripped my arm. "Why have you sent for me? Is it true that my daughter wishes to see me?"

"Yes, Lord Priest Potiphera, Asaneth has agreed to meet you." Even to myself, I couldn't explain how seeing Simeon had caused her change of heart.

"Then let us go." I understood his anxiety as he squared his shoulders outside her door. My heart pounded in anticipation and hope.

"Remember what you told me – that you love her and regret the mistakes you made?" For the first time, I gave him a quick embrace.

The door was opened by Sarah. She led us to where Asaneth sat with needlework in hand. I saw that she was not working on it, but holding it tightly crumpled in her hands. She was nervous, too, about the meeting. Quickly I crossed the room to drop a kiss on her forehead.

"Here is your father, dearest one. He has come at your request."

The man stood uncertain in the center of the room waiting for a response from his daughter. They gazed at each other for a long time, each afraid to make the first move. Then Asaneth dropped the needlework and ran to her father. He held open his arms to receive her. Tears sprang to my eyes and I heard Sarah sob as priest and princess were reconciled and became a family again. I left them together to make up for the many lost years.

When Asaneth sent Sarah for me much later I entered the room to find that my bride had ordered a feast prepared. Father and daughter sat next to each other and my sons were somewhat hesitantly getting to know their grandfather. My wife rose and came to me. "Thank you, my love. You have shown me how to forgive," she told me after a welcoming kiss. Taking my hand, she led me to sit next to her.

Potiphera had a demeanor of peace as he clumsily played with the boys. He smiled at me.

"Zaphenath-Paneah, you have worked a miracle in my life this day." It was the closest he came to a thank you, but I understood.

Much later after the children were sent to bed, the priest bid us goodnight. Set escorted him to the guest chambers. Asaneth cuddled in my arms.

"Are you content?" The question was unnecessary for she snuggled happily against me.

"My love, I pray that your brothers return soon and that your God will remove the shadow from your eyes and heart." Her response was soft. "You have given me back my father…" She stopped as tears trickled down her face.

"Don't cry, beloved," I begged, kissing the tears from her cheeks.

"I am crying for joy," she insisted continuing to sob. I held her until the tide eased.

The gods seemed willing to heed her prayer, for the next day word came that a caravan of Canaanites had crossed into Egypt to buy food.

I gave Set orders, "If these are indeed the men who came before, they are to be brought into my private dining chamber. I will eat with them."

"*With* them! My Lord Governor, you will be defiled! *Eating* with filthy herdsmen!" He was scandalized.

I hid a smile. "Have a separate table for me then." With that the butler had to be satisfied, although he was still shaking his head.

"Also, I want them seated in a certain order. Here it is, all written out. If the youngest brother, Benjamin, is indeed with them, he will have special portions of the food." My voice cracked with the deep emotions I was holding inside.

Curious but obedient, Set left to put the orders in motion. I retired to my room with Adam and Kevak to prepare myself. Nervously, I paced until Kevak begged, "Good master, I cannot complete the dressing and makeup if you continually move around."

With an apology, I sat before the mirror but my hands continued to fidget. At last Set brought word that the men had arrived.

"It is the oddest thing, my lord," he told me. "When they came in they tried to give me two pouches of silver. Some story about finding their earlier payment in their sacks of grain."

"How odd," I replied without a change of expression. "Adam, see that the prisoner is brought to rejoin his brothers."

With a low nod, my faithful guard left the room.

"Is the youngest brother with them?" Anxious to learn if my brothers had brought Benjamin, I could not wait until I saw them.

"Yes, my lord, there are ten men. One said his name was Benjamin."

"Is the interpreter there? And the meal is ready?"

Set gave me an odd look and I caught myself.

"Never mind, I know you have all in order."

Adam's return prevented further conversation. Set left with a bow but I saw him shake his head just before he left the room.

"I fear Set thinks I have run mad with all this for some Canaanite herdsmen." My laugh sounded hollow even though Adam smiled slightly in agreement.

"The men fear you have brought them here to entrap them. I heard them talking when I took the prisoner in."

"Then let us go."

This time I entered through a side curtain thus catching them by surprise. My eyes sought Benjamin. I would have known him even had he not been seated in his place. He was staring around the room in awe, taking in the ornate carvings, hangings, and golden images. The eyes and face were my mother's. He must have felt my look, for it was Benjamin who first noticed that I stood in the room.

"Great Lord Governor!" He fell prostrate followed by the rest.

Not trusting my voice, I turned and left the room. Adam found me leaning against the cool wall, resting my head on my arm.

"They are your brothers." In sympathy he dared to put his hand on my shoulder.

"Yes, but they do not know me. I am a stranger to them. They are strange to me. Even Benjamin is a man now, not the boy I remember." I was embarrassed by the raw pain in my voice.

"My lord, they think you dead long ago. You have changed into an Egyptian prince," he spoke encouragingly.

Gathering myself together, I squared my shoulders. "Of course, you are right. It was foolish of me to expect them to see in me the youth they last saw tied to a camel." I could not prevent the bitter acid in my voice.

I returned to the chamber to find my brothers in a panic. As soon as I entered, Reuben stepped forward.

"Let not my Lord, the Great and Noble Governor of Egypt, be angry. Behold, we have returned with our youngest brother as you commanded."

He pushed Benjamin forward. I gripped the young man's shoulders and stared deep into his eyes. He stared back bravely until I turned to look at the others. Slowly, he bowed backward to his place.

"And your father? He is well?"

"Yes, Lord Governor." The interpreter condensed the several responses into one.

"Then, I must believe that you are truly brothers." I turned my back on them and walked to my chair.

Reuben followed me nervously.

"Let not the Wise and Mighty Lord be angry with his servant, for I am as a worm in your sight. Great One, here is the silver for the last grain we purchased and," he hurriedly added, "the money for more grain. We do not understand how, but our silver was found in our grain sacks when we opened them."

He fell to his knees and held the pouches out to me over his lowered head.

"Nonsense, I received your payment myself. Perhaps your God gave it back to you."

"Please, Lord Prince, accept this then as a gift." He laid the pouches at my feet. "Also, Most Noble One, our father, Jacob bar Isaac, has sent you offerings from the meager fruits of the land of Canaan."

With a twist of his head, he indicated that his brothers should bring forward the chests and baskets they held.

"Here are dates and figs such as you will not find in the land of Egypt. Also nuts and rich, sweet smelling balm from Canaan."

I had to swallow the lump in my throat before answering. "Give your father my thanks." My father had sent gifts to a governor not knowing that he actually sent them to his long lost son. To cover my emotion, I ordered, "Let the food be brought."

My words signaled a procession of servants with platters of meat, vegetables, bread and the sweet honey wine that was part of each meal in Egypt. From the huge roast presented to me, I sent a large portion to Benjamin. His open-mouthed astonishment made me smile. At the end of the meal, I sent for Seth.

"You will accompany these men to the storehouse as before." I told him. Through the interpreter, I instructed the men to gather their donkeys and meet the lad by the gate. They left with many bows and expressions of gratitude. After the door closed, I handed Seth the money pouches as before.

"Return the silver as you did a year ago," I told him. At his excitement, I could not suppress a smile. He grinned in response and turned to go.

"Wait." The boy turned back. I held my silver goblet, slowly turning it in my hand. "This cup must go into the sack of the young man, Benjamin. Be sure it is not visible when the sack is opened." The chalice was placed in the boy's hand and I gripped my hands together to stop their shaking.

"Yes, my lord," he replied, his eyes full of questions but he said nothing.

"Get fresh grain sacks from Set. They will cover what you hold."

He scurried from the room with a cocky bow and a grin. The secrecy and adventure appealed to him. I leaned back in my chair and released my breath in a sigh. Looking at Adam, I responded to his curious look. "I need to be sure they are indeed all honest men now. Or will they sell out Benjamin to save themselves?" Leaning forward I held my head in my hands.

"I wanted to tell them who I am, Adam, but I could not. I was afraid that they would reject me again. God of my Fathers, help me."

Adam stood silently sympathetic as I struggled with my fears. Seth returned to report that all eleven were on their way back to Canaan.

"The cup is safely in the man Benjamin's grain," he reported in response to my question.

"Now, my faithful Adam, your part in this masquerade starts. Send for Set."

The steward entered. "Was everything as you wished, my lord?"

"The meal was fine. But my silver goblet is missing. I fear one of the guests may have taken it." The passion in my voice could pass for anger.

"That is awful, my lord!"

"Adam, take a troop of men and accompany Set. Stop the men and search their baggage. Bring the guilty man to me."

When Adam and Set left, I fell to my knees in longing. "God of my Fathers, why must I torture myself with these endless tests of my brothers? Am I still so afraid of their anger that I don't dare trust myself to them? I have risked all by sending them away again. Will you bring them all back or will they sacrifice Benjamin in order to save themselves? My God, you saved me and brought my dreams to reality. Why cannot I trust your plan for me? I still doubt. God of Abraham, Isaac and my father Jacob, forgive me. I desire reconciliation but when you offer it, when my brothers stand before me, I push them away. Please, my God, give me courage."

The shadows lengthened as I prayed. At last I heard a commotion. Set came in looking as dusty and disheveled as I had ever seen him. In his hand was my silver cup. "My Lord Governor, we have indeed found your goblet." He held it out to me. "It was in the youngest man's sack of grain."

"Good man, where is the culprit now?" I took the cup and turned it around in my hand while he answered. The answer would tell me God's answer.

"They all came back. Each one refused to leave the young man. Adam has them under guard in your audience chamber."

My heart leapt with hope when I heard that my brothers had not deserted Benjamin.

"I will deal with this crime," I told Set. Standing, I took a deep breath to calm myself.

Ever the butler, he adjusted my collar and tunic before handing my staff to me and then opening the door. Watching him striding ahead of me down the hall to the audience chamber, I was amused at the outrage on his face.

"The Lord Governor, Zaphenath-Paneah, Interpreter to the King and Preserver of the Land." Flinging the door open he announced my presence.

Fear-filled silence greeted my entry. Feigning disdain, I barely glanced at the eleven men as I strode across the room to the chair on the dais. I was actually afraid that I would not be able to continue the charade if I looked at them. Dramatically, I placed the silver goblet on the table. "Did I not say that you were spies and thieves? Did you not think that I would know by divination that you had stolen this cup?"

Only then did I turn and look at my brothers. They all lay prostrate on the floor. After a long silence, I spoke one word. "Well?"

The interpreter waited for their response. Finally Judah spoke. "Let the Great and Noble Lord Governor of Egypt hold me responsible."

"So you took my divining cup?" My voice was rough.

"No, Mighty Prince!" He was aghast at my words and bowed his face to the floor. "The lad would not do such a thing either. Someone must have put the cup in his sack."

"Why?" I decided that monosyllables were best.

"Mighty Lord," he moved forward with hands held open pleading. "I do not know who or even why such a thing would be done. But Great One, the boy is innocent, I would stake my life."

"Really?"

"Sovereign Lord Governor, Wise Ruler, know this: our father's life is bound up in this boy. His brother, as we told you, is dead. Their mother only bore two sons to our father. We dare not return without the lad or we will surely cause our father's death."

"So?" It was hard to speak around the lump in my throat at Judah's pleas.

Falling to his knees at my feet, Judah held up his hands.

"Take me, take all of us as your slaves. Only let the boy return to our father."

The others added their voices. Once again, all were kneeling before me. Benjamin lay flat on the floor, surrounded by my brothers. They were all pleading for his life. My tears and cries for mercy had been ignored, but now these same men were begging for my brother's life. It seemed that in the lifetime that passed, they had learned compassion and honesty.

Seeking to gain self-control, I moved to the window. My heart was breaking with the desire for reconciliation, but the words would not pass my lips. With my back still to them, I gave judgment.

"Only the guilty man needs to stay as my slave. The rest of you are free to go." My voice was rough edged from the feelings pounding in my heart.

"No, Lord Governor, we will not leave Benjamin. We will remain until he is acquitted." Judah's reply didn't surprise me.

My fingers were white as I gripped the staff praying for peace. As clearly as if someone spoke, I heard "Only you can make the peace." I barely heard the rest of my brothers offering their lives for Benjamin. The breeze from the Nile seemed to give me the courage and words I needed. Suddenly I spun around to face the room.

Everyone fell silent and my brothers threw themselves to the floor in petition.

"Leave me! Let all those of Egypt leave me!" Curious and surprised guards and slaves left me alone in the room. Adam was last to exit and he saluted my courage.

Only after the tall doors closed did I step off the dais and move toward my brothers. They scrambled backward, cringing from me and barely daring to raise their heads.

"Look at me." The voice barely sounded like my own. I spoke in Hebrew.

Fearfully Judah raised his head when I stood beside him.

"Come close and really look at me." I pulled the wig and cornet from my head and exposed the dark brown and forever wavy hair of a Hebrew not an Egyptian. I moved from brother to brother, raising them up and forcing them to look in my face.

"Am I still strange to you? Don't you see that it is I, Joseph, your brother?" My cry rang in the room. "Can't you recognize me?"

"But how can that be?" Levi voiced everyone's confusion. "You are the Lord of Egypt."

"You sold me for evil, but the God of our Fathers preserved my life to bring good." The statement made them all step back, fear apparent on their faces. I stood still praying that they would see that I was their brother and meant them no harm.

"Can it be?" Judah came close and peered into my face.

"Is it truly Joseph?" The others too finally began to grasp the reality. Benjamin hung back as the other ten gathered around.

"Benjamin, my brother, I see in you our mother's eyes and her face. Can you not see that I am your brother Joseph?" I drew him to my breast with tears brimming in my eyes.

"I believe you must be my brother." His arms returned the embrace. The emptiness in my heart began to ease.

I held out my arms to the rest of my family. One by one, they conquered their fear and allowed me to enfold them in my arms. Tears flowed as I held my brothers. Twenty-two years of pain melted away from my heart.

"You must now all return to Canaan and bring my father and your families here to Egypt. There are five more years of famine yet to come. I will speak to Pharaoh and you will get land in Goshen where there is good grazing." Already my mind was moving on to plans. The eleven men still stood silent stunned by the turn of events.

"You will dine with me tonight and meet my wife and children. Then, in the morning, I will see you on your way with wagons for your little ones!"

Hurrying to the door, I flung it open. Adam and Set stood together, uneasy at the long silence from the audience chamber.

"My lord, are you all right?" Set's eyes traveled from my bare head to my rumpled tunic. He hurried forward to try and repair the folds of cloth.

"Yes, never mind," I brushed his hand away. "My brothers will be dining with me tonight."

"Your brothers?" The astonishment made me smile.

"Yes, Set, these men are my eleven brothers from Canaan. See to their needs. I must tell Asaneth."

Leaving the butler standing with mouth agape, I rushed toward my wife's apartments. Adam hurried to catch up.

"They have recognized you my lord?" he asked deferentially.

"Yes, Adam," I paused to look at him. "They know I am their brother Joseph, and they will eat with me tonight."

"I rejoice for you, my lord." The guard, who was more than a slave, smiled in delight at my joy. Then he held out my discarded wig and coronet.

"My friend, thank you. I should put this on before I see my wife." He helped me repair my appearance before we continued on to Asaneth's room.

She was sitting quietly with her women when I burst in. Her musicians played softly in the corner and the fan bearers languidly moved the heavy fans. Sweeping her up, I whirled her around until she squealed.

"My love, you will meet all my brothers tonight."

When I set her down, she took my cheeks between her hands and looked into my eyes. "The shadows are gone! You have made peace with them, haven't you?"

"Yes, sweetest love of my life," I punctuated the words with many kisses.

"They will return to Canaan and bring my father and their families here to live out the rest of the famine."

"Does Pharaoh know?" Her question recalled me to duty.

"I am going to him now."

"Wait." With her gentle hands she straightened the wig and adjusted my garments. Then with a final kiss she sent me on my way.

My mind tried to find words to tell the King of my brothers. But Ctah's greeting informed me that the Lord of the Two Lands already knew and was pleased.

"Your joy is my Lord Pharaoh's joy," the butler said. Then he opened the tall ebony doors and announced, "The Lord Governor, Zaphenath-Paneah."

Pharaoh came forward to embrace me. "We are pleased that your brothers have come and made themselves known to you."

I knelt before him. "I crave a boon, Mighty King."

"What is this groveling before us? Zaphenath-Paneah, you know that in all but the throne we hold you equal."

"Yet, I crave a gift from that throne, my Lord Pharaoh." Stubbornly, I stayed on my knees, ignoring his outstretched hand.

"Speak on then." He sat with a sigh. "We believe we know your desire, Lord Governor, but speak on."

"Wise King, my brothers have indeed come from Canaan for the famine is severe there also. This is the second time they have come, as my Great Lord knows. The first time, I kept Simeon in prison as hostage for their return. Although my heart yearned for them as brothers, I did not trust myself to them. This day my heart broke open with desire for reconciliation and I made myself known to them. I was reunited with my brother Benjamin, son of the same mother, for whom I have yearned greatly. Not only that," I hurried on when he started to speak. "Great Lord of the Nile, I have promised them land in Goshen, for they are herdsmen with many sheep and cattle."

"It is our desire, Lord Governor Zaphenath-Paneah," Pharaoh gripped my shoulders and drew me to my feet, "your family shall indeed have the finest land in Goshen. Wagons and supplies will be provided for their journey. We rejoice with you for it is time and more for your family to be reunited."

I would have knelt again to kiss his feet, but he held me still around the shoulders.

"We would meet your father when he comes. Now return to your family. Take them our blessing." Pharaoh gave me an affectionate shove toward the door.

"Mighty Lord King, you are a wise and noble ruler." I bowed from his presence with my heart lightened by his acceptance of my plans.

Ctah stopped me in the hall. "My Lord Pharaoh has ordered his cooks to send portions to your kitchen to help with this joyful feast."

"My Lord is kind," I replied, humbled again by the kindness of those around me.

With lovely Asaneth on my arm, I entered the great hall. A bath and clean tunic followed by Kevak anointing my body with oils and applying the makeup and wig made me presentable. I was more proud of the lovely picture my wife made. Her hair was ornamented with rows of beads and pearls that danced when she moved. The gown of finest Egyptian linen shimmered in the lamplight. Out of consideration for the desert customs, she wore an additional scarf draped around her body. Manassah and Ephraim walked hand in hand behind us. They curiously and eagerly looked at the men who fell to their knees when we entered.

"Introduce me, Jo-seph," she asked.

Together we went from brother to brother. She carefully repeated each man's name and kissed him on the cheek. Her pronunciation made me smile, but her acceptance and welcome of my kin brought tears to my eyes. I knew they were uncomfortable with her presence but as the meal progressed, we all began to relax.

We talked late into the night. The boys were sent away with their nurse after the meal, but we continued to talk. I learned that even Benjamin was a father of four. No one spoke of the past. Rather, I told them of the land of Goshen. Watered by the Delta and winds from the Great Sea, there was always grazing even in this time of famine. The royal herdsmen had land there, as did the priests. It would not do for the palace or temples to go without meat.

"Pharaoh has graciously agreed to give you plentiful land," I announced when we finally rose to seek our beds. "Wagons are being provided to bring all your families here to Egypt. In the morning, all will be ready. I will ride with you as far as the border. My duties to Pharaoh prevent me from following my heart and going with you to tell Jacob, my father, of all the blessings God has given to me and to this family."

Parting from my brothers was hard.

"Make haste on your journey," I urged. "Bring my father to me. Tell him all that has been granted me by God. For the God of our Fathers has made me a great ruler in this land for the saving of our family."

I hugged each man and gave him a final caution, "Do not fear to return and do not quarrel on the way." Already, I had overheard arguments regarding what to tell Jacob about my miraculous return from the dead. I knew that they would spend the trip to Canaan disagreeing on the story to tell.

With many a bow, my brothers moved off ahead of the wagons full of gifts and supplies for my father's comfort. Benjamin hung behind for a final embrace before hurrying to catch up.

My sight blurred, I prayed for their safe and speedy return. When they were out of sight I took the reins from Adam. With a final salute to the border guards, we headed out for a tour of the storehouses. Asaneth was returning home with the boys, so only silence awaited me in my apartments. It seemed a good time to visit all the supervisors.

Chapter 19

As we rolled down the road toward the river and the waiting barge, Adam ventured to ask the question that had been troubling him for many months.

"My lord, Great Governor, forgive my presumption. I seek to understand." He spoke with head bowed, looking at me from the corner of his eye.

"Go on." With a nod, I encouraged him.

"Is it true, my Lord, that you are not Egyptian, but Hebrew?"

"That is true."

"But, then ..." He paused, unsure how to ask the question.

"I told you once that I was a slave in the house that, by Pharaoh's generosity, I now own." Taking pity on the Syrian's confusion, I started my explanation.

"I remember."

"The rest is an amazing gift from the God of my Fathers. The God of Abraham, Isaac and Jacob kept me alive through slavery and prison in order to fulfill the promise he made to Abraham, 'you will be the father of many nations, and in you, will all people be blessed'." I looked at my companion; his brow was furrowed as he thought about my words.

"Through the will of God and the dreams sent to Pharaoh, not only Egypt, but the entire world is saved from this famine." Pointing out the obvious made him look at me, a sad smile on his face.

"My father claimed ancestry to Abraham also," he confessed. "To Ishmael, the promise of a mighty nation was given, too. But I stopped believing in gods when the traders killed my father and harassed us to the hills. God deserted us and I deserted him." The bitterness of the words reminded me of my own struggles with God.

"Yet, the God you claim to have abandoned preserved your life to be part of His plan." At his confused look, I smiled and explained. "In the depth of prison, I swore there could not be a God. Why, if there was a God, why was I – the princeling with the dreams – brought to the dead end of life in prison in a foreign land? Long days and nights I cursed God and my brothers in my anger. It seemed that once again hope had been snatched from me. My master, Potiphar, had become like a father to me and gave me privilege above my fellow slaves. Then he turned against me and believed his wife's lies over my loyalty."

"And," Adam prompted me when I stopped, remembering the dark prison cell and the darker emptiness in my soul.

"And then, there in the prison, even with my hands bound and bars on the walls, I learned that God had not abandoned me. But it was not until I gave up fighting God that I found Him."

"What happened?" Adam leaned forward.

I drew rein and stared for a long minute out across the river to the temples on the far shore and beyond that to the western desert. The Egyptians believed that a person's *ka* went to a land beyond the western desert to be with Osiris and Ra when they died. Unity with the gods was the ultimate desire of every Egyptian, either by their own merit or as servants of a noble house. The God of my Fathers, however, gave me assurance of His protection now and not in some vague eternity. I responded to my friend. "There was a peace and serenity that I cannot explain. I know it came from God and assured me that He had not abandoned me. What mattered was not where I was, but who I was. I knew I was chosen for His plan and that God would bring it to fulfillment. I gave up wanting my dreams of power and authority. In that moment I was freed, even though I was still in prison. God even gave me back dreams in the night and the ability to interpret them."

Adam was silent as we boarded the waiting boat. We didn't get to talk again until we were floating upriver toward Thebes.

"My lord, I don't see how what you say can relate to me." Adam sighed, standing by my side and staring at the hippos in the water near the reeds.

"God kept you alive and kept your family together even through the fighting and capture," I pointed out. "I saw you and, in compassion, took you from the slave market. You are more than a servant to me, you are a friend." My hand rested on his shoulder. "Adam, you must come to your own terms with God. What I can give you is freedom from man's slavery. I will petition Pharaoh for a 'writing of freedom'."

"My Lord!" With tears in his eyes, the man reached for my hand. Emotionally, we gripped hands. To break the tension, I pointed to the baby hippo playing with his mother.

That night, alone in my room at Thebes, I had time to think about our conversation. More and more I realized that God had indeed kept His hand on me each step of my journey, even in my relationships with the priests and officials. We had just spent the evening discussing the conditions in Egypt and the surrounding areas. I assured them that the storehouses would continue to supply all needs. Each man had to admit that there had been no complaining about the distribution. The priests were gratified that people continued to attend the yearly festival when the god was brought from his place deep within the temple to answer questions of the populace.

Morning saw us moving upriver. The constant travel distracted my mind from my family. Only when we returned to the capital to meet with the King did I stop to calculate when my father and brothers could be expected.

In response to Pharaoh's question, I replied, "A full moon cycle to reach Canaan but it will take longer to return for they will have loaded wagons, little ones and flocks to care for."

"But you think that your family will be here before the Inundation?"

After consideration, I responded, "Yes, Great One, they should have crossed your border by then or possibly sooner."

He was pleased with my report of the status of the storehouses. His many questions about the amount of grain left I was able to answer. I was happy to report that there seemed to be no corruption among the supervisors. Content with my summary, the King sent me home to Asaneth.

"Take time to be with your wife and sons before the Inundation and before your brothers return."

Gladly, I agreed. Before I left the palace, I sought a private audience.

Ctah announced me. Pharaoh looked up in surprise from the game of Foxes and Hounds he was playing with the Queen. "Zaphenath-Paneah, we thought you would be on your way to your wife."

"A petition to the Lord of the Two Lands." With a bow, I waited for his response.

"What is it you desire that cannot be requested at our daily audience?" The man was irritated at being disturbed.

"As you wish, Mighty One." I turned to leave.

"No, stay. We are but annoyed from hearing many complaints. Your desires, Lord Governor, are ours. State your petition."

"Only this, Most Noble Lord King, I would give freedom to my faithful slave and guard, Adam." He raised an eyebrow and I explained. "I should have asked this of you when he saved my life before the famine began." Kneeling before him, I could almost hear Pharaoh reviewing in his mind my service to him and Adam's to me. He tapped one of the playing pieces in his hand.

Finally, he spoke. "It is our will to grant this petition. We would order, however, that the man, Adam, remain your servant even as a free man." A smile softened the command.

"I, too, would desire that, Most Wise King." Bending I kissed the ground in gratitude.

"Write the paper and we will sign it. Then your man will be as free as anyone in Egypt."

"Thank you, Gracious Pharaoh."

"Now, get up and quit groveling. Go to your wife before the Queen accuses us of being heartless and breaking up your family." He winked at her and grinned. I knew he was pleased with his generosity both in freeing Adam and in sending me to Asaneth.

The Queen held out her hand. "Zaphenath-Paneah, tell the lovely Asaneth to take good care of our noble governor. Give her my love," she added.

I bowed from the room. Adam was waiting in the courtyard.

"You will be free as soon as Pharaoh signs the scroll," I told him.

"My lord!" He fell at my feet in gratitude. "I will not leave you, but I thank you for my freedom."

Slightly embarrassed by his display in the middle of the courtyard, I said somewhat gruffly, "Get up and let us be going."

The interlude with my family was full of joy. During the weeks with my sons, I told them about their uncles and the grandfather they would soon meet.

"Your grandfather, Jacob, is an important man in Canaan where he lives." I told them. "He is rich in flocks and herds. With all his sons, your uncles, they have more sheep and cattle than anyone else in the area. They are all going to come and live in Egypt, in Goshen, because of the famine. They had no wise Pharaoh to plan for storing the grain to give to the people."

Manassah looked at me with curiosity. "Aren't shepherds awful, smelly people? My tutor says that is why all Pharaoh's herds are in Goshen, so they don't contaminate everyone."

"My son," I crouched to be at his level. "To God nothing and no one is detestable. People sometimes call others names. That makes them feel better or more important than someone else. I would not have you believe that anyone is worse than you, even a slave. Remember I was a slave, even though I am son of Jacob, sheik of Canaan and am now Lord Governor for the King. Being a slave is not a crime. Hurting another person is worse. Do you understand my son? Love, not condemnation, is what the God of Israel wants from us."

"Yes, father." He was quiet, thinking about what I said.

"Papa," a small hand tugged mine.

"Ephraim, my son." I swooped him into my arms and over my head so that he laughed.

"Will I get to ride a camel?" The question came from the giggling urchin in my arms.

"We will talk to your uncles," I promised. "I'm sure they will have a camel for you to ride."

Asaneth was waiting for me each evening when I returned from my time with the boys. After a goodnight kiss, she sent them off with their nurse. Then we sat side by side or strolled in the garden before retiring to bed. I shared my fears with her. "Do you think my brothers will tell Jacob the truth? Will they confess that his son is not dead, but a ruler in Egypt?"

"My love, what have they to lose? They will bring good news to your father and they don't have to explain how you came to be here in Egypt. Indeed, you have given them a refuge in the famine rather than exacting the vengeance they had every right to expect." Her vehemence surprised me and I drew her close.

"Do you think they understand that God's hand is behind all that has happened?" With a gentle hand on my cheek, she turned my head.

"Look at me, beloved. What they believe or understand is between your God and your brothers. Is it not enough that you have come to peace with your past and your brothers?"

I kissed her nose. "Wise and beautiful, God has truly blessed me with such a wife. You are right, the God of my Fathers will bring my father to me."

"They will come, I know it, my husband."

Once again, she was right. Barely a week had passed when a runner brought word that the Canaanite caravan had been sighted.

"They will cross into the Black Land tomorrow," he reported. Hard on his heels came a message from Pharaoh. I unrolled the scroll and read:

"To The Lord Governor, Zaphenath-Paneah, Interpreter to the King and Preserver of the Land from Pharaoh, King of all Egypt and the Lands Beyond. Greetings. We have been petitioned by a delegation from south of Nubia for food. Hearing that your family is even now crossing our borders, I have sent these men to you rather than order you to come to the palace. Deal with these men as you know best. Then, may your God give you all speed to greet your family. Welcome them in our name and direct them to such lands in the Delta as we discussed."

I barely finished reading the words when Set announced that the delegation had arrived.

"Have a canopy set up in the garden," I ordered. "I will meet with them there."

Kevak helped me dress in the full regalia. The gold trimmed breastplate and helmet reflected the sun as I came down the stairs. Striding to the chair placed under the canopy, I took my seat with Adam at my side and slaves stationed to fan me. It was an impressive sight. Suitably awed, the ambassadors bowed to the ground.

"Pharaoh has told me of your request. Therefore, speak."

Before they could continue, Set appeared at my side.

"My Lord Governor, forgive the impertinence. One of your brothers has come."

"Await my return," the delegation was told. Hurrying to greet my brother, I was aware of the curious looks following me.

"Judah! Where is my father?" Eagerly, I searched the road behind him.

"He sent me ahead to tell you we have come and to get directions." My older brother nervously shifted from foot to foot.

Disappointment surged through me. Stiffly, I told the man, "Proceed toward Goshen. I will meet you when I have finished my meeting." I had to pause for a moment before returning to the delegation. Mixed feelings of anger, hurt, and fear that my father no longer cared whirled in my mind.

"Prepare my state chariot!" I ordered Set, determined to meet my family as Lord Governor of Egypt. If not love, I would at least command respect.

Absentminded, I listened to the petitioners from Nubia and gave them a scroll detailing the amount of grain they were entitled to. Ignoring their protestations of thanks, I strode through them and saw that my chariot was waiting. Set was thorough. Trumpeters and guards were stationed to accompany me. The whole household gathered to see me off. They had never seen the entire impressive entourage and the ostentatious chariot gilded with gold embossed shields that were my governor's due. Clep and Nukor were standing with the rest of the staff. I walked to them.

"Who would have dreamed of this day?" I asked, giving each old friend an affectionate embrace. "My family coming to me rather than my return to them."

"My lord, I always knew that you were special," Clep said with tears in his old eyes.

"It is as I once told you. Your God has great things for you," Nukor added.

"I thank you both for your faithfulness," I told them before turning away.

Asaneth, too, had tears in her eyes. "Your joy is mine, my husband," she said with a kiss. "Beware of your pride, my love." She added in a whisper for my ears only.

Vaulting into the chariot, I took the staff Set held for me. Adam leapt in behind me and at my signal the charioteer set the horses in motion. Trumpets sounded and the guard fell in behind. In a grand procession, we moved down the road toward the border.

Asaneth's words echoed in my head. What was my motive for this grand display? Was it what I had told my wife when she questioned the pomp? I remembered the words but now they sounded hollow. "My love, I want my father Jacob to see how I have prospered here in Egypt."

She had said nothing. Perhaps that very silence was more eloquent than an argument. Now, standing in the gilded chariot as the pair of horses trotted along the highway toward the border, I reconsidered.

"Pharaoh would think such an array the only right and correct way to welcome such a man as Jacob," I mused. "But," my heart replied, "your father is a simple man for all his wealth."

I was no closer to a solution when we paused to water the horses with the sun high in the sky.

"Adam, walk with me." Removing the gold ornamented helmet that was part of the elaborate official armor, I stepped out of the chariot. The rest of the group took advantage of the time to soak hot feet and take a break in the cooler shade of the palm trees by the small oasis.

"You are troubled, my Lord Governor." His statement did not surprise me.

"Look at this crowd. Do you think it is too much for a reunion with my father?" I waved vaguely in the direction of the trumpeters and soldiers lounging and talking.

"Are you trying to welcome or overwhelm your brothers?" The Syrian's answer made me turn my head away in shame.

"You are right and so is my lady Asaneth. This display is only to prove how great and powerful I am. My pride was wounded when my father did not rush to my side, but sent Judah instead." My shoulders slumped and I sighed. "Once again I have acted like the youth who had to learn humility in slavery and prison. God of Abraham, Isaac and Jacob, forgive my pride and arrogance. It was only by your grace that I survived to become the man I am. In my fear of my brothers' contempt I have again been foolish and pompous. Help me, God of my Fathers, to be unafraid of this reconciliation."

I stood with my head bowed for a long time letting tranquility seep into my soul. Finally, I looked up. Purposefully, I strode back to where my retinue waited. Each man sprang to attention at my approach. I had to smile for some stood with a sandal dangling from their hand or water dripping from their faces. "You will all return home," I ordered. "Adam and I will proceed alone."

None dared question my command, although a few curious and scandalized glances slid my way when they thought I did not see. I knew that my actions would be the topic of conversation for days. My heart told me that I was meeting my father, as I should, with only the power of God to shield me.

"I will drive the chariot. You will return with the others." I sent the charioteer to join his companions. He jumped from the vehicle to salute and turn back down the road.

So, it was that Adam and I set out together on the last leg of the journey. My eyes strained for signs of the cloud of dust that would signal the approach of many carts and people. It never materialized.

As we topped a sand dune, a scene of turmoil greeted our eyes. One of the wagons had lost a wheel. It sat, tilted at a drunken angle onto the side of the road. Animals milled around the edges of the wreck. I noticed as my glance slid over them, that they were very thin. Carried on the slight breeze was the sound of my brothers' quarrel. My stomach clenched in memory of the many times I had been recipient or observer of the same anger. The endless wrangling and contention among the men had always been upsetting to me. I never understood their need to wrangle for Jacob's regard. Secure in my father's favor, I felt no need to vie for his attention, a fact that turned my brothers' rage onto me.

Now, my hands tightened on the reins causing the horses to toss their heads and dance restlessly. Jaw gritted; I searched the crowd for my father. As always, he distanced himself from the fray. Long ago, he had stopped trying to intervene. But, still they strove together, a habit unbroken for forty years.

Benjamin, I noticed, was working with some of the servants to jack the wagon up in order to replace the wheel. For a moment, I wished for a trumpet fanfare to announce my arrival. Adam had the same thought for he grinned.

"A trumpet to call a charge would bring a halt," my faithful friend suggested with a chuckle.

Trying not to laugh, I replied, "I'm not sure that even Phari's trumpet would break through their bickering." My dreams of family unity seemed destined for failure.

"Do you see your father?" He deftly turned the subject.

"See the old man standing to the left of everyone?" My heart broke to see the whiteness of his beard but there was no mistaking Jacob. He still stood tall although I saw that he leaned more heavily on his staff than when I last saw him.

I voiced my concern: "Twenty-two years is a long time. What other changes will I find?"

As usual, Adam cut to the heart of my fear. "A father's love does not grow cold. Would your love for Manassah and Ephraim end just because they were far away? Or would mine for Seth and my other children fail?"

"Thank you, Adam." Humbled by his wisdom, I gripped his shoulder. Taking a deep breath, I signaled the horses. "Let us go."

The lump in my throat grew larger the closer we got to the stranded travelers. One of the little boys saw me first.

"Look, a gold chariot!" His cry alerted all the children.

Eagerly, all the youngsters ran into the road. I pulled to a halt before the team could step on anyone. Over the heads of the excited children, I saw my father turn. In a corner of my mind, I heard my brothers' exclamations.

"It is Joseph."

"The Lord Governor is here."

"Children come away."

I paid no heed. In Jacob's eyes I saw the hope that had brought him this far. Even my Egyptian armor, wig, and makeup did not prevent his recognition.

"My son." I saw his lips move and waited no longer. With tears blurring my sight, I leapt from the chariot leaving Adam to deal with the horses. The children parted to form a path. I saw only my father. He moved toward me, energized by love. When we met, I fell into his arms, the lost child safe at last.

"My son, Joseph, my son!" His words were balm and healing. How much time passed while I held him and we wept I don't know. At last I drew back.

"Welcome to Egypt, my father." I knelt to the man who gave me life.

"My son." He did not seem to tire of the words. "God has truly blessed you in this land. I see that what your brothers said is true. You are indeed a Great Prince. Stand up, my son, it is not fitting for one of your station to kneel to me."

At his insistence, I stood up. Finally I turned to the eleven men standing silently. Their dejected faces told me they feared that I would now turn on them.

"Brothers, welcome to Egypt." I dropped my father's hand and went to each man with an embrace. "Pharaoh has given you land in Goshen. Fine grazing for the flocks and room for your tents." Reassuring them, I saw their faces relax.

"Has the wagon been repaired?" The question made them look guiltily at each other.

"Come my brothers, let us get it done. You can camp on my land tonight. Tomorrow, I will show you the way to your new home in Goshen."

It seemed, however, that the servants had completed the job as we talked. With a lightened heart, I helped Jacob into my chariot.

"Ride with me away from the dust," I persuaded him. As we drew closer to On, I pointed out the temples on the Nile bank. At last we stopped and I pointed to the house where I once served as Potiphar's slave, the home that I now owned as Pharaoh's Lord Governor. "My father, not only has God given me freedom and favor in this land, but look at the home and lands I have here." My hand pointed out the land and pillared estate where I knew Asaneth and my sons waited. "You are welcome at any time. All that you see is mine and all that I have is yours."

His eyes roamed from the fields barren now in the famine to the riverside to the house and gardens spread out and gleaming gold in the setting sun.

"The God of our Fathers has been gracious indeed to you, Joseph, my son. No one can deny that you have found favor with God and with man. Although my heart broke when I heard from your brothers that wild animals had killed you, I prayed that they were wrong. And you were not destroyed..." His hand reached out to touch my arm, assuring himself that I was real.

"Not destroyed by wild animals or by treachery or slavery or imprisonment," I replied. "For God preserved my life to fulfill his promise of blessing given to Abraham and to Isaac and to you, my father."

"Blessed be the Lord God. I prayed to God at Beersheba to bring me in safety to you, my son. And he has. God also renewed the promise given to me at the Jabok crossing when I wrestled with his angel. 'I am the God of your father; do not be afraid to go down to Egypt, for I will make of you a great nation there. I myself will go down with you to Egypt, and I will also bring you up again'." Jacob's face took on an exalted look as he repeated the words of God.

I bowed my head and stood in silence knowing that God would indeed accomplish what he promised. "Come, I want you to meet my beloved wife, Asaneth, and your grandsons,

Manassah and Ephraim." I gave the horses rein to trot the last short distance to the house.

Asaneth was waiting. Her welcome was all any father-in-law could wish for. With graceful homage, she welcomed Jacob into the house. At her signal, Set offered him the welcome cup and water to wash his feet and hands. Then she led the way into the dining hall. Slaves had spread Syrian rugs on the floor and cushions were piled on them. I saw a tear in my father's eyes as he saw the care taken for his comfort. Set carefully settled the old man. My wife made a quick motion and Sarah entered with Manassah and Ephraim. Together we presented them to Jacob.

"My sons," I told him.

Tears slid down his face, "I never thought to see you, and now God has shown me your sons." He held out his arms.

Shyly, the boys hung back from the exotically dressed stranger until he drew from his robe a handful of sugared dates.

"I know what lads like," he said with a grin.

Sure enough the sweets overcame the awe. Soon he had a boy on each knee. I was glad they knew enough Hebrew to talk to their grandfather. Manassah and Ephraim were sent off with their nurse when Set announced the arrival of my brothers.

Clep and Nukor had seen that the tents were set up and then escorted the men to the house. More than a little awed, eleven pairs of eyes stared around at the murals and gold embossed shields on the walls. Slaves brought out dishes especially prepared under Sarah's direction with the help of Adam's wives. Rather than the ornate Egyptian dishes, simple delicious meats and vegetables were set before us. Fresh, warm, flat bread, staple of all nomadic tribes was heaped on a platter. Asaneth and the slaves retired to leave us in peace. Even Adam left me alone for this reunion with my family.

Jacob gave a brief prayer of thanksgiving and blessing. My brothers, cautiously at first, and then more eagerly, began to eat. Seated at my father's side, I rejoiced in serving him. I barely tasted what I ate for my heart was too full to need food.

In their reserve, I sensed that my brothers still feared retribution. Trying to set them at ease, I questioned them about the families they brought. All had wives and children, and some of my brothers had grandchildren.

"In all, my son, the total number of persons that God has granted respite from the famine is sixty-seven. You and our sons bring my family to seventy," Jacob said, leaning back finally replete and satisfied.

"God has already made of you a great people," I remarked. "Pharaoh has asked to meet you, my father. Tomorrow we will travel south to the capital. Nukor and Clep will guide my family," I savored the word, "to Goshen. Reuben, Levi, Simeon, Judah and Benjamin will accompany us to Pharaoh." I knew that my choices made the men uncomfortable, so I continued. "When the King asks what your profession is, you must tell him the truth. Say that you and yours have always been shepherds and herdsmen. Then he will not press you to settle in the cities but will give the rich grazing in Goshen."

Looking around at the circle of brothers, I smiled and explained, "It is all part of the formality of court. Pharaoh will make public his favor and grant you land. It will be inscribed on a scroll and become part of the permanent record of the land."

I noticed that Jacob was nodding off, although he tried to hide the fact.

"Tomorrow is time enough to talk more. Let me show you to your room, my father. Unless you would feel more comfortable in the tents." I hesitated at the door to the chamber prepared for him.

"I will sleep in my son's house this night." He embraced me for a long time before entering the room. My brothers stood uncertain in the hall.

"Let me walk with you to your tents. I want to be certain that you lack for nothing." Linking my arm with Benjamin, I led the way through the house. The stars shown brightly in the Egyptian night, reminding me as always of God's faithful promise to his chosen people.

"I will give you descendants as the stars of heaven," I quoted to Benjamin. "The God of our Fathers is ..." I searched for the word.

"Amazing," my younger brother supplied. "I barely remember you, but I know that God has done wonderful things in your life. You are the Ruler here in Egypt, second only to the King. God is amazing."

"Yes, and He has given me back my family." I spread my arms to embrace the whole encampment spread out in the fields between the house and the river.

We talked little more before I returned to my house and the cool rooftop where Asaneth waited for me.

"My husband is content?" She smiled at me.

Swinging her around in my arms, I replied, "What does my lovely wife think?"

A kiss was her response and we nestled happily together while she listened to me babble on about the trip to meet my father. She smiled when I told her how I sent back the retinue and laughed about the scene at the broken wagon.

"My father is here." I repeated the words.

"Jo-seph, my love, I am glad to see you so happy."

We sat quiet until I carried her to our chamber to kiss and caress her and finally to fall asleep sated in her arms.

Chapter 20

The barge waited at On to take us to Pharaoh. I bid Asaneth goodbye and walked up the road to find my brothers. I heard Leah's sons before they saw me.

"Do you think he means to turn us over to Pharaoh now?" Levi's voice was edged with fear. "Why were we singled out?"

"He could have killed us or turned us over to the King before." Judah was trying to be rational.

"Unless he was only waiting until Benjamin and our father were safely here," Simeon interjected.

"Did we not wrong Joseph once before by believing that he stole our father Jacob's affections?" Reuben spoke up now. "Let us not make the same mistake again. Indeed, our brother has reason to want to see us all punished, but I believe that the welcome he has given us is genuine."

"Of course Joseph does not mean us harm." Once again Judah spoke. "He would not have included Benjamin if he planned punishment."

"We will see," grumbled Levi, still unconvinced. "And this Goshen land he speaks of. How do we know it is as rich as he says?"

Simeon said, "You fool! That is true. Have you never heard the traders talk about the grazing in Goshen that saves their pack camels after the desert trek?"

Silenced, Levi turned away. Sorrowed, I turned aside to find Benjamin. With my younger brother, I returned to the house and brought Jacob to the camp. Clep and Nukor were supervising the packing and loading of the rest of the family for the trek to Goshen. My father was impressed by the speed with which the Egyptians worked.

"Let us see the travelers off," I suggested, trying unsuccessfully to put Levi's words out of my mind. Feeling like an outsider, I watched my five brothers bid their children and wives farewell. My father hugged each grandchild and the six sons heading for the land in the Delta. Every daughter-in-law received a kiss on the cheek. I was not surprised that they all loved the old man. Age had gentled his crafty striving into wisdom and gentleness.

"The barge is ready." Adam's timely arrival with four chariots prevented conversation. The drive to the dock was brief and allowed me little time to consider my brothers' concerns.

"God of my Fathers, how can I convince them that I mean no harm?" I prayed silently as I steered the chariot through the traffic of the streets of On. My father said nothing, overwhelmed by the sights and sounds of the metropolis dedicated to the sun god.

Early morning light sparkled on the water when I led the way on board. I knew none of the men with me had ever been on a boat before. Gently, I assisted my father into a seat. Reuben, Levi, Simeon, Judah, and Benjamin stared in surprise at the boat, unsure if it would stay afloat. I remembered the same feelings on my first boat trip. The papyrus reeds seemed unsuitable for supporting men and animals on the water. Now, I knew that they were sturdy and rarely sank even under the weight of the massive blocks of rock floated downstream for Pharaoh's temples.

The captain saluted me, and after Adam boarded, he gave orders to cast off. Poling out into the deeper water, the oarsmen took up the rhythm and set to work rowing upstream to the capital. Benjamin stood beside my father, his eyes wide as he looked at the massive pyramids and temple complexes. The other four stood together silently watching me. They had not moved since they boarded the boat.

"The river is almost to shallow for oars," I told my brothers. "See the water line above the bulrushes? That is the normal river level. The drought has lowered the lady Nile by three cubits so far. Four years remain of the famine." For a moment my thoughts drifted from my family to the people of Egypt. I knew that there was enough food still in the storehouses. Even after three years, the level of the grain was barely lowered. Still, I knew the people were worried about the continuing lack of water and crops. Potiphera talked to me of the priestly fear that the people would desert the temples if the famine continued. I planned to talk to Pharaoh about some way to reassure the nation.

Now I turned to speak to my brothers. I pointed out the tombs of the earliest Pharaoh's. Even the interest of my wary brothers was caught by the grandeur of the construction. The brilliant paintings on the temple pylons and the gold-capped obelisks, even the white limestone facings on the pyramids, were all designed to reflect the sun for miles around. In this way Ra was invited to remember the people of the Black Land.

When we drew up to the landing at the palace, the four men were almost relaxed. I felt their tension return as we disembarked and were greeted by Pharaoh's personal guard. We settled into the litters he provided. It was a mode of transportation I rarely used, preferring to walk from the river to the palace. My brothers were obviously leery of getting into their litters.

"I have heard of such things but never thought to see and ride in one!" My father was eager as a child as I helped him into his seat. My brothers carefully followed suit and then I climbed into mine. With Adam striding beside me, the bearers started up the path to the palace followed by the others. I heard muttered oaths from my brothers as the litters tilted slightly on the incline.

I saw Ctah hovering anxiously in the background as the door steward presented me with the ceremonial cup. After a touch of my lips to the rim, I presented it to Jacob and each brother. Ctah then bustled forward.

"I will take the Lord Governor, Zaphenath-Paneah, and his father directly to the King of Egypt," Ctah announced, somewhat pompously, I thought.

Smiling a little at the affronted look on the door steward's face, I returned the cup with a brief nod.

We walked down the long tiled hall. I remembered my first visit to the palace as Potiphar's scribe. I saw in my brother's faces the same disbelief and awe at the myriad painted and gold embossed panels portraying Pharaoh's life and god-ship.

We stopped at the familiar ebony door. So many times in the past ten years I had come into this audience chamber to report on the storehouses and supplies. This time my heart beat uncomfortably in my chest. Ctah turned to me.

"Lord Governor, the Mighty One awaits you and your father. The Great King rejoices with your joy." Then with a flourish, he opened the doors and announced, "The Lord Governor, Zaphenath-Paneah, Interpreter to the King and Preserver of the Land, second only to the Great and Wise Pharaoh, has come with Jacob, Sheik of Canaan, Father of the Lord Zaphenath-Paneah and his sons." The last was added almost as an afterthought when Ctah saw my brothers standing together behind their father.

"Come, our Lord Governor is welcome." Pharaoh stood to greet me. Leaving my father and brothers standing as though turned to stone by the audience chamber and magnificence of the King himself, I crossed the room to kneel and then accept the royal embrace.

"We would meet your father." With a smile for me, he looked at the men standing in the doorway. Resuming his seat, he picked up the staff and flail of his office.

Ctah bowed to Jacob and indicated that he should proceed. My father proudly walked across the room to kneel and offer the Bedouin salaam in homage to Pharaoh. I was surprised that he did not prostrate himself but greeted the King as he would a visitor to his tent. Pharaoh acknowledged the greeting with an incline of his head.

"Do you speak Egyptian?" The question surprised me.

"Poorly, Great One," my father replied slowly, sounding out the words.

"Let our Lord Governor interpret then." A majestic nod in my direction gave the order. He continued, peering again toward the door. "These are your sons?"

"Half of them, Mighty Lord," Jacob replied, signaling for my brothers to move forward. They came slowly, fearful of words and customs they did not understand. Prostrating themselves at Pharaoh's feet, they lay immobile behind my father until he introduced them. Each man briefly raised his head as his name was announced only to flatten it to the floor again. Benjamin alone remained kneeling, staring straight at Pharaoh after he was introduced.

"This is Reuben, my first born. These are Simeon and Levi and Judah. They are all sons of one mother, Leah. Benjamin, my youngest, and the son I know as Joseph, your governor, are sons of my beloved Rachel, Leah's sister. The sons of the serving women have stayed with the wagons and children."

"What is your occupation?" The King started the official questioning.

"Your servants are herdsmen and shepherds. This we have been since our father, Abraham of the Promise, left Ur of the Chaldees."

"Then you have great wealth in these flocks?" The King tilted his head to wait for the answer.

"Few and weak are the animals left to your servants. There has been but poor grazing in Canaan these past years."

Satisfied, the King nodded.

"What is your age?" I was surprised by the next question. "For we see that you have lived many years to attain the wisdom and wealth you have."

"Let my Lord Pharaoh know that few and hard have been my years compared to that of my fathers. I have only seen one hundred and ten springs. Meager and useless are my flocks and herds next to your riches, Mighty One. My true wealth comes from the God of my Fathers and in these my sons and other children."

I was proud of my father's answers as I translated. A small smile tugged the corner of Pharaoh's mouth as he glanced at me.

"And, Father Jacob, tell us how many is this wealth in number?"

With a bow and sweep of his hand, Jacob replied, "besides these six sons, I have six others. Together with wives and children our number is seventy, if it please My Lord, the King of Egypt."

Pharaoh stood and my brothers who had dared to raise their heads during the conversation, dropped to the floor again. Jacob, too, knelt and Benjamin bowed to the floor again.

"It does please us. We rejoice with our Lord Governor, Zaphenath-Paneah, who you name Joseph. It is our joy that his father and brothers have at last been restored to him. Of our gracious favor and love towards Zaphenath-Paneah, we will give you a rich portion in the land of Goshen for your flocks and herds and families. If any of your sons are especially good herdsmen, we would have them tend the royal flocks. Goshen is the least affected by this famine but grazing is still less abundant than usual. Our Egyptian shepherds are not as adept at finding good grazing as you and your sons no doubt are."

"Lord Pharaoh, I am at your service, as are my sons." My father again touched forehead, lips, and heart in the Bedouin salute.

"It is good and will be written. We bid you a safe journey. Ctah will show you to a room to refresh yourselves. Before you leave, we will give you a feast to honor your son, our wise governor."

The court burst into polite applause while Ctah escorted my family from the hall.

"We will speak to our Lord Governor in private." By stepping from the dais, he indicated that the audience was ended. He linked his arm with mine and we walked to the library to talk.

"Your father is well and a fortunate man in his sons." Pharaoh spoke first.

"Yes, My Lord. My God has been gracious in reuniting us all, with your help, Great One."

"Yet, I sense you are not satisfied." He probed the wound.

I turned away and rubbed a hand across my eyes to forestall the tears that threatened.

"It is but foolishness, Mighty King." I hedged.

"Tell us." Pharaoh sat at ease, ready to listen.

Pacing the room, I finally blurted out what bothered me. "My brothers all fear me. I heard the four oldest talking this morning. They are afraid I plan to entrap and punish them."

"Zaphenath-Paneah, my friend, it is their guilt talking. Surely you know that."

"God did not preserve my life to wreak vengeance, but to save lives." I turned to the man, despair written on my face.

"My friend," he stood and put his hands on my shoulders. "They must come to know you again. When they look at you, they are reminded of their betrayal. Your brothers do not see the hand of your God, yet. You have come to find the good in their actions. They fear the powerful man you have become with the favor of your God and with my favor."

"Yes, I know. It is just that I had hoped for a fresh relationship with my family. But they are the same – bickering among themselves and vying for the best and most." The weight of the world seemed to be on my shoulders. I groaned, "They are just as jealous of me as ever and hate me just as much."

"Perhaps more," Pharaoh pointed out. "You are now greater than your brothers can ever hope to be."

I resumed my pacing as I still struggled. "It is true that God has fulfilled the dreams I had in my youth. I dreamed that my brothers and father would bow to me and they have. But what seemed sweet then is bitter now. How can I make them love me?"

"Can love be forced?" His question made me stop and consider. Before I could answer, he continued. "Love must grow over time. Surely your God will soften their hearts as they get to know you."

"I pray you are right," I sighed. "Though my heart yearns for them, I will be patient."

After a final turn around the room, I turned to my friend. "Thank you, Wise King, your wisdom is higher than the stars." My reply was accompanied by an exaggerated bow and a flourish of my hand in imitation of the priests' extravagant homage.

Pharaoh laughed at my antics and changed the subject. "No flowery phrases, Lord Governor. Now tell us what you hear from the delegations. Is the famine as severe in the surrounding lands even south of Nubia?"

"Yes, Mighty Lord, from all reports the lands around the Black Land are indeed drying up. Even south of Nubia in the Dark Places they have had no crops for over a year, and the pastures are shrinking. I provided food as they had money."

"Show us on the map the extent of the drought," he ordered.

I unrolled a scroll onto the table. "From the Jordan to the Great Sea, from Haran in the northeast to south of Nubia, and from across the Sahara, people have come seeking food." With my finger I traced the outline of the area from which ambassadors had come.

"Yet Egypt has stores enough for the remaining years?"

"Let the Lord of the Two Lands be assured that there will be no lack of food. However, the people are running out of silver to buy the food. Some have already offered their animals. Then they will offer their land and even their lives into your service. Egypt will belong to you, Most Powerful Pharaoh, before the famine ends."

"So we are enriched to save my nation?" He considered aloud, not entirely pleased.

"Yes, my King." My reply was accompanied with an incline of my head with my hand over my heart. I too was burdened by the thought that Egypt would no longer be free.

"Then raise the price to foreigners and lower it to our people." The decision was brusque.

"It shall be done." Again I lowered my head. We both knew, without discussion that this measure would only postpone the sale of animals and land to the crown in exchange for food.

I wrote out the scroll to be copied and sent with Pharaoh's seal to all the storehouses. A little more business was discussed before the King bid me farewell.

"Take your father and brothers to Goshen. See them settled. Place those who you think wise over the royal flocks and herds."

"Yes, Mighty One, it will be as you say. I will then tour all the storehouses to ensure that the supervisors have put into practice your decree," I continued as we left the library.

"Bring us a report. May your God grant you peace with your brothers." He gripped my wrist and then gave me an embrace as I left the royal presence.

Jacob and my brothers were waiting in the chamber Ctah had prepared for them. The remains of an elegant meal were on the table. When I opened the door, their heads turned.

"Come my family, the day is nearly over. We will stay here tonight in my apartments. Early tomorrow, the barge will take us down the river to meet everyone else in Goshen."

The evening passed quietly. In response to his questions, I told my father of my duties under Pharaoh. My brothers listened but made no comment. Benjamin sat on one side and my father on the other. If not for the wariness on the other four faces, I would have been content.

The early morning light saw us dismounting the litters and boarding the boat. The dawn gilded the white temples with golden light as we moved out into the current. Oars were applied until we were well underway, and then we floated smoothly northward toward Goshen.

My father seemed content, as if tired from his interview with Pharaoh and visit to the royal residence. "The King of Egypt is a wise young man," he remarked. "God has shown favor to Egypt by providing such leadership. Someday, you must tell me how you came to be the Lord Governor and second only to Pharaoh."

"Yes, my father, I will tell you all." Reuben's eyes met mine with apprehension. "But not now. Rest and enjoy the sights of the land," I settled him onto the cushions provided by the captain. Then I started pointing out points of interest as we passed.

Two days later, we reached the Delta. Wagons and horses were waiting. Adam reported that Clep and Nukor were only a day's journey away.

Jacob grew more and more enthusiastic the more of Goshen he saw.

"Joseph, my son, this is indeed a place green even in the famine and drought. Our flocks and herds will prosper. I suggest you put Gad and Dan and Napthali in charge of Pharaoh's herds. They are wise shepherds and know how to use the land and not overgraze it."

With joyous relief, I saw my father settled into his tents in the best of the heart of Goshen. My brothers were given land nearby for themselves. The tents were erected and the children began to explore their new homes in the timeless freedom of children. I smiled to hear the women singing as they arranged their pots and baskets.

Too soon, I had to bid Jacob farewell and return to my duties as Lord Governor. A brief stop to see Asaneth was all I allowed myself before setting out with Adam on my tour of inspection. Up and down the Nile, the people needed reassurance that when their money gave out they could still buy food with their cattle. The announcement that the price was lowered was greeted with great relief.

"But still our money reserves grow slim and the people will starve." I heard plaintive words at every stop. The councilors, with their allotment, feared that they would not be able to purchase the extra grain they had enjoyed.

"The grain supply is plenty for the remaining famine and the Great Lord of the Two Lands has reduced the cost to Egypt." My words failed to reassure them.

"But when there is no money for grain, what good will full storehouses be?"

"Pharaoh will not let any of his people starve. Allowance will be made for those with no money to trade animals or land for food."

With that they had to be satisfied for half the famine remained. By the time the famine ended, Pharaoh was indeed enriched by the animals, lands, and lives of all Egypt. Only the priests still had their own land.

Then, one spring in the eighth year, the Nile began to rise for the yearly Inundation. The Dog Star once again foretold the start of flooding. The people rejoiced and the priests called for a celebration. Pharaoh sent word to plant and harvest, saving, as always, a fifth for the throne. With joy, the people sowed the fields. The crops came up and flourished. The Nile had resumed her place in the life of Egypt, just as God had said. The seven years of famine were ended.

In Goshen, my family prospered and the royal herds increased. Many times Pharaoh spoke to me of my brothers.

"We are fortunate to have your brothers watching our flocks. Never have such fine animals been seen during a famine time. How does your relationship with them prosper?"

"Great King, I fear they will always see me as the Lord Governor rather than their brother. It is true that they no longer seem to fear me, but all my attempts to be their brother are met with stiff formality as due my office."

"Zaphenath-Paneah, we are sorry," he replied to the resignation in my voice. "But we would rather have you as our Lord Governor and Advisor than loose you to your desert kin."

"Yes, Mighty One, my life is for your service." I took his offered hand as a sign of mutual affection.

"And your father?" He asked one evening.

"Does well." I replied. "For a man of his years, he is strong. I would crave, when you, Great King, can spare me, to travel to Goshen and spend time with my father. He has asked often to hear of my adventures."

"We too, would like to hear the whole of your story. After the harvest, this first since the famine ended, we will travel with you to see your father!"

Epilogue

"So that is how I came to Goshen, to you, my father. You have now heard how great are the promises of our God." The governor finished his story by bowing his head onto his father's lap.

"My son, you are chosen of the Lord. I knew you were special from the moment the God of our Fathers opened Rachel's womb to bear you." The old patriarch caressed the bent head. "Joseph, God has indeed added to you His promises and grace."

Finally, the man turned to Pharaoh. "My Lord King, you now have heard the story of my life and why I believe that the God of my Fathers has preserved me." He was surprised to see tears in the royal eyes.

"Our Lord Governor, you are indeed blessed of the gods. We were wise in giving you that name when you became our chief advisor. Zaphenath-Paneah, you have touched us with your story." He held out his arms and Joseph knelt to receive the embrace of the king.

"These brothers of yours?" The question made ten hearts beat faster with fear. Pharaoh turned to look at the men crouching near the tent. His face wore a frown and he tapped the flail in his hand as though desiring to use it.

Joseph stood and faced the King. Calmly, he repeated the truth he had learned. "Great One, what they did from evil and jealousy, the One God has turned to good not only for me, but for Egypt. I have no anger left toward them."

With these words, the son of Jacob turned to his brothers. "Will you not believe me now that you have heard from my lips how God's promises have been fulfilled?" His voice was pleading.

Slowly the men came forward to embrace Joseph and accept his forgiveness. In their hesitancy, Joseph felt the apprehension they still clung to. He sighed and prayed again that God would heal the rift built from years of guilt.

Jacob smiled, happy to see his family reunited. With the clap of his hands, servants were summoned to spread out the banquet prepared for the King. Later, the young women would perform the tribal dances for the Ruler of Egypt.

"My son," the old man held Joseph near him, "I have been blessed that God has allowed me to see you and your sons before I die. The God of my Fathers has let me see all my children in harmony again."

"Yes, my father." Joseph smiled, too, content that his father was with him and that the recital was done. There was time enough to continue to heal the distance between the brothers. He looked up at the stars and knew that he was indeed Joseph, the son of Jacob, sheik of Canaan, and of Rachel, the most beloved wife. For the first time, he acknowledged that Joseph was also Zaphenath-Paneah, Lord Governor, Interpreter to the King and Preserver of the Land of Egypt and that a part was still Hebiru, slave of my lord Potiphar, Captain General of Pharaoh's Army.

"God of Abraham, Isaac and Jacob you took me from Canaan and brought me through slavery and prison to be part of your plan for the saving of the nation and of my family. I am your servant and you are my God." His heart breathed the prayer into the night sky, and he felt a deep peace and assurance that all was well. With great happiness, he joined the conversation and feasting.